PRAISE ~~FOR~~ ~~LEE~~

"*An exhilarating and original organized crime thriller that delivers big time on atmosphere, intrigue and fun.*"

BESTTHRILLERS.COM

"*A taut emotional tale.*"

KIRKUS

VICIOUS RIPPLES

THE DESIRE CARD BOOK FOUR

LEE MATTHEW GOLDBERG

ROUGH
EDGES
PRESS

Vicious Ripples
Paperback Edition
Copyright © 2022 Lee Matthew Goldberg

Rough Edges Press
An Imprint of Wolfpack Publishing
5130 S. Fort Apache Rd. 215-380
Las Vegas, NV 89148

roughedgespress.com

Paperback ISBN 978-1-68549-140-6
eBook ISBN 978-1-68549-139-0
LCCN 2022941643

VICIOUS RIPPLES

"No man, for any considerable period, can wear one face to himself and another to the multitude, without finally getting bewildered as to which may be the true."

—— Nathaniel Hawthorne, *The Scarlet Letter*

"Before you embark on a journey of revenge, dig two graves."

—— Confucius

GRACIE

Nine going on ten but Gracie Stockton feels like she's pushing thirty. Demanding private school that doesn't allow for subpar. Plus ballet school, even more demanding since she chose that as her future career. She doesn't have time for boys yet, barely a second for friends. Already after her parents' divorce, she has to shuttle between their apartments, only separated by Central Park. The weekly walk through nature providing her a few moments of calm. Heavy backpack of books digging into her shoulder blades, the fall light tilting through the crisping leaves. Sometimes earbuds in her ears, on a group text with girls from her ballerina class since the girls at Chapin are juvenile. Today she plays "Dance of the Blessed Spirits" from her upcoming performance of *Orpheus and Eurydice*. She's no longer a chorus girl after her last *allegro* wowed her teacher. Now she's with the twelve-year-olds in the front of the line, not the lead, but she knows she'll make it there soon. She will not be satisfied with anything less.

The light wanes as she makes her way through the

Ramble. Soon her walk will be in the dark, something her mother and father should frown upon but they're too busy to notice. After surviving his liver transplant surgery, her father started a new job and has recently been traveling to Haiti. Her mother had to go back to work as well, not as a volunteer at UNESCO like before, but a full-timer, causing her much stress. She's also become swept up in a new romance with a man named Peter who Gracie likes because he has very nice and clean teeth. After the divorce, her parents swarmed with an overabundance of adoration so she wouldn't feel like she was at fault, which she knew. Their separation wasn't a surprise. Her father had never been home and kept secrets from her mom and her mom got pissed. But now, the newness of the split having passed, her parents have resumed their former ways. Gracie doesn't mind. She's always been independent, unlike her brother Brenton who needs attention every damn minute. He's always making fart jokes, making her wonder how they're even related.

The sky flashes a weird indigo color, clouds thick as soup, rain on the horizon. Sometimes when she walks this route other people pass by. Today there are none. She's cold in her thin sweater and wraps the sleeves around her hands, but it doesn't do much to stop the chills. The park full of wildlife, astounding and frightening. She once saw a hawk and imagined it landing on her head and pecking at her brain. She's also seen raccoons with their sharp teeth and scary yellow eyes. When she hears a rustling behind her, she tells herself it's not a hawk or a raccoon but a robin, there to make sure she arrives at her destination safely. She turns around and sees nothing.

This has been happening more and more. She used to think she was being followed, despite never seeing any evidence to justify her paranoia. The thought of a crazy person waiting to attack occasionally invaded her nightmares, but she figured she was acting silly. Still, in New York City, you always had to stay on alert. From a very early age, her mother warned her of kidnappers and wouldn't let her walk by herself until she was satisfied that Gracie understood the rules. Gracie knew to go for help if anyone was bothering her, especially to a woman rather than a man. She always carried her phone and should call the police if ever felt threatened or even uncomfortable. She was confident that she'd handle herself well should the situation ever arise.

Hearing a *snap* from off in the distance, her left ear picks up the sound, tilts toward the source. She gazes in the direction, but the park is full of camouflage and it's difficult to make out anything suspect. The *snap* mutates into a rustling of leaves, a nearby bush the culprit. She peers closer hoping for that robin singing its cooing song. But the sound was so loud she heard it through the crescendo of "The Dance of the Blessed Spirits," louder than a robin could ever hope to be. She unplugs one earbud, crouching over the bush. Hands dart out, pulling her inside, the branches slicing her face, drawing blood. She lets out a scream but it's muted by the enclave she's descended into, this new world of prickly leaves and a bed of dirt, of uncertainty and stoked fear. A handkerchief gets pressed over her mouth, the smell of chemicals sharp. The arms that hold her are strong and powerful. She squirms, kicking her assailant, bucking against the body, but it's no use. She's so sleepy. She just wants to rest. Her eyelids close even as she tries to fight. Barely conscious, she's lifted out of the bush, the air stinging against the cuts on her cheeks. It's the last thing she feels until sleep completely consumes and she lays against the powerful arms carrying her out of the park, as if she's this predator's child, too tired for her little legs to walk any farther.

DETECTIVE MONICA BONNER

NEW YORK HAS PROVEN A RESPITE FROM THE Pacific Northwest. Detective Bonner landed right before the rainy season began in Seattle, a perfect time to flee. Instead of dampness, she was met with crisp. The air full of smog but her clothes rarely soaked. Sunshine even as it ticks toward November. She's happy she can only recall opening an umbrella once.

The transfer to the 20th Precinct Missing Persons Division relatively smooth. Her partner, Aldon Ramirez, supportive and without the macho buffer that she imagined of New York cops. Three weeks in and she'd already been invited to his home where his wife Irulan cooked *mofongo* that was dripping with garlic and delicious. Monica tried to play with their son Emilio, although it was difficult. Not the boy, he was sweet and giggled and sang songs. She plastered on the smile her mother told her to wear before she left town and made sure it stayed firm until she left with a doggy bag to her studio apartment by Hudson River where a slew of boxes waited to be unpacked that she knew would stay unopened.

"Bonner, you heard of what went down in Killenroy?" Ramirez calls out, his lean face popping over their partition. His caterpillar eyebrows floating upwards. "Is that near Seattle?"

It has been a slow day at the precinct. What a cop always wishes for, but usually something terrible turns up to sour any premature celebrations.

"No, that's way up in the woods," she says. "No man's land."

"Weird ass quintuple homicide."

"I remember. It was right before I left town. All over the papers."

"Case is still wide open. No leads a month in. Just wondered if your buddies back home were close enough to have jurisdiction?"

"Nothing I've heard."

"Let's grab dogs."

They head outside to the hot dog guy. Ramirez gets two piled with relish, onion, ketchup and mustard. Bonner nibbles on one, the bread stale. Didn't New Yorkers always say how good their hot dogs were, or was that just the pizza?

She takes a bite, gets a dab of mustard on her suit.

"Fuck."

She wipes at the stain but only makes it worse, now absorbed into her sleeve.

"How's your place coming along?" Ramirez asks.

"Haven't unpacked yet," she says, and immediately wants to take it back because his caterpillar eyebrows raise again.

"Damn, what you waiting for?"

"I just like to take my time."

This wasn't a lie. Since Monica was a girl, she'd always been meticulous. It used to drive her mother crazy at dinner when she'd cut her food into tiny little bites and chew each one until the food was pulverized. Drove her husband Jim nuts too. Jim with the ability to demolish a plate in seconds, always eager to move onto the next thing. While Monica ate carefully, never rushed. A trait that made her good at her job. Prudent consideration. People went missing, but there was always a crumb, someplace to begin. Pick them up one by one. Don't dictate the crumbs. Let the crumbs speak for themselves. Relationships were more complicated.

"I could come over sometime and help–"

"*No.*"

She snaps at him, unaware the force of her venom. Her teeth hurt from the hiss. For a year she barely brushed them, wondering what was the point. Now they throbbed uncontrollably.

"Whoa, settle down. No need to pounce."

"I'm sorry."

The thought of Ramirez entering her apartment turned her stomach. The bite of hot dog not helping the situation. It's not the unpacked boxes. It's because of the only thing she *has* unpacked. The shrine she knows she needs to get rid of, but the shrine is all she has to get her through the day. The anticipation of pictures taped to the wall. The smell of a light blue blanket never washed.

She runs her hands through her short hair still searching for the phantom length. She'd cut it right before she left, the first time since she was a teenager. Jim had been shocked when he saw her off. She'd already moved to her mother's house, but there were a few of her things left at their place. He said he didn't recognize her at first. He reached out to touch her new long-bob-short-bangs hairdo. She told the young girl at the salon she wanted to look like Uma Thurman from *Pulp Fiction*. She said to Jim that she didn't recognize him either because he'd become a deflated version of himself. The air sucked out, the skin left pale. The life, gone. They had met as very different people: hopeful. They emerged now, weathered and beaten. In their final hug, she realized he hadn't showered, possibly not at all that week. If she didn't leave, she'd vanish into nothing too.

"I'm sorry," she says again to Ramirez because he's a nice guy and means well. And she could've been saddled with a dick for a partner. "I'm private."

"Yeah, I can tell."

"Just give me some time. I like to take my time."

"You know anyone here?" he asks. She shakes her head. "Irulan can be a good friend. I mean, if you need one."

She smiles that plastered-on smile. Delivers it with enough conviction to make him forget any awkwardness before.

"I'll reach out sometime. I will."

"Good. She likes you. My last partner... Whew, he was something. Racist motherfucker. The force let him go. Took long enough. He literally got in an argument with my wife about Puerto Rico not really being a part of America."

"What an asshole. There are so many assholes out there."

"Tell me about it. And we picked the wrong profes-

sion, since we gotta deal with all of them on the daily."
He turns to a bedraggled man humping a brick wall.
"Like this asshole. Stop humping that wall, homes," he
shouts. "It don't love you back. There's no consent!"

She smiles for real this time and whispers "thank
you" to Ramirez because she knows he's acting funny to
uplift her mood. Because she gets in funks she can't
swim out from.

Her police radio buzzes.

"Bonner, Ramirez, we got a 10-57 we want you to
check out."

"10-4, we're right outside the precinct grabbing a
bite."

"Little girl reported missing. Only been a few
hours, but the parents say she's never even been late
before. Stockton is their name. I'm patching in the
address."

"Right away, Chief. We'll take care of it."

She puts her radio away.

"You better finish those dogs, Ramirez."

He swallows them in two gulps. Just like her
husband would.

3

GABLE

"I see," Gable says, into the phone, not his encrypted one, but the cell number given to his family. He runs his fingers through a swoop of chalk white hair. He'd come to Audrey Hepburn's studio to destress. Hepburn rolls over in her bed, blows a puff of cigarette smoke at the ceiling, and wanders into the bathroom. Leaving the door open as she showers so he could watch, still wearing her mask.

"Helly, we will find her," he tells his distraught daughter. His only granddaughter Gracie has gone missing. A serious child, his DNA in her blood.

He can hear Helene mopping up her tears. She tells him the police are on their way. "Good, good," he says. "I will see what else I can do. I am sure she is fine."

"How can you be?" Helene asks. "Hold on, I'm getting another call."

"Take it, darling," he says, in his most calm and assured tone. He doesn't like to see Helene, or any of his family, show vulnerability. To win at life, one must always remain in attack mode. He knows who has

Gracie—the rogue James Dean. The difficulty will be getting her back without implicating the Card in the matter.

He hangs up the phone, observes Audrey Hepburn soaping up. She gives a show in the muted fluorescent light. He debates joining her, but will need to recharge first. One of the worst things about being seventy.

Macau had been success and a disaster. He'd removed his competitor Hasan Bouchtat from building the tallest casino in the providence so his could reign supreme, but James Dean, a.k.a. J.D. Storm, a.k.a. Marcus Edmonton, or whatever the hell he calls himself now, killed more operatives in a short period of time than ever in the Card's history. Rita Hayworth—iced. Jimmy Stewart—with a bullet to his brain. Cary Grant too. Garbo dead on a plane. The list goes on. Gable still has operatives left; he'll always have reserves. But he can't deny the Card has taken a hit.

To make up for the losses, he must lean on Laurence Olivier, the head of the international office, and siphon some of his operatives. Though Olivier technically works under Gable and the international office is not as huge as the domestic one, they've always run rather independently from each other, a deal the two came up with after the Card's inception in the 1970s and practically going to war over who'd be its Boss with a capital B. A split down the middle meant restructuring and also expanding its outreach beyond the borders. At the time, Olivier had agreed to the stipulations.

But weakness is something both men understand well. If Olivier ever showed vulnerability, Gable would pounce and oust control over the international office, putting in a more loyal figurehead. He'd expect nothing less from Olivier. So, certainly a bind, yet he needs operatives to help find wherever J.D. has taken Gracie.

The water shuts off and Audrey Hepburn emerges in a white towel. Thin like the starlet, her collarbones seeming to reach out and grab him.

"Did they find her?" she asks.

Hepburn was one of his favorite actresses, why he chose his lover to hold the honor of wearing her mask. Films like *Roman Holiday, Breakfast at Tiffany's* and *Charade*, lighthearted to mask the darkest times. Hepburn a bright force with a sweet cadence that had the ability to lull. He'd met her actual presence at his lowest: before the Card, before any seized power, when he was ordinary and only dreaming of becoming more.

He holds Audrey's face in his hands, kisses the masked lipstick lips. Loosens the towel and licks from between her breasts to her bush. Kisses her again with the taste of her on his tongue.

"Any news?"

She always has a pep to her voice, like the real Audrey Hepburn. A permanent beacon of positivity, at least while wearing the mask. He's aware when it's removed she must crumble, her real face shattered from plummeting through a windshield after a car accident as a child that left the rest of her family dead.

"He's playing a game," he says.

"James Dean?"

Gable touches his nose.

"Ungrateful," she says, practically quaking with anger. "What you've given him. All of us. It makes me murderous."

She says this all in her sweet baby voice, which lends it an even more chilling nature.

"Let me help you," she says, in his lap.

"This is how you help me."

"I want to be out in the field again. My trigger finger itchy."

He places her index finger between his lips, sucks all the way down until it disappears.

"I *am* low on operatives."

"Then let me leave this apartment, this glass house you keep me hidden."

"It's because I couldn't bear to have any more harm come to you."

"I. Am. Fine."

She goes loose in his arms, crawls off. There'd been a close call over a year ago. An assignment that put her in peril. He'd had Cary Grant covering the operation, a hit that seemed simple. But the mark proved ruthless. Grant needed back-up. Hepburn was called in and there'd been a shoot-out. She took a bullet to her chest.

Gable runs his aged hand over her scar now that looks like a Buffalo nickel, hates how she winces whenever he touches too close. When he had held her in his arms covered in blood—her breaths getting less and more spaced out—he anticipated them stopping completely. But then the magic doctor they had on retainer brought her miraculously back to life. It'd been the first time he'd asked for God's help, immediately regretting that he'd sold his soul to the wrong deity's side, even though he had his love back. He built her this glass house afterwards, a studio in the clouds, and made sure she barely left.

"I'll think about it, Audrey."

He can tell she's upset, but the mask hides it well. He knows her so closely; every tiny movement a signal. He enjoys his lifelike puzzle.

"So, what's the next step?" she asks.

He doesn't want to show vulnerability, but she's aware of his contention with Olivier. So when Gable grimaces, she knows the cause. They are not married like he and Vivien, but this woman understands him more than his wife of forty-odd years.

"Olivier will allow you some of his operatives," she says.

"Allow me?"

"I mean, he'll be happy to comply for a greater cause."

"My granddaughter is one of the few I'd sacrifice anything for."

"I know this, Gable."

"She is like my arm. When I am in the ground, someone must continue this lineage. She is not yet ten, but she has the aptitude for such a job. I can tell. I can always tell."

"Should I leave you alone to contact Olivier?"

"You don't want to see me grovel?"

Hepburn doesn't know how to respond, never wanting to tick him off.

"I'm kidding. I don't grovel to anyone."

"No, you don't."

She curls into his lap again, presses against him until he grows hard.

"But first...?" she asks, letting the anticipation dangle. Leaving him always wanting, never completely satisfied. His beautiful Audrey Hepburn, the adoration of many long ago, when a flash of her smile was all that was needed to ease someone's troubles, the mournfulness beneath her glamour relatable.

Although he'd never admit it out loud, even to her, this is the lowest he's felt since those dark times, when his mother... well, what would be the use of opening any locked boxes in the recesses of his brain? The Card has only seen a meteoric rise since its start, the setbacks few and limited. There was bound to be an era of a dip.

The addictive power the hardest to lose. With each operative added, he swells, balloons into a greater presence. The many arms of Gable as he calls them. The prongs of the Devil, that higher being he favorites. He visualizes James Dean's face on a bulls-eye, the dart piercing the one eye that remains. The freed child returned to Helene. A Card rebuilt better than before, tweaking any mistakes. Maybe he'd been too swept up in revenge? His son-in-law's messy quest for a liver, followed by Hasan Bouchtat's underhanded business venture, and James Dean's desire to leave. His strongest operative only wanted freedom, which he could never grant. They'd all want to leave eventually once they no longer needed his therapy. He is a healer, yet they'll never know how much they all heal him in turn, his masked men and women, passing their souls over in an attempt to be whole.

Those same broken pieces of himself that he's spent years collecting, piecing the dispersed parts together into a distorted creature like Frankenstein's monster.

4

SIR LAURENCE OLIVIER

AT HIS OFFICE IN BRUSSELS ALONG THE RUE d'Aerschot, a hotspot for the city's underground nightlife and famous brothels on the edge of the Turkish quarter, a well-placed location with enough seediness to distract from his own sinful undertones, Sir Laurence Olivier smokes his fifteenth Benson & Hedges of the day, the brand that launched Olivier's own tipped cigarettes back in the 1950s. The mask he wears is the finest and most expensive in the Card's oeuvre, even more than Gable's since Olivier nips and tucks his until it achieves perfection. The mustache sewn in from his own follicles, the jet-black hair as well. In real life, he used to be dashing, a *charmer* as all his ex-wives would say, movie-star looks, never gaining too much weight in his belly like most men in their middle-to-declining years. Brussels' gastro scene never seduced him to excess and he swam a hundred laps every morning in his private pool in Saint Gery.

His cell phone rings, the encrypted one he shares only with Gable. While they used to speak once a day earlier in the Card's history, now their calls are regulated to fires that need to be extinguished.

"And to what do I have the honor?" Olivier asks, stroking the fine hairs of his mustache.

"Were you updated about Macau?" Gable asks, always speaking in the form of a dog barking. Maybe it was Olivier's European sensibilities, but he always found Gable's American ways boorish.

"Yes, Cagney reached out."

Olivier lights another cigarette, sucks in a good third.

"Massacre to put it lightly."

He can picture Gable back in States, knocking around in his unwieldy body, gearing up to making this call. The man certainly wants something, and Olivier would only grant any wishes after a good squirm.

"I never did trust James Dean," Olivier says. "Ah, that's not entirely true. I didn't trust him because he thought too much like you and I. He was never destined to remain an underlining like the rest."

"Yet you never expressed concern?"

"Would you have listened? About your protégé?"

"He wasn't my protégé!"

"Forever searching for your Errol Flynn. It's been forty years, Gable."

"How dare you bring him up..."

"You seem like there's more you want to say to me."

Olivier could hear the man's teeth grinding.

"I do not have the time."

A pause lingers between them, vicious and bereft of any human decency. The two imagining ideal ways for the other to die, or at least cause immeasurable pain.

"My granddaughter has been taken."

"I am putting two-and-two together," Olivier says, giving a final suck before lining up the cigarette along a ring of others in the ashtray. "James Dean is responsible?"

"Correct."

Olivier can visualize Gable touching his nose like he often does when making an assertion.

"You need operatives."

Olivier does not pose this as a question, for that would mean he's willing to offer an answer.

"I do."

"Cagney told me we lost some of our best. Garbo, that was a surprise. Her brutality matched that of a samurai warrior. She was an enigma I was never able to solve."

The red light from the theater outside slants through the tiny frosted window by Olivier's desk and he thinks of a night they shared in Stockholm in the Gamla Stan, drunk off vermouth, eating reindeer with lingonberries at an outdoor restaurant on the Stororget, her head relaxed in his shoulder as they walked along the water after fulfilling a wish of a billionaire who desired his wife to disappear. By the lapping waves of Lake Malaren, she removed her mask with much difficulty because he had asked, which he never did because he respected his operative's former personas. Unlike Gable who preyed on their weaknesses, Olivier prided himself on their rehabilitations; but she acquiesced to his curiosity. Peeled back her face to reveal a travesty only Picasso could love, the features out of whack: nose askew, eyes unaligned, lips folded inwards. She blinked up at him in her alien form and he made love to her pre-butterflied stage on a wooden dock strewn with empty liquor bottles formerly filled with their bad decisions. He cried for her then and he sheds a lone tear for her now. Only Audrey Hepburn had given him more powerful nights than that one.

"I have to ask for three," Gable says.

Olivier rushes back to the present, the lump in his throat a bulging golf-ball.

"Three? Yes."

A knock on the door and Alain Delon slips inside the office dressed as if he stepped from out of *Le Samourai*: a cool, grey suit and trench coat, light grey fedora with a black band around the brim, gun in his breast pocket.

"*Gable*?" Delon mouths, and Olivier nods.

"I can give over three," Olivier says, into the receiver.

"I'll have you rephrase that," Gable says.

"Come again?"

"You say, you *can* give over three, but I think you mean you *will*."

"Do you really want to get wrapped up in semantics?"

A cackle echoes from the outside streets, the local brothel opening for business as the sunlight dims.

"It's a question of authority," Gable says.

"We are equals," Olivier says, always believing the initial spark of the Card to be his idea. Gable the facilitator more than the creative.

"Yes, back during those ruptured late seventies, our brains fried from Vietnam and psychedelics, who remembers who came to who with the rapturous suggestion?"

"Even on two dabs of acid I know it was me."

"More importantly, it's about who was able to make the Card soar."

"I'm not getting into a dick-wagging contest with you, Gable."

"Then you do not really know me after all these years."

Olivier looks over at Delon who rolls his eyes and reaches into his coat pocket for his gun. Olivier taps his nose with a Gable-like gesture.

"I'm agreeing to three of my operatives," Olivier says. "Will there be anything else?"

"No, I spent long enough with your blather today."

Olivier wants to bash the phone into the wall, but he summons his ability to be composed. It used to be out of fear, now he's simply waiting for the precise time to attack, just like Gable would do.

"Good day then."

"What is the mission?" Delon asks, once Olivier hangs up.

"Ice time."

Delon runs his fingers across the brim of his fedora, a sign between the two when a kill has been ordered.

"Then it is done," Delon responds.

Outside the cackles from the brothel reach a crescendo, the street full of their debased mirth. Delon's face shadowed red from the flashing neon glitz, like a devil winking.

5

MARCUS EDMONTON

THE GIRL HASN'T CRIED YET, ODD FOR SOMEONE her age under these circumstances. She might be more like her grandfather than Marcus could've imagined. He rented a basement apartment paid full in cash with soundproof walls that he told the landlady were necessary to record his podcasts. She was Polish, could barely speak any English, and only cared about the money. The place sparsely furnished, visible piping instead of crown molding. The tiniest sliver of a window and a stream of people walking by. A hotplate so he could make food for them both with rows of Chef Boyardee cans along the kitchen wall. A half fridge stocked with Capri Sun and apples. A TV so he could keep track of the news. The kidnapping hasn't made headlines yet.

Gracie awakened from the chloroform but refuses to speak. He tended to the cuts on her cheeks and left an apple by her side, now starting to turn. The water bottle hasn't been touched either and he worries she might be suffering from dehydration.

"You need to eat...drink."

Her eyes cut into him.

"I don't intend to hurt you. You do not have to worry."

She looks away as if she's done with him and this whole charade.

"If you speak, this will go a lot faster."

Nibbling on her lip, she considers.

"You don't have to be scared."

"I'm not."

He's caught off guard by her voice, picturing that of a child. She sounds like a forty-year-old with a stressful job.

"This is about your grandfather."

Her brow furrows. "Papa Jay?"

Hearing Gable's true name makes Marcus's limbs icy. The blood stops running.

"Jay?" he says to himself, bewildered that a monster can have such a normal name.

Gracie watches him carefully, digging into his soul. Gable has done it before; his granddaughter with the same honing ability.

"Your grandfather, what's his number?"

She checks for her phone in loose pockets, but he holds it up.

"His number's not in my phone."

"Are you lying?"

"Papa Jay doesn't like talking that way."

"Do you know his address?"

She nods. "It's in Connecticut. Greenwich."

"I'm not surprised."

"222 Conyers Farm Drive."

Removing a pair of scissors from his pocket, Marcus creeps toward her.

"What are you doing?"

Before she can fight it, he's snipped off a lock of her hair. When she squirms, she realizes her feet are tied to a cord connected to a weight ground into the floor.

"I need to mail this to him."

Tiny teeth emerge from her bottom lip, seething and ready to chew him apart.

"Your grandfather, he's not a good man."

"That's your opinion." She traces a circle around her sore ankle. "We love him very much."

"You do not know him. He's a very bad man responsible for many people dying. It's all due to his business. He tried to kill me too."

Her eyes go wide, a trace of tears finally developing. "That's not true."

"Your mother and father don't know about him either. I need him to shut down his business. That's why I've taken you."

Picking up the apple, she bites in and spits it out.

"Too mealy."

"You need food—"

"Fuck you."

Not expecting her to curse, he has no idea how to respond and can tell she enjoys this new power dynamic.

"Papa Jay will pay whatever it costs to get me home."

"This isn't about money."

A sly smile stays on her face, dripping upwards.

"It's *always* about money. That's what Papa Jay says."

"Your Papa Jay is wrong. He has to pay for his greed."

She lets out a sad yawn, bored of this conversation, already tucking herself into a ball. Such a bony body, her spine visible.

"I'm sorry you're caught up in this," he says. "Can I make you some Spaghetti-O's?"

"I don't eat that kind of food. It's disgusting."

"What would you like?"

"Not something out of a can."

"That's all I have."

"You can't even kidnap right," she says, her back vibrating from laughing. "So what's your plan?"

"I will give you back if he ends the Desire Card."

"That's Papa Jay's business?"

"It's a card that facilitates people's darkest wishes. Not good ones, evil."

"You used to work for him?"

Marcus studies his hands that once were responsible for these unspeakable acts.

"You did those evil deeds?"

He doesn't want to get caught in her judgmental gaze, but she lures him in. And then he's stuck.

"Many. But I'm trying to make up for it now."

"By doing more evil deeds?"

"You are a means to a goal."

"My ankles hurt." She rubs at the sore spots again. "Is this really necessary?"

"You'll try to run, kick me."

"Probably."

"So then I must keep you tied."

Now the tears begin, quiet at first, building in force.

"My parents will be worried."

"Yes, that is the point."

"They'll think I'm dead!"

He finds an envelope after rooting through a desk along with a pen and a stamp. He places the lock of hair inside and scribbles a quick letter before sealing the envelope and adding the address. He almost writes Clark Gable.

"What's your last name?"

"What if I won't tell you?"

"I can just go in your phone and find it out. You have a fingerprint password."

"Oh yeah, true. It's Stockton."

"Jay Stockton," he says, stretching out the name, feeling its presence in his mouth.

"Papa's last name is Howell. My mom's dad."

"Of course."

He finishes writing the name, in awe of the trauma this man has caused, who sounds no scarier than a golf pro at a country club.

"It's crazy how ordinary he seems... You wouldn't understand."

"What name did he tell you?"

"He was always Gable."

She scratches her chin in thought. "Like the movie star."

"Yes, how did you know?"

"Papa Jay and I have watched *Gone with the Wind* many times. My brother Brenton found it boring and never made it to the end. But Papa Jay and I always did, even if it was way after my bedtime."

Marcus has understood for a while now that Gable has a family, one he actually did love. But to hear this family spoken about, an indication of humanity in the midst of what he forever deemed was a rotten soul, he needs to hold onto the counter so as not to be shaken to the ground.

"You look white," Gracie says. "Maybe you should eat that apple?"

He wipes the apple off on his sleeve and bites in, finding it mealy just like she said.

"I told you it was a bad apple."

"Do you ever remember your grandfather being mean? Yelling at you?"

"No, maybe at my dad. They never got along. But I could do no wrong."

"Some of us have two faces."

"What do you mean?"

"I need to mail this," he says, picking up the envelope. "If I got you food, would you eat it?"

"Depends."

"Hamburger, fries, and a soda. There's a place up the block."

"Maybe."

When he's at the door, Gracie wobbles to her feet.

"Mister, what's the most evil thing you've seen Papa Jay do?"

He could explain the time Gable ordered an operative to peel off a mark's face. Stretched it back until it flapped over the man's skull. But how to reconcile that with a child?

"He has ordered much death," Marcus says, zeroing instead on Annie. Cagney firing a bullet that soared through her skull while she blew him a final kiss.

"Someone you loved?"

"Yes, and he took her away from me right before my eyes."

He reaches under his good eye to flick away a lone tear.

Gracie blows out her cheeks. "I hate that he did that to you."

"Let me get you that burger," Marcus says, fleeing out of the door, because of part of becoming Marcus permanently means shedding all of J.D., Annie included. Keeping her rattling around would only shift him off his game.

And to win this war he needed to be sharp as a scythe.

6
DETECTIVE MONICA BONNER

HELENE HOWELL LIVES ONLY A FEW BLOCKS FROM the 20th Precinct so Detectives Bonner and Ramirez head over right after they receive the call from their chief. A high-rise, two-bedroom with a converted office into a third, seemingly unlived. Boxes still decorate, and Bonner finds a kinship. The whole family is there: Helene and her ex-husband Harrison, a match that seems suspect even though the relationship ended. Helene radiates wealth, making Bonner recall *The Great Gatsby* and how Daisy is described by Nick with a voice "full of money". Helene's chunky pearl necklace and diamond earrings furthering the evidence. Harrison couldn't be more opposite, a sad-sack with a yellow hue to his skin and fat black sacks under his eyes. Granted, their daughter is missing, but those fat black sacks have taken up residence for some time. Between them sits Peter Chambers, an aged hippie with greying hair down to his shoulders and Zen beads on his wrists. A loose tie and blazer at war with his more spiritual side. Peter holds Helene's hand as if she might be cast out to sea if he lets go. Harrison with no one to hold. The grandparents are present too, having just driven in from Greenwich, Connecticut. Vivien Howell, who resembles an even more aged Daisy, white hair pulled taut into a ponytail, a lightning vein on her temple. She dips her nose into an inappropriate martini, but people tend to handle upsetting situations differently. And Jay Howell, his arm around a sad boy of fourteen, the missing girl's brother who seems to be summoning every bit of courage not to cry. Jay, the patriarch, a man with milky hair and a ruddy face with a permanent grimace. He wears an expensive suit and throws his weight around from the start. The gatekeeper of the family.

"Who was the last to see or speak to Gracie?" Bonner asks.

"It was breakfast this morning," Helene says, composed at the moment, but a hair away from losing it. She twists a Kleenex in her lap, leaving behind a discarded moist trail. "I made eggs for Brenton and Gracie. Brenton had soccer that afternoon and was missing a cleat. He and I were hunting for it."

"And Gracie?"

"Yes...Gracie," Helene says, as if she's already resigned herself to the fact that they've lost her.

Bonner wants to shake her and yell: "YOUR CHILD MIGHT STILL BE ALIVE. YOU DON'T GET TO GIVE UP YET. FIGHT!"

"Gracie was finishing up her homework at the counter. She's always been a diligent child. Very studious. Very into ballet. It's her passion."

This Helene tells to Ramirez so he feels included in the conversation. Before they entered, they agreed to let

Bonner handle the questions, the first time she'll take the lead since arriving to the city.

"Was she headed to ballet school today?" Bonner asks.

"No, Wednesdays are her one day off. I was finishing up later than I expected at UNESCO so Gracie and Brenton had spare keys. I left snacks in the fridge but texted her that I would bring dinner."

"We're contacting the phone carrier for a record of any calls and texts to and from her cell."

"Thank you," Helene and Harrison say at the same time and then frown at one another. Peter squeezes Helene's hand harder.

"Does she ever hang out with friends after school?" Bonner continues.

"Usually not," Helene says, glancing at Harrison again, waiting for him to corroborate. "She spends so much time at ballet school she has little left over for friends from school."

"Would you say she's friendly?"

"Why do you ask that?" Jay barks. This isn't his first interruption, yet Helene seems to welcome his gruff interrogation.

"Would she be nice to a stranger is what I'm asking," Bonner says.

"No, she knows better. Since she started walking alone–"

"And when would that be?"

Helene glances at Harrison. "Uh, I would say a year, no maybe two years ago. We lived close to her school. It was an easy walk. And now with us both back at work..."

"She's nine?"

"Yes."

"Turning ten," Harrison adds. "She'll be ten by Christmas."

"We felt it okay for her to walk by herself. Especially between our apartments. The park separates..."

Bonner could hear Helene's voice becoming shrill.

"Ms. Howell, I'm not judging you whether it's appropriate for a child of ten to travel in the city on her own, at least before dark. I must ask a broad range of questions."

Helene fingers her necklace and breathes a sigh.

"Now, would you call Gracie friendly?"

"Well..."

"Not particularly," Harrison says, and the whole family turns on him with disapproving stares. "I mean, she's a quiet child. Serious. She never gets in trouble. Rather adult-like, an old soul."

Ramirez writes all this down. Bonner thinks how she was similar at that age. Of course, she didn't have an upbringing like Gracie Stockton. Her father ran out on them when she was five, the day he left burned into memory. A fight between her parents that sent dishes flying, her mother screaming *"Get out,"* over and over, tempting him, so he took her at her word. He gave Monica a final strangling hug, so tight it hurt her little bones. She asked a million questions that never received answers. She waited up all night for his car to pull into the driveway. When day broke, her mother stumbled in with a bottle of something and told her to give up hope.

"He ain't returning, baby. I really messed this one up."

For a while, Monica got postcards. He'd sold his mechanic business and traveled up and down the

Caribbean, hopped over to Mexico, wound farther down south. The last card she got from him was Argentina sometime in high school and then they stopped, as if there was nowhere further for him to go, and therefore, no need to update her anymore.

"And how is your relationship?" Bonner finds herself asking, clutching onto her throat like it's hard to swallow.

"Our relationship?" Helene chirps. "Well, good. I mean, her father and I divorced recently. Harrison also went through a recent health scare."

"I had a liver transplant," Harrison says.

"But Gracie seemed...seems to be handling the divorce fine. She spends weekends at her father's, in fact their relationship has gotten closer."

"Why is that the case, Mr. Stockton?"

Harrison coughs into his fist. "My work situation has changed dramatically so I have more time for my kids now. While she was growing up, I have to admit I was not able to be there. Work dictated..."

"Do you have any leads on my granddaughter?" Jay interrupts, and Brenton puffs out his cheeks and expels some tears.

"Brenton, honey, why don't you go to your room?" Helene turns to Detective Bonner. "Is that all right? He's had a tough day."

"Sure, if we need to ask him any questions, I'll pop in before we go."

Brenton lumbers into his room, wiping his sleeve across his eyes.

"Now, Mr. Howell," Bonner begins. "Gracie has only been missing for a few hours. We have officers searching the areas nearby. There is nothing more I can tell you at the moment, but I will keep you updated with any developments."

Jay mumbles something derogatory under his breath. Bonner decides it's likely misogynistic. His wife pats his wrist with a slight scold that he ignores.

"I can't believe this is happening," Helene says, starting to be overcome by grief. Bonner knows that parents have a window where they're helpful, which dissolves once reality sinks in.

"Here," Peter says, handing her a pill. She gulps it down without water, squeezing her eyes as it makes its way down.

"I apologize," she says. "This morning she was here and now..."

"We're going to do everything in our power to bring her home, Ms. Howell. I just want to circle back to the questions I previously asked. Is there any reason to think she may have run away?"

"Run away?" Jay scoffs. "That's ludicrous! She was taken."

"That is probably the likelihood. We have to cover all our bases."

"Like I said," Helene begins, "we've had a trying last year. The divorce and Harrison's health. We even did some family counseling. But the children appeared very adjusted to the situation. In Gracie's class alone, over half of them come from divorced families. It's sadly commonplace, at least in New York."

"It's the tight quarters we live in," Peter says, looking around with a wry smile. "That's my theory. Outside of New York, people have larger homes and aren't on top of one another as much..." He trails off when no one seems to respond.

"She would not run away," Helene says, and Harrison continues for her.

"She was very loved and had everything a child could desire..."

Harrison's voice hangs on the last word, *desire*, something about it causing his face to scrunch up as if he had a light stroke.

"Are you all right, Mr. Stockton?"

"I'm overdue for my medications." He removes a baggie from his pocket filled with colorful pills.

"Detective Ramirez, please take Mr. Stockton into the kitchen."

"Yes, I could use a break," Harrison says, quietly.

Ramirez helps Harrison up and leads him away.

"Is there anyone else in the family that might offer some insight?" Bonner asks.

"My brother," Helene says, and Jay's eyes sweep down like vultures after victuals. "Yes, my brother Chip has been unreachable for some time."

"Have you reported this?"

"Chip's done this before," Jay says. "Wanderlust has often taken hold."

"That's true," Helene says. "Although this time is longer than the rest."

"Even when he was living in ashram in India?" Vivien adds, and goes right back to her drink.

"That was longer," Helene says. "Anyway, you brought it up, Detective, so I thought I would mention."

"We'll look into him too. I doubt there's a link."

"What more can we all do right now?" Peter asks, trying to be helpful. The new boyfriend, relegated to white noise in the background.

"Wait by your phones. Keep me posted with any

developments, or if you can think of anything else related to the case."

Bonner rises and hands them all her card.

"This is my direct line. Any time of night do not hesitate. We will be reaching out to all of her class-mates, those at her ballet school too. If they noticed anyone suspicious hanging around. Does your daughter have a diary?"

"I...I don't think so."

"Will you allow me to look in her room?"

"Of course."

Bonner shakes all their hands. "I am going to do everything in my power. That I can swear to you."

"Thank you, thank you so much," Helene says, and engulfs her in a hug that catches Bonner off guard. She pats Helene on her back and passes the woman over to Peter.

In Gracie's room, she turns on the light, picks up a wind-up ballerina and lets her twirl on the desk. Much like the rest of the house, the bedroom feels unlived, although according to her notes the family has only been here a few months. Gracie's schoolbooks are lined up neatly on her desk. A black and white poster of a ballet slipper takes the place of what would normally be on a nine-year-old girl's wall, some heartthrob she could pray to every night. Bonner goes through the desk draw-ers, checks the clothes drawers next, finds what could be a diary and bags it up.

She hears sniffling coming from the room next door. The brother lies in bed, his arm tossed over his red face. She knocks and he sits up.

"I wanted to see how you were doing," she says.

"Fine."

"I know this is scary."

"Was she taken like Papa Jay said?"

"We don't know yet."

"I always picked on her, but I really miss her now. I feel bad for calling her names."

"That's what older brothers usually do."

"Really?"

"You made her tough. She'll need to be tough now. And you need to be tough for your mom. Because she's having a really hard time.'"

"I will." He points at the bagged book under Bonner's arm. "What's that?"

"Might be a diary Gracie kept."

"Do you think it'll tell you where she is?"

"No, but it might help me get to know her better. And that could help me find her."

"What makes someone want to spend their life finding kids who are lost?"

Bonner is thrown off, never expecting that to come out of his mouth. She goes to answer, but her voice box stays closed as if a substance blocks the pain from being released. This boy, who could be a future version of her own, had he been given the chance to grow. Weak in the knees, she hovers by the door, grasping onto the doorknob like it's a buoy, tethering her. The boy observes her curiously, waiting for an enlightened answer. Finally, she's flung back into reality enough to give a quick quip.

"Someone has to do it," she says, receding into the dark recesses of the hallway, the comfort of shadows until she's her steady self once again.

7

VIVIEN

AFTER THE POLICE LEAVE, VIVIEN DASHES TO THE bathroom to freshen-up. The day causing much chagrin, not intending to come into the city. She and Jay had dinner plans with their dear friends the Reinwalds at Jean Georges' The Inn at Pound Ridge, which had to be canceled. Not that she minded. Her granddaughter would always come first, although she found Gracie a rather curious child. The two having a very civil relationship lacking warmth, although she's as much responsible as Gracie for their icy distance. Neither being the type to ever give into smothering kisses and hugs.

In the bathroom, she sorts through Helene's soaps and lotions, finding them of the Bed, Bath & Beyond variety. Choosing an eye cream that seems the least pedestrian, she dabs away and emerges into the hallway slightly refreshed. Passing by the kitchen, she listens in on Jay talking with Harrison, a strange occurrence to hear them saying more than two words to one another, even when Harrison was still married to her daughter.

Jay always had a disdain for Harrison that bordered on obsessive.

"Is the *Card* responsible?" Harrison asks, trying to keep his voice down but Vivien can tell his anger makes it hard.

"How can you even ask that?"

"The illicit things..."

"We will speak of this no more. Really, Harrison? That you would even ascertain—"

"I don't know what you're capable of."

"I am capable of exiting from this horrid conversation."

Jay flies out of the kitchen in a huff, practically bumping into Vivien. His eyes all over the place.

"That son-in-law of yours has a screw loose," Jay says, whisking by. "Let's get our coats and go."

Vivien finds herself mouthing the words to ask what they'd been speaking about, but Jay already has their coats slung over his arm and he's embracing Helene who's weeping into his shoulder.

"We're only an hour away if you need us," he says. "Are you sure you don't want us to stay?"

"It's too crowded here."

"I want updates with even the slightest news."

"Of course, Daddy."

Vivien winces from Helene devolving into a little girl around her father. She always saw it lacking in character. And Helene *never* regards Vivien in that way, her mother always a secondary figure. But Jay has the ability to wrap those he chooses around his finger. Vivien had certainly been guilty of falling prey to it herself.

He beckons her to come. From the corner of her

eye, she catches Harrison folded over the kitchen counter, his face twisted with the expression of his guts spilling out. What secrets do these men hold? She receives her coat, pecks Helene on the cheek, and follows her husband out into the night.

———

In the car back to Greenwich, Vivien refuses when Jay offers to play music and she finds the podcast on NPR dull. She inspects her lipstick in the rearview, hating the wrinkles bursting from her lips, and occupies herself with the sweep of trees. But the image of Jay and Harrison in the kitchen nags. She never likes to pry into her husband's life. She tells her friends she loves him from afar. He's just that type. Get too close and his stinger might prick. From the amount of money he's accumulated, she's aware there might be a few suspect business dealings in the bunch. Every year she's unsettled after signing her taxes, wondering if there might be some kind of fraud she'd been blind to, but Jay always assured her everything he did was legit. She'd asked their accountant once a few years back when the amount on the taxes was so high she couldn't believe that anyone could make that kind of profit. And their accountant echoed Jay. Everything had been "above the line," an expression she never heard before but could guess its meaning.

She had grown up wealthy, Connecticut wealthy. A white colonial house in New Canaan, not far from where they lived now. Her father had been a successful businessman in the city, much like his father before. She went to prep school, attended Radcliffe, and met a boy her senior year with shoulders like a linebacker, and the thickest hair she'd ever run her fingers through. He was a few years out of Yale, and ordered dinner for her when they went out, taking her virginity on a cold winter night in his hotel room in Cambridge during a terrible blizzard that kept them locked inside and forced to rely on room service. He hadn't been brought up like her, raised in the outskirts of Boston with the faintest trace of an accent. She questioned if he came from Newton or Chestnut Hill, and even though he was cagey about his origins, she knew he came from money like her. The sixties were ending with a dramatic explosion of assassinations, and a war she wasn't sure about, and Civil Rights and free love, and a festival called Woodstock her friend Eden was attending. She'd smoked exactly one doobie, been drunk off cherry cordial twice, and been felt up by a co-ed with eczema all over his hands. The world was spinning too fast and she needed an anchor. So she latched onto Jay, and they were married by the decade's end with a baby girl on the way. During the 70s, she stayed at home tending to Helene and then their new baby Chip while Jay built his empire. And she was in awe of his startling accomplishments. The business expanding beyond the borders and into Europe and South America. She never questioned her decision to be with him.

"What were you and Harrison speaking about?" she asks, tapping a front tooth that started to throb.

"What?"

He stares at the road ahead, avoiding looking at her.

"In the kitchen, darling. I overheard, couldn't help myself. Harrison seemed quite upset."

"His daughter is missing. I can't see how else he would be."

"He asked if you were responsible. What a curious thing to say."

Their car winds off the highway onto a dark road with hovering trees blocking out the moon. Vivien closes the top button of her sweater.

"Harrison is a *curious* person," Jay says, and then gives a rat-a-tat laugh that gooses her skin. "What Helene ever saw in that schlump."

"Could there be any business associates, someone you burned–"

Now he looks at her, eyes like lasers.

"That I burned?"

"I mean, who may not be pleased with how a transaction ended, or felt they got stiffed? And wanted to exact revenge."

"By kidnapping my granddaughter?"

"The detective said to think of *any*thing that could be of help."

"Dear, none of this has to do with me. Harrison's always looking to point the finger away from himself."

"What does that mean?"

"I'd heard from Dougie at Sanford & Co. about the kind of boy our Harrison was. A girl on the side..."

"When did you hear this?"

"It was part of why he and Helly broke up."

"An affair? Really? While he was so sick?"

"Skewed priorities. Anyway, he knows I know and never wanted it revealed to the family. So, there's my secret, darling. I covered that carouser's tracks. Why I do not know. I guess it's due to a man-to-man type of loyalty. You know how it goes?"

"But Helene knew?"

"Never the extent. So he harbors resentment towards me, always has. Looking for ways to cut me down."

She pinches the top of her sweater so her neck is closed off, the chill from outside unbearable.

"Oh," she says, so softly she wonders if it's even spoken aloud.

He switches on the radio, a classical concerto that rocks the foundation of their Benz. She tries to ask him more, but her words are drowned out by the swells of violins shredding, her husband lost in the notes until they arrive at home.

At the foot of the door, Jay collects the mail, frowning at what appear to be bills.

"Are you worried about Chip?" she asks.

"Chip's fine."

"It's true this is the longest we've gone without hearing from him."

Jay takes out his keys and opens the door. The house smelling of apples, the maid baking a pie.

"Vi, I've learned over the last forty-odd years not to concern myself with the comings-and-going of our Chipper. The boy is made from stock different from us. He taps to his own beat."

"Still, a mother has worries. The last we heard was in Macau."

He kisses the top of her forehead, a way of silencing.

"If we don't hear soon, I'll start reaching out. I left him to cool off in Macau. I didn't want to bother you with trouble he'd gotten into."

"Drugs?" she says, with a shudder.

"Drugs and an incident. Anyway, he's drying up there. I told him his trust will be revoked and the PR company sold out from under him if he doesn't clean up."

"And you think that's enough of a threat?"

"He's wandering the world searching for himself, for a clean version of himself at least. I warned him not to return until he found it."

She places her purse down on the table in the foyer and spies a business card wedged in the groove. She thinks of what Harrison said. He'd asked Jay about a card, emphasized the word as if it had a capital C.

"I smell Esmerelda's pie," Jay says, his nose directing him into the kitchen. "I have little appetite but I think we deserve a bite after the trying day."

"I'll meet you there, darling."

She gives him a radiant smile that's enough for him to leave her alone. Once he's gone, she yanks the business card from the groove, nervous to read. But it's only a card from their landscaper, who appears to have gotten a new address.

"Come, Vi," she hears Jay calling from the kitchen. "While it's still a touch warm."

"Coming," she replies, but will search the house after he's gone to bed for any other cards.

She can never tell if he's lying because a sliver of her wonders if lies are all he knows.

8
GABLE

GABLE WAITS UNTIL HIS WIFE GOES TO BED BEFORE using his earpiece to contact Brando and Astaire, two of his few remaining operatives still alive. Vivien had pestered all night with vaguely accusatory questions, usually smart enough to keep a wise distance. That's how their marriage lasted for almost fifty years. But the dual shock of her granddaughter and her son going missing might be too much. Knowing exactly where Chip is, he'll have him contact his mother soon, but there are more pressing matters to deal with first. Namely Harrison. Of course, the Desire Card was involved with Gracie's kidnapping, and Harrison likely didn't buy any of Gable's assurances. Soon the dumbass would crack to the police.

"I have an urgent job," Gable says, into the earpiece. It's a secure line he keeps for both Brando and Astaire, since the two work together often. Out on his manicured lawn, the night revealing few stars, he debates Harrison's fate.

"My ex son-in-law is making accusations."

"You want him iced?" Brando says, whose voice is a higher pitch than Astaire's.

"No, just spooked. Apparently, he didn't get the memos I previously sent. My mask washed up on a beach in Punta Cana warning him that I am always watching."

"Then why not get rid of him for good?" Astaire asks.

"Again, I can't do that to my daughter, my grand-children as well. You two are part of my close circle. You know my family dynamics."

"What about James Dean?" Brando questions.

Gable spits on his lawn upon hearing the name. In his hand, a letter from the traitor. He hasn't opened it yet.

"Olivier is sending over operatives from the international office. And I will use Cagney. You two take care of Harrison."

"And what do you want us to say?" Astaire asks.

Gable lights a cigar, puffing away.

"Tell him this is his last warning. That I've been patient. That I am innocent related to Gracie, but I do not appreciate the third degree. He must know his place."

"It is done, Boss."

The signal clicks off. With the cigar between his teeth, Gable opens the letter from James Dean.

Asshole,

I have Gracie. I don't intend to cause her any harm, but if you do not comply I will have no choice.

It is time for the Desire Card to end. I need assurance of this. ALL your operatives disbanded. The phone lines for the Card disconnected. Then we go our separate ways. I've taken a lock of her hair. The next cut will be a finger. Here's the number for my throwaway cell to set up a meet.

(917) 555-7676
-Marcus Edmonton

Gable lets Gracie's lock of hair float to the grass and crunches it under his foot. As much as he loves her—one of the few things in life he actually holds dear—he'll be damned if he ever disbands the Card. It will outlast his own life and generations beyond. A footnote of the future.

He dials the number.

"Hi, asshole," Marcus says.

"So, you're Marcus Edmonton now?" Gable asks, with a derogatory laugh. "Still searching for yourself?"

"No, I've finally found who I am."

"Cheers to that." Gable takes a long puff, holds the smoke between his cheeks before exhaling at the sky.

"Do you agree to my requests?"

"I'll do whatever to get my Gracie back. Let me hear her voice."

A rustling sound as the phone is passed over.

"Papa Jay?"

"Gracie," he says, a tear the size of a millimeter at the corner of his eye. "Did he hurt you?"

"No, I just want to go home."

"And you will, darling. I'm coming to get you."

Marcus gets back on the line. "Satisfied? She hasn't been hurt...yet."

"Yes, I'm aware of your threats. Do you really have it in you to snip off a child's finger?"

"You've made me into the kind of person able to do that."

"Under other circumstances I'd be proud."

"The meet point will be by the horse stables on West Fifty-second Street. Can you get here by midnight?"

"I'll leave in a moment."

"Just you. No tricks. Any deviation from the plan, and I start taking fingers."

"You have my word. But let me ask you, Marcus. Even if I tell you I'm disbanding the Card, how can you be sure? We exist in the cracks and crevices, in areas you least expect."

"If that's a threat, then I might as well start snipping fingers."

"It's a reality. You worked for us for years. You know how far our tentacles reach. You know it's impossible for us to be completely silenced."

A pause from Marcus's end that simmers between them.

"I do."

"So why continue this foolishness? You wanted me to leave you alone. Fine. You made your point. As a granter of wishes, that wish is guaranteed."

"It's not enough anymore."

"That is greed speaking, Marcus."

"Even if I'm safe, the fact that your brand is out there, wreaking havoc... I couldn't live with myself knowing I didn't do everything in my power to stop it all."

"I love my granddaughter very much," Gable says,

being honest for once, his heart swelling with memories. "But I don't love anything more than my Card."

"I don't doubt that."

"Then we are in a pickle. And all the severed fingers in the world won't change that."

"There must be some agreement we can come to."

"It's an hour drive into the city. Give me the time to come up with a solution that satisfies us both."

A crackling from Marcus's end. "That's fair," he finally says.

"See you in an hour…Dean."

Gable hangs up before Marcus can refute being called his former name, all he'll ever be known. Make a pact with the Card, bloody one's hands, and there's no shedding that skin. Gable has been responsible for much death, aware of the hell that awaits at the end of it all. Someone like James Dean is in for a rude surprise once his life is snuffed. However much good he does from now on, it can't make up for the very bad.

He puts his earpiece back in and dials.

"Yes, Boss?" Cagney says, his number one station agent.

"I have Dean's location. Meet me at the horse stables on West Fifty-second Street."

"Shoot to kill?"

"Always," Gable says. He rips the receiver out of his ear, practically crushing it in his fist.

He checks to make sure that Vivien's light hasn't been turned on. Seeing the bedroom shrouded in darkness, he gets in his Benz and turns on Led Zeppelin's "No Quarter," singing the lyrics of his youth.

Walking side-by-side with death

The devil mocks their every step
The snow drives back the foot that's slow
The dogs of doom are howling more
They hold no quarter
They ask no quarter

9
LE SAMOURAI

"There is no greater solitude than that of a samurai unless it is that of a tiger in the jungle," a quote from Bushido that has stuck with Alain Delon since his childhood in the north of Marseilles where poverty, drug dealing, and assault rifles marred the region. Father, a scoundrel, mother a prostitute, the two welded by a love that resembled masochism. Beaten daily, sodomized, a childhood full of booby-traps. While he waits for Gable in the man's Mercedes, he recalls a time he was chased down a back alley by neighborhood bullies who flung lit matches. This was a chronic fight he endured, usually being forced to miss school to avoid a broken limb. Often, he fought back with his words. Screamed for help. Cursed his assailants. But the day before, he had snuck into a movie theater playing Jean-Pierre Melville's *Le Samourai* starring Alain Delon who had a cool confidence he could only dream of possessing. The next day in the alleyway, he morphed into a super machine.

As the rain fell and soaked, he'd no longer seen his

tormentors as boys, but targets. He'd taken a brick with him that morning. The first boy who put his hands on him was met with that brick to his forehead. Blood spurted out like from a squeezed ketchup bottle and another boy shrieked. He silenced the shrieking nuisance by shoving the brick into the kid's windpipe, cutting off his air. Two boys now remained. One had foolishly gone to help his fallen comrade and he leaped down upon him, driving the brick into the boy's skull that opened up upon impact revealing bits of bone and brains. The forth boy backpedaled, wise enough to give up the fight, fleeing into the downpour until he could no longer be seen. The samurai had been born.

Now he must make a choice between two bosses, but it's an easy decision. Olivier was European like himself where Gable was a rude American. When he initially trained for the Card, he strived for a position under Gable, only to be told he lacked the "right temperament." Fearing his English was shaky, he asked Gable to elaborate only to discover that Gable never intended for him to work at the American offices, which were reserved for its prime operatives. Alain Delon, the actor himself, had a bigger following outside of American audiences, and therefore, this reemerged Alain Delon would serve where he best fits.

"It's a matter of gelling," Gable had said.

"Gel-ling?"

Gable locked his fingers together. "You and I, I don't foresee us meshing. I envision friction."

"Why is that?"

"For the very reason you are questioning me now. What if this was a test? The operative I'd want under me would've acquiesced. Been happy for the position they received rather than the one they didn't. You will work better with Olivier because he does not require as high a standard."

Even thinking of this now in the backseat, ten years later, still causes much anger in Delon. Since then he'd placed subtle hints to Olivier about offing Gable, but Olivier always said it had to be the right time. With someone like Gable, you only get one shot.

Gable enters the car and Delon goes still. He's practiced becoming the samurai before, not moving a muscle, even expelling a breath.

Led Zeppelin's song "No Quarter" plays as the car shoots out of Gable's driveway onto a backroad. The sky dark as tar, very few pinpricks of stars. No lights except for the headlight beams. He clutches the wire between both fists, then leaps up and wraps it around Gable's neck. The car veers to the other lane but rights itself—Gable's hands tight on the wheel. Delon pulls back, the wire cutting into flesh. Delon can't fully wrap it around due to Gable flinging his head into the seatback. But the wire digs in, droplets of blood leaking onto his fingers.

He can see Gable glancing in the rearview in an attempt to see his assailant. The grey fedora shrouds Delon's face, but it should be obvious. The car bucks from lane-to-lane, hugs the shoulder, decelerates before slowing into a dirt bank.

Delon jumps onto his knees to use his weight. In the millisecond he lessens his grip, Gable wedges two fingers between the wire and his neck. He attempts to thrust it away, but his two fingers aren't strong enough. The wire slices through his digits prompting an agonizing cry.

"Delon," he yells, spit flying from his lips. "You don't have to be Olivier's stooge."

Wrong thing to say. Le Samourai is no one's stooge. Delon has made his choice where to align and won't be swayed by any of Gable's maneuvers.

"What...is...it you want? I can make it happen."

"So can Olivier."

"Really?"

"I am his station agent."

"A number...two...position. Rather impressive. What if I...made you *my* station agent?"

"That's Cagney's job."

"There is room for two."

"Lies!"

Delon pulls the wire tighter, feeling the sensation of it slicing through skin, reaching towards bone.

"There...has to be...something else. What have you always...*desired*?"

"Your tricks won't work."

The Zeppelin song reaches its end, switching over to "The Ocean" and its jaunty bounce.

"It's...no secret...the Card is struggling. We are down more operatives than ever before. What will... killing me accomplish?"

"An overhauling of the American office. Olivier will be in charge and I become more than a station agent, number two of the whole operation."

"I can grant you that too."

"Bullshit."

Gable slips a third finger between the wire and his neck, gaining momentum.

"It will be...much easier to fold the international office into my own rather than vice versa. I am a wealth of knowledge...about the Card. Without me and the passcodes for the whole operation here, you'll be starting from scratch."

Delon slightly lessens his grip allowing Gable to insert a fourth finger between the wire, using his palm as leverage.

"I have operatives Olivier does not even know, clients I've never told him about. This information isn't on some fucking computer, it's all in my head! You'll be bankrupt in months."

"I'm sure Olivier has thought of this."

"No, because he never thinks two steps ahead. Unlike myself."

Gable stomps on the accelerator as the car goes flying forward. Delon flung into the front seat, loosening his grip even more. Gable rips at the wire, dislodging it from Delon's hands. He spins around with the bloody wire and leaps on top of Delon.

"No, no!"

Gable wraps the wire around Delon's neck: once, twice, cutting off circulation, Delon's skin turning purple. Delon weeps at the fact that he did not act like the tiger in the jungle; he allowed his opponent to usurp. He attempts to wedge his fingers between the wire and his neck, but Gable has wrapped it around twice and it's too tight. The car seems to speed forward at an unprecedented rate, spelling an impending doom for them both, a hallucination on wheels. The world gets very bright for Delon before turning extremely dark. He can smell fire, feel his body cooking. A cackling hovers from above: Gable, or a more malevolent force. He visualizes gates opening, swallowing the Benz whole. The tormentors from his youth cheering. All the deaths he caused lined up to welcome him into the fold.

And then, Gable vanishes. Delon alone is in his torment, no greater solitude than that of the samurai, as giant red hands with sharp, black fingernails collect his fallen body, remove his fedora and grey trench coat, strip him naked to place him over a bonfire that chars his limbs to a crisp, rotating until not an inch remains free from burns and the only thing left of him is a dark, eternal scream.

10

HARRISON

Harrison will never escape the Desire Card entirely, a penance for the choices he's made. The liver he tried to obtain through them, which never worked out, and how he's beholden to Jay for successfully getting him a clean one. The menace of the Card's giant unwieldy thumb. He's accepted this, even given up on Naelle so as not to endanger her. It hasn't been easy. After his work in Haiti finished, he visited her in Punta Cana with the intention of declaring his love, but then Gable's mask washed up on the beach. Its eyes telling him he'll always be watched.

He should be happy with his life. The liver transplant has been a success after death seemed so inevitable. And then, a second chance. A rebirth. But nothing matters if Gracie is gone and Jay responsible. The thousands who Jay fucked over have returned to enact revenge by taking his granddaughter. Even if Harrison hadn't descended down a morally suspect path, anyone connected to Jay always ran a risk—Gracie forever in jeopardy.

He's worked so hard at becoming a better person but none of it meant anything. The threat would be there even if Gracie survived. How to go on living in constant fear? At his lowest, when it seemed like he didn't have a chance at a new liver, he contemplated suicide. A freeing aspect to the idea. He'd stuffed himself with pills in Mumbai but couldn't go through with it. Could he do it now? If anything happened to Gracie, he'd belly flop in front of a bus. But then he curses himself for thinking so weakly.

Truth is, he has no one to confide in. Helene wouldn't care. Brenton too young. He lost any friends he had when he was fired from Sanford & Co. and the divorce took the rest. He imagined if he could be with Naelle, she'd ease his woes. Take him in her powerful arms, let him sleep against her bosom. He's written letters to her he's never sent. Keeps them in a box at his bedside. Reads them occasionally when he wants a good cry. If they can get Gracie back, maybe he and Naelle could flee with her somewhere the Card would never find them? Get new names, start a new family even. Brenton too—God, how could he forget his son? Helene would never be open to it. She could come too! Bring her new boyfriend Peter along because Harrison actually liked the guy. Although, Helene would want her mother and father—definitely her father—to come along. And she doesn't even know that he's the very person they're trying to get as far away from as possible. Not even worth fantasizing about, since it's near impossible.

He's headed back home to sleep. It wouldn't have been healthy to stay at Helene's. She had Peter and they agreed to keep Harrison in the loop should any new developments occur. It's two in the morning and his weighted body can barely take another step. He lives on the sixth-floor of a walk-up on York Avenue because it was cheapest he could find in Manhattan. His entire floor filled with post-college twenty-some-things who divide up their one and two bedrooms and live like kings from all the money they make. Half of his paycheck goes to rent for a place big enough to fit the kids on weekends. He knows he'll be crushed to go home and see anything of Gracie's.

The block is empty because it's a work night and York gets isolated from real traffic noise. Every sound amplified. A garbage can rattles. He turns toward the sound and is met with a fist to his face. The punch hard enough to cause blood to gush out. He stammers back-wards and is captured from behind. Someone has their arms around his waist, wrestling him to the ground. He fights out of instinct but becomes overpowered, his head plowing into the curb as it begins to feel like some bits of brain are leaking out. He sees his assailants confer-ring with one another before darkness arrives. Out of the black hole, Naelle shape-shifts into her human form. She's toweling off after a shower like the first time they met in her hotel room at the London. She sings a Spanish song that's always stayed in his head. The words too difficult to latch onto, but the melody present. She's humming it to him because if she doesn't he'll die. The only thing still connecting him to the world in danger of being cut. And then she starts to fade: her long mouth, her surprised eyes, her dark caramel skin. The black hole swallowing her as she reaches out a beautiful hand, fingernails painted with silver star decals like he remembers, and he reaches out too. But they slip through each other's grip and nothing remains of her, vanished into smoke.

This is not death but a purgatory in-between, one he may never wake up from.

11

BRANDO AND ASTAIRE

THE OVERWEIGHT GUY WENT DOWN EASY, BARELY A struggle. But from the way his head hit the curb and the *amount* of blood oozing out, he may be dead. Brando and Astaire hear him groan but then he stops. They lean down to check when a light on the street turns on, a head popping out of the window along with a muffled voice. They dart into the shadows offered by a tall tree. "Who's out there?" a voice asks. "What is going on?" Another light turns on, domino effect. Soon the block will be lit up with eyes on them. Must escape. The Boss ordered Harrison Stockton spooked, not killed, but there'll be no way to stay and find out.

They dash to Carl Shurz Park amongst the few homeless sleeping on benches. Catch their breaths. The masks made them more suspect so they remove each other's (always easier to have someone else doing it for you, since the masks tend to stick), and place them in their tiny backpacks filled with a gun, an emergency passport, and a wad of bills in various currencies.

"I think he's dead," Brando says. "When I leaned close I didn't see him breathing."

"It was too dark to tell," Astaire says, the more practical of the two. Brando tending to freak-out easily.

Without the masks, they couldn't be further from their other personas. Brando, an albino, his face pale as the moon. White hair shaved to a buzz cut. Eyes sunken-in. Astaire, black with vitiligo spreading across his face in the shape of Australia, covering his eyes like a patch. Both in their mid-forties working for the Card most of their lives. Gable snapping them up as teenagers.

"What do we tell Gable?" Brando asks, his voice shaking.

"Exactly what happened. We attacked, the mark hit his head on the sidewalk. We had to leave before we'd get caught."

"He will not be pleased."

"No."

They shiver because it's cold, an extra chilly November night. A light snow sprinkling. Brando and Astaire know you are only as good as your last job in Gable's eyes. Meaning they are a failure should the mark die. Especially since this mark is the Boss's ex-son-in-law.

But what may save them is the Card's precarious position. Get rid of Brando and Astaire and who will Gable have left? His mistress Audrey Hepburn and the freelancer Mae West, along with a few others who're only used for specialized jobs. Other than the station agent Cagney, Gable would be at a loss without them.

They do not have to say this to one another, but both know what the other thinks. Twenty-five years of missions together will fuse one's brains symbiotically. Sometimes it's as if they've shared a womb, the bond that close. They live in the same apartment in an isolated section of the Bronx. They keep no attachments in this apartment. There are two beds, yet sometimes they share one. The kitchen full of cookery so they can stay in as much as possible when not working. And of course, the device that connects them to Gable. They are ready to be called at any time. Pleased to be able to help in any way they can. Oftentimes when not working, they live in silence like monks. Their neighbors unaware that anyone resides at their place. Life is the job and nothing else bares importance. If not for Gable, both are certain they would've been dead a long time ago.

Brando's body covered in burns. Crackhead father torched their apartment in the projects with him in it. Father died, Brando unfortunately survived. Astaire's wounds self-afflicted. Tired of being harassed because of his skin ailments, he walked directly into a blazing fire one day. A house on his block crumbling and he wanted to join. To his chagrin, firefighters saved him. Both of their burns still hurt terribly. Skin occasionally peeling off. They have each other to rub salves into the wounds and bandage up their bodies. Gable also provides drugs that soothe as well: keep them sharp, but the pain at bay. They are fully addicted now. If Gable cut them off, they'd cut each other's throats.

What makes someone into a killer? They've often thought about what has led them down this wretched path. At times, they've broken their silence to ask one another. Deciding it's from lack of caring about anything. Their souls excavated in their mutual fires, never to return. Brando sometimes laments this, since his fire was unplanned. Astaire proud of his decision, glad to make others feel as awful as he does.

"Let's walk home," Brando says. "We don't want to get a taxi that could corroborate us being at the scene of the crime."

"Good idea. You are always thinking."

So they make their long walk back to their isolated place in the Bronx. It's after three in the morning and the light has shifted the night from complete darkness. The city remains still, pure. They breathe it in. When they reach home around six, garbage trucks are huffing down the street. They walk up a spiral staircase to their apartment. Take off their boots, their feet soaked with sweat. Sit on their adjacent beds and patch in a call to Gable, but he does not answer. It's rare of him not to pick up and they would be concerned, yet they are pleased since they do not have good news to deliver. They take off their clothes and unravel each other's bandages. Brando's burns are worse today so Astaire gets the salve and rubs it in good. Then he gently wraps his partner up in fresh bandages and can see Brando is relieved. He crushes up the drugs Gable has given them and they snort dual lines of medicine. Then they unravel Astaire and cover his body with salve before wrapping him up again. The sun has risen now and they must sleep so they pull down the window shades. They go to lie in their respective beds, but Brando can't sleep and crawls into Astaire's. Usually he is the one to do this. Astaire never kicks him out and welcomes Brando by wrapping his arm around Brando's body, pulling him close. They stare at the ceiling in silence, minds flooded before the drugs kick in and sleep yanks them into its peaceful embrace.

When they wake hours later, they put in their earpieces and try Gable again but he still doesn't respond.

This time, they are way more concerned.

12

DETECTIVE MONICA BONNER

Morning four hundred and sixty-two of sleepless nights. Monica used to dream about Kellan and wake up sobbing. She'd heard of ways to control her dreams and spent money on devices. Jim silently called her a fool. She tried special lights, fistfuls of herbs, books on tape. She wanted to hug Kellan one last time, even if it was just in dreamland.

He'd been a dream baby: happy, playful, kind. Barely cried while friends' infants wailed. As a kid, he loved baseball. Jim had played for the minor leagues and Kellan inherited those genes. She loved to watch his little legs running for a ball in the outfield. Her heart pinched every time his bat connected. The two were closer than he was with Jim, even though she worked insane hours. She never believed in soulmates, but she was tuned to her child in a way that others were not. They enjoyed the same things. Salt on their ice cream. The first breath of morning in Seattle that was always a little wet and rainy. And old black and white movies.

Jim was serious, not much for entertainment. Her

work was so serious, so when she was off she wanted freedom from anything upsetting. Audrey Hepburn was a favorite of both. Kellan always wanting to watch *Roman Holiday*. He made friends easily but would rather spend nights with his mom after she got home from work. All in all he was a good kid.

The cancer came swiftly. He'd talk of aches, of being tired. Jim brushed it off. Baseball season stretched these kids, and she figured she'd be tired too. Then Kellan started throwing up and never stopped. They put him through chemo, but it was clear to see it wouldn't help. They met other parents who had been through many stages with their sick kids. Some going into remission and then the cancer coming back. Kellan was gone in less than a month. It all happened so fast it didn't feel real. Phantom images of him appearing throughout the house, her mind not ready to let go. And the dreams. His face hazy. Too far away to hug. She never got to wrap her arms around him again, not for lack of trying.

She has a ritual before her day begins involving her shrine. It starts with spending a few minutes on each of her favorite pictures of him, culling the memories from their far-off locations. They were receding farther into the universe, ready to untether. She'd be damned if that happened. Then she watches a video of Kellan where he talks about his favorite day when he hit a home run and his teammates cheered and they went to the ice cream spot that had salted chocolate chip and watched *Roman Holiday*. She loved him because he was far from the average kid, this miraculous being she created. No one would ever be like Kellan again.

———

Detective Bonner takes the 1 train down to the precinct and doesn't allow thoughts of Kellan to creep in. She has Gracie on her mind. Today she'd organize a task-force to search and spend her time at the Chapin School for Girls and Gracie's ballet school to uncover any other leads. How easily the most important person in your life could be snatched away. Yet she's envious for the Stocktons. They have a chance to get their girl back.

When she arrives at the precinct, a woman in a tattered house dress with multiple plastic bags at her feet waits by her desk. Ramirez says the lady has infor-mation about a missing girl, but he spins his finger around his ear to indicate the lady may be crazy. Still, he thought Bonner should ask the questions.

"Thank you, Ramirez," she says, and squeezes his elbow, thanking him not just for that but also for being her friend.

"I'm Detective Bonner," she then says, reaching out a hand. The woman studies it curiously. She pinches her fingers together and offers her own as if she's royalty.

"Pleasure."

There's a ripeness to the woman's scent, citrus mixed with garbage. A dirty sheen covers over any exposed skin. She has beautiful blue eyes that seem as if they came from someone else's face.

"I was told you might have info about a missing girl."

"Well." The woman chews her lip. "Maybe. That is, I don't know what I saw."

"Where was this?"

"Central Park."

Okay, Bonner thinks. *That's a good start.*

"I was doing my walks. With my bags. I walk with my bags. These bags." She indicates the ones at her feet filled with empty shampoo and water bottles. The plastic clangs around when the woman gives it a swift kick. "Ex-er-cise. Anyway, I had just taken my meds. So sometimes things get fuzzy. But I saw these hands reach out of the bushes and grab this girl walking though the Ramble. You know that area?"

"I've heard of it."

"Winding paths. Good place to lose yourself. That's what I do. And ex-er-cise! That's what I do too. I walk with my bags, see?"

"What happened then?"

The woman yanks at a long hair on her chin. "Well. That's where the fuzzy comes in. I hid. Cause it scared me, but I could still see. There's a big knotted tree I peered out from."

"What did the girl look like?"

"Little wisp of a thing. Couldn't be more than nine-or-so. Hair in a ponytail, large backpack. Rich. Cause she had on a school uniform."

"Do you remember the name of the school?"

"I wrote it down. Cause my memory ain't so hot. So I write things down. Hold on."

She digs in her pockets and pulls out crumpled-up balls of paper. "It's in one of these."

She opens one that simply says, *kitty.*

"Now that's not it."

She opens another that says, *I See You.*

"That one was from God Himself."

"Let me help you," Bonner says, smoothing out a third that reads, *Chapen.* Close enough.

"Ms...?"

"Darla. Darla Farquarth."

"Ms. Farquarth. Did you see whoever took the little girl?"

"Not the face." She yanks at her chin hair again. "But I waited and he emerged."

"A he?"

"Yes, oh definitely. Strong man since he was carrying the child like a doll. And I didn't see the face except that he wore an eye patch."

"Are you sure?"

"Sure as shootin'."

"And then what?"

"Well, he hoofed away. And I was tired, so tired, on account of my meds. So I rested on a bench. And then it was morning and I came here."

"Thank you, Ms. Farquarth, this is very helpful. I'd like you to make a public statement with this. Would that be all right?"

Ms. Farquarth yanks her chin hair one final time until she pulls it out by the root.

"Sure as shootin'."

13

MARCUS EDMONTON

It's been a bruising night for Marcus. Gable hadn't shown up at the horse stables. Marcus anticipated this, which was why he didn't bring Gracie. But he expected another operative to be sent in Gable's place to go through with the hit. Amongst the whinnying snores, he waited for hours with his gun trained at the night for the sign of any movement. Cagney could be ready to pounce, or the one-two punch of Brando and Astaire, possibly the freelancer Mae West, or an operative from the international office since Gable was running out of henchmen.

By sun-up, Marcus headed back, cursing the fact that he'd have to send another letter since he didn't have Gable's number. Gracie was already asleep upon returning. He was glad to see she drank a little water and ate some of her hamburger. He caught about an hour of sleep before his internal clock reminded him he's only allowed to rest once this is all over.

He turns on the news to find a crazy woman talking

about a little girl from the Chapin School of Girls who was taken by a man with an eye patch.

"That's you," Gracie says, pointing. He didn't know she'd awoken. The girl stealthy, like a spy. "Look what you've done," she says. "And I need to go to the bathroom."

"I left you a bucket."

"Really? A bucket? Are you serious?"

"I'll leave you privacy."

"That's disgusting. You're disgusting."

"I know. I'll pick you up breakfast."

In an alternate life, Gracie could've been his daughter if he never went to Iraq. He would've married Annie after their whirlwind week falling in love and have their own Gracie. He'd still have both his eyes, and more importantly, never taken someone's life. He'd have a normal job, maybe in the logging industry if they stayed in the area around Killenroy. After work, he'd have his buddies he'd drink beer with at the local bar Trigger Happy. Annie raising their daughter, maybe another kid or a whole bunch. She'd go back to teaching little kids because he remembers she said that was what she wanted to do. Little kids with disabilities. Those whose lives she could really affect. And their family would be happy. Not rich. Not changing the world. Just simply content. But isn't that what everyone strives for? Certainly not a life spent hiding amongst the shadows like he's chosen.

He exits the basement apartment that leads to a poorly lit back alley. Realizing he's wearing an eye patch, he removes it out of fear of being spotted. As he places it in his pocket, a gun presses into his back.

"Gable," he says, whipping around but is met by

Cagney punching him in the face. He's dragged back to the door, keys swiped. Cagney flings open the door. Inside Gracie's pissing over the bucket and screams, then loses her balance and topples over, urine spilling all over the floor. Marcus waves away the stars in front of his eyes, coming back to life. Cagney stands over him with his ugly mug, the gun at Marcus's nose.

"I followed you from the stables, you stool pigeon," Cagney says, slapping him across the face. "You never showed with the girl."

"Gable didn't show either."

"He intended to but got in a jam."

"That's bullshit. He has no intention of honoring our deal. I won't let you take back his granddaughter until the Card is finished."

"You dirty yellow-bellied rat. I'm gonna give it to your jaw."

Cagney whaps him with the gun, blood gushing from Marcus's chin.

"Stop it, stop it," Gracie yells.

"Quiet you," Cagney says. "I'm rescuing you."

"No, you're a bad man too."

She's sniffling and holding onto the pissing bucket like it's her wet blanket.

"The Boss man always had an affinity for you, Dean. But I thought you were gutless."

When Marcus looks in this cold man's eyes, all he sees are Annie's. She'd betrayed him, sure, but who connected to the Card hasn't betrayed someone along the way? Burning in his mind is the last kiss she ever blew as she fell to the ground.

"You want me dead, don't ya?" Cagney asks. "For what I did to your sweetheart."

Marcus doesn't respond, not wanting to allow Cagney any power.

"Sure you do." Cagney grins. "But I don't die, see? I've been a bruiser since I was a kid, a trail of bodies in my wake."

He presses the gun between Marcus's eyes.

"I believe I shot your honey through the brain. You can meet the same fate too."

He turns to Gracie. "Sweetie, you might want to close your eyes and ears."

Gracie screeches and chucks the metal bucket at Cagney, coming into contact with his head, covering him in piss. He loses balance and slips to the floor. Marcus is on top of him instantly, fists pummeling, Cagney's face smeared with blood. Cagney raises his gun, gets off a shot that breaks a lamp, the silencer muting the sounds. Marcus opens his jaws wide and bites at Cagney's neck, chewing off a chunk of flesh, spitting it to the side. The wound spouting blood like a sprinkler. Out of instinct, Cagney goes to cover the gaping flesh with his hand holding the gun. Seeing this moment of vulnerability, Marcus knocks the gun out of Cagney's hand. It spins across the room to Gracie. She's trembling as she holds it up.

"Sweetie, don't shoot it," Cagney says, his hand clamped over the spurting wound. He and Marcus sit up as she moves the gun between the two.

"Gracie, hand me the gun," Marcus says, looking like a wolf after a kill with blood around his mouth. "It's dangerous."

She's crying and Marcus steps closer, almost begging her to shoot and end it all. A fantasy of reuniting with Annie and fighting through the flames of Hell together.

"Shoot him, little girl," Cagney cries. "He's a dirty rat. He took you from your family. I'm just trying to get you back."

"You're the bad gangster," Gracie says, her lips blue.

"The what?"

"In the movie. The one I watched with Papa Jay. You're so mean in it, so bad."

"Kid, that's not me."

"But it looks just like you."

"It's a part I play, you see? An act? It's not who I am. Now put down that gun!"

"Then take off your mask," Gracie says.

"He can't," Marcus adds, knowing Cagney got a new kind of surgery that none of the other operatives have done yet. His face completely replaced with James Cagney's. There was no mask to pull off anymore, the two one and the same.

"You work for my grandfather?"

"Yeah, kid, I do. To bring ya home to him."

"Prove to me you're wearing a mask."

Cagney sighs, so loud Marcus can feel it deep in his own chest.

"I can't," Cagney mumbles. "It's who I am."

"And you've chosen to be bad?" Gracie asks, her finger squeezing at the trigger.

"Bad is all relative."

"Gracie don't," Marcus says, and he's crying now too because he doesn't want her to become him. Because firing that gun will mean it's too late to ever return to who she was.

But Cagney envisions his fate. "Ah, you're cut from the Boss, kid," he says. "I can see that—"

His voice interrupted by a bullet blowing a hole in his cheek. His eyes wide in surprise. Marcus runs to Gracie, takes the gun away because she's too shell-shocked to notice. Her mouth in a perpetual O. He hugs her tight. He collects her tears. He removes the chains from her legs and lets her lie down sobbing on the couch. Then he reaches into his pocket for the Desire Card and his eye patch to place over Cagney, while he figures out a way to dispose of the body so not only this dirty gangster gets blamed for Gracie's kidnapping, but the true target in his crosshairs.

14

HELENE

WITHOUT A WINK OF SLEEP, HELENE FACES AN apartment full of police officers assuring her that they are doing everything they can to find Gracie. The news outlets had already run with the story of a homeless woman who identified a man with an eye patch taking a little girl in a Chapin uniform out of Central Park. A manhunt has been issued to find him. She looks for Detective Bonner only to be told that Bonner is currently at Chapin talking to students and teachers. Bonner had asked for a list of everyone Gracie knew so Helene sits at the kitchen countertop and writes down family and friends, neighbors and acquaintances. She's given coffee and thanked.

She had tried to reach Harrison when she woke but it went to voice mail. She calls again and leaves an angry message along with an angrier text. Here his daughter had vanished and he can't bother to pick up the phone. She curses the stupid girl she used to be who decided to marry him. They were never right from the start—upbringings being the most obvious difference. She never liked to say it out loud but Harrison came from white trash, plain and simple. His father was a drunk and his mother medically induced even before the cancer struck. At first, this boy from another world intrigued her. She'd met too many rich Connecticut boys that seemed content with floating from their parents' savings. Conversely, Harrison was certainly a go-getter. He threw himself into his work at Sanford & Co., so much it nearly killed him. And when he needed a liver, he was determined even if it meant sinking his morals. But he also was the kind of person bad things happened to, walking around with a permanent doom cloud. She knows he's not responsible for Gracie's disappearance, but it's easier to target her anger at the situation on him.

She hears the clinking of Peter's Zen bracelets. He sits beside her at the countertop, takes her hand. She doesn't want to hold hands now. She doesn't want to be comforted. She wants to scream until her throat bleeds.

"We'll get through this," Peter says, flipping his wild gray hair away from his eyes. He reaches into his pocket and pulls out a rubber band to tie it up. Something she would've found charming yesterday, but today she hates it so much it causes her teeth to grind.

"Harrison is unreachable."

Peter shrugs his shoulders. So aloof about everything. Peter never had children. At fifty-five, he's lived a selfish life and nothing ever gets him worked up. She finds that pathetic.

"I've called. I've texted. Mean texts. Here his daughter–"

She's ready to go into a rant but doesn't have the

energy. The coffee has somehow made her more drained.

"You said how unreliable he was when you were married."

"This is a crisis. It's common sense not to turn your phone off."

Her phone beeps and she checks it to see a text from a friend, one of a thousand. Once the news story went live, her phone hasn't stopped buzzing.

"Can you deal with this?" she asks, handing him the phone.

"Of course. Do you want me to answer everyone's messages?"

She's about to say she doesn't care, but to keep him occupied she nods instead.

"Where's Brenton?"

"In his room."

"Should I send him to school?"

"It might be best to keep him busy."

"Where's my baby?" she asks, the tears rushing forth. Every time she tries to quell them, she's less successful. A cop comes over and hands her a tissue.

"Ms. Howell," the cop says, an Asian woman with short hair fanning her face. "You need to stay strong. We're gonna get your daughter back."

This had been the slogan of the morning. Everyone in blue reiterating the same cliché. But the statistics weren't helping right now. The majority of missing kids taken by a family member, not a stranger. And while a high percentage percent of those kids return home, of those taken by a stranger, just over fifty percent survive and the rest killed. Surfing the web for these facts had consumed Helene's night.

"She was taken by a stranger," Helene tells the cop. "There's no one I can think of who would do this."

"Sometimes it's an ancillary person in your life," the cop says. "But due to technological advances, ninety-nine percent of children are found."

"And the one percent?"

"Those are good odds, Ms. Howell. We've already issued an Amber alert."

"Oh God."

Helene starts to shake so much she spills her coffee.

"Let me get that," the cop says. "Maybe take a shower. The simple things we do every day can help us cope."

Helene wants to yell, SHOWERING WILL NOT BRING MY DAUGHTER BACK, but she knows she'll sound unhinged.

"I'll get Brenton and bring him to school," Peter says. He goes in for a hug but Helene doesn't return his affections. She hangs there limply and then escapes into the bathroom.

She turns the water on full force to drown out the sounds of people in her home. She strips down and lets herself be slaughtered by the hard spray of water. She doesn't have it in her to use soap, she just wants to stand under the water hitting her in the face. A flood of memories pummel. Gracie at her last ballerina recital. She'd practiced so hard, strived to achieve perfection. Helene readied herself for a disaster, a missed step, a forgotten twirl. She was anticipating consoling her frazzled child, but Gracie excelled. This tiny being she created who once fit in the nook of her arm. Who giggled when Helene would touch her nose. Who could stand on her tippy-toes when she was two without wobbling or falling. Who deserved to dance until she was ninety, not be outlived by her parents.

The memories now shift to a funeral with a small coffin being lowered to the ground. The ache of never being able to see someone again, that's what scared Helene the most. That she would always be the woman whose daughter had been murdered, branded for life. She'd carry around a type of pain no one should ever burden.

A knock at the door. The water had filled up the tub and she splashed out, wrapped a towel around her body.

"Yes?"

"Ms. Howell," a voice says from the other side of the door. Helene recognizes it as the cop. "It's your husband."

"Is he on the phone?"

"I'm afraid not."

The voice prickled with uncertainty.

"What is it?"

She flings open the door, startling the cop.

"He's at Mount Sinai right now. In a coma."

She feels herself falling backwards. Never having fainted before, her body goes light, ethereal. Like she'd taken a fistful of Xanax. The tiles cold and wet under her head. And the police officer hovering above, going in and out of focus, until she's joined by a sea of others: Peter, her son Brenton, more blue uniforms. After not sleeping all night she desires just a moment, a reprieve from reality, so she closes her eyes and gives in to the pull of unconsciousness.

15

GABLE

AFTER NEARLY BEING KILLED BY ALAIN DELON, Gable opted out of meeting James Dean at the horse stables on the west side to rescue his granddaughter. He had every intention of going and using Cagney as a buffer while he assessed the situation. Instead, he lumbered over to Audrey Hepburn's place on Riverside Drive. He didn't want to talk, just sleep, and she never questioned him. She gave him her bed and took the couch.

In the morning, she makes coffee and he wakes to the smell of the beans, his old limbs aching from the fight with Delon.

"You weren't sleeping soundly," she says, handing a steaming cup. "Like you were in a fight."

"I was reliving last night," he says, accepting the coffee. Thick sludge as it spills down his throat, culling him back to life.

"Your bruises." She touches each one: grape-sized on his shoulders, spreading across his neck like a terrible rash. She disappears into the kitchen and returns with an ice pack.

"This was Olivier sending a message," he says.

The ice pack slips from her fingers, creating a wet stain on the bedsheet.

"More than a message," he continues. "Delon was out for blood."

She chews on a fingernail. Her mask doesn't allow worry lines, but he can sense them forming underneath.

"What happened to Delon?"

"Dead. It was him or me."

She gives a soft yelp. Had she formed a relationship with Delon over the years during any international trips? He frowns upon operatives intermingling, but he'd rather them be with each other than anyone outside of the Card.

"Did you know Delon well?" he asks.

"No. How well can any of us know each other under the masks?"

"So, you are not upset?"

"I am processing the news," she says, confident with her answer. "How do you know it was Olivier who called the hit? Maybe Delon went rogue?"

"Because he admitted it." The ice pack becomes too cold to continue to press against his bruises. "Enough of this."

"I don't see why Olivier would do something like that."

"You are naïve, Audrey. I almost respect him for attacking at such an opportune time. I've never been as weakened as I am now."

There had been times over the years when Gable

thought of striking Olivier first. But losing the figurehead of the international arm of the Card would have put a huge dent in their widespread capabilities. Olivier always seemed a nuisance he could eventually extinguish. Never a true power broker with the ability to usurp.

"What is your plan?"

"Nothing less than an all-out war."

"But it could decimate the Card."

"Then we will rebuild. There is a cancer eating away at us that must be dealt with."

She chews at another fingernail.

"You're really gnawing at those nails, Audrey."

"I am scared."

He wraps his arms around her. "Oh, baby. Oh, doll. Fear is good. Fear keeps us primal, engaged. I have become too complacent."

"Which operatives are definitely on your side?"

"Cagney, of course. He was on a separate mission last night. I haven't heard back yet, but I'll pull him off that detail for the time being. Brando and Astaire. Sinatra, Gary Cooper and Mae West, the freelancers."

"I've never worked with them."

"Newer to the Card. But vicious, just as I like 'em. And, you of course."

"You'll let me out of this house?"

He can't see her true eyes, only that of the mask, unsure if there's hopefulness or trepidation flashing in them.

"Would you like that?"

"I've told you, very much so."

"You are ready?"

"I can be if you need me."

"Do you want to hear that I need you? Is that what you desire?"

He cups her chin, caressing her cheek. Their lips meet, tongues dance. She nods in that melancholy way she often does.

"I don't need anyone," he whispers into her ear, making her shiver. "That's how I'll survive at the end of all of this. Because even those I care about are expendable."

He's never voiced this so honestly. Up until now, he hadn't visualized the destruction of his beloved Card. An impossibility, he decides.

"Will you be going to Brussels?" she asks.

"No, Olivier will come to me. On my turf. That's where I will squeeze him."

He clutches the ice pack until it bursts in his hand. Audrey Hepburn gives a shriek and he laughs. The blue dye splattered across her chest.

"Look at you. You're a mess."

"I'm sorry."

She removes her nightgown covered in blue, naked underneath.

"I should check in with Cagney," he says, fiddling with her nipples, his wind-up toy.

"I'll leave you to it." She gets up to leave.

"No," he says, grabbing at her to stay. He strips off his clothes from last night, soiled and stained with drips of blood, until he's naked with her too. His body surprisingly fit for a seventy-year-old, betraying his age. He's strong enough to hold her down while she squirms. Like a cat, she prowls beneath, her rosebud asshole presented. He dives in, hopped-up on pills he chronically takes from Madagascar that can make him hard whenever he requires.

"Tell me you'll kill Olivier," he says, with a fist of her hair in his grip, doing her from behind.

"Yes."

"Don't just agree. I want to hear you say it. Then I'll let you free."

"Olivier is dead," she says. He turns her face so she's looking him in the eye.

He slaps her on the ass. "Again."

"Olivier is dead," she says, with more conviction this time.

"Again! Wake up the neighbors."

"Olivier is dead," she yells, and he comes inside of her, a pittance but still enough to fuck away all the anger he's been storing. He pulls out, a ball of sweat, and nestles into her form.

"From your lips to the devil's ears, baby. And he's listening, cause that's the deal we made, he's always listening to Gable's desires. Cause he and I are attuned, baby. Locked for this life and beyond. Us and the cockroaches at the very end of it all."

His nose at the back of her neck, breathing like a bull, blistering hot.

16

DETECTIVE MONICA BONNER

"Hello?" Bonner says into the phone before she looks at who the caller might be. She'd spent the day at Chapin interviewing all the girls in Gracie's class plus her teachers. She learned Gracie was dubbed a loner (one girl called her stuck-up) with few close friends and no desire to make more. They spoke of how much she loved ballet dancing, all they heard her talk about. The teachers echoed the same sentiment. Gracie did her work on time, participated in class. She was intense, and her teacher said she had the tendency to pluck out her hairs. It usually indicated stress in the household, but the teacher knew of her parents' divorce and her father's illness so she didn't think it too serious.

"Mon?"

Forgetting she'd even answered the phone, Bonner's brain replays the conversations of the day for a hint of a clue.

"Mon? Monica, you there?"

"Yes? Hello? Who is this?"

"It's Jim." Dead silence. "Did you erase my number already?"

Jim had never been good at humor, his jokes always landing flat. She can hear him trying to laugh it off before he goes silent again.

"No. I'm on a case. It's the first I'm leading. Missing girl."

"Oh. Well, that's great, Mon. I mean, horrible for the girl but—"

"It's not a good time."

She pictures him walking around in his boxers through an empty house he's trying to sell. His sandy hair getting whiter at the edges. The same bushy mustache he had from the day they married. A Mariners game on in the background.

"I just...well, Mon, we haven't talked since you left for New York. Wanted to check in."

It always bothered her how he'd say her name over and over in conversation, like she might be confused who he was speaking to.

"I'm..."

She's about to say good, but that would be a lie. She'd never be *good* again, the word erased from her vocabulary. She could maintain. That's what she strives for.

"I'm settling," she finally decides. She gets in her police car to head back to the station, puts him on speaker.

"I didn't mean to bother you, Mon."

Traffic is a nightmare and she can't do anything but creep so she honestly has the time to talk.

"It's fine, Jim. How are you?"

"Oh me? Oh, well, trying to get bids on the house."

"I know. Any luck?"

"They say there's a boom in Seattle, but I'm not seeing it yet. Gonna drop the price."

"Just move it. Even if the price is under."

"I want a small place in San Juan Island. Away from the bustle, ya-know? To fish and just breathe, I guess."

"That sounds nice."

"Here you moved to the bustle and I'm trying to get away from it!"

"Did we ever have anything in common?" Bonner asks, and then she regrets it. "I didn't mean it that way."

"No, Mon, no I don't really think we did. You always wanted to be bigger, brighter. I held you back."

Jim was forever down on himself. It got worse when the minor leagues dropped him, no hopes of ever playing pro. He lost a chunk of himself. And if Bonner really thought about it, he never had that much to begin with.

"You didn't hold me back," she says, even though it's partially a lie.

"No, it's true. You're kind to make me feel better."

"We'll always be friends," she says, because it's something her former therapist suggested she should say to help ease the pain of the separation. Because she'd been done with the marriage before Kellan got sick. There was no chance of leaving someone when you were spending all your time in hospitals. Even though she'd never admit it out loud, Kellan's death allowed her to be free.

"Yes, that's true, Mon. I understand you don't want anything more than a friendship."

"I can't."

"You see his face in mine, don't you?"

Her throat feels gripped by a vice.

"It's not only that—"

"See, I see you in him, but I find that comforting. Cause I'm losing him a little more every day. Memories feel farther and farther. But if we were together..."

"I'm in New York now." She sighs, mostly so he'd get the hint but Jim was never good at picking up signals.

"I guess this is where we differ the most, Mon."

"I guess so."

"I hope you find your missing girl."

"I hope you... I hope you're well. Bye, Jim."

She hangs up before he can keep her on the line any longer. A call is coming in from her radio and this reunion has diverted her focus.

"Bonner?" the radio squawks.

"Yeah, Ramirez?"

"You ain't gonna believe this. Man just washed up in the East River. And get this, he's wearing a fuckin' eye patch!"

———

Blustery by the East River, the wind tousling Bonner's hair despite its short length. Ramirez and cops from the 9th precinct surround a body. She's introduced as the lead officer on the Gracie Stockton case. Slips on gloves and leans over the bloated corpse. The face recognizable, although she can't quite place it.

"Is he wearing a mask?"

"I thought the same thing," Ramirez says. "'Cept it doesn't budge."

"It's James Cagney," a cop behind her says.

"What?"

"The movie star. It's a dead ringer."

The cop pulls out a phone and brings up James Cagney's picture, the two so identical it's as if Cagney washed up himself.

"That's bizarre," Bonner says.

Ramirez holds up a plastic bag holding what looks like a business card.

"We removed this from his pocket," he says.

"That's all he had on him?"

"Yup."

She holds the bag up to the sunlight to read its contents.

THE DESIRE CARD

Any wish fulfilled for the right price.
PRESS below to inquire.

"The Desire Card?" she asks. "What's that?"

Ramirez shrugs. Bonner presses the button through the baggie but only hears a crackling noise from the other end.

"Water must've fried it," Ramirez says. "You think this eye patch guy is a coincidence?"

"It's never just a coincidence."

17

MARCUS EDMONTON

AFTER WRAPPING UP CAGNEY'S BODY IN THE RUG and hauling him down to the East River, nobody looking at him strangely because you really need to go out of your way to attract attention in New York City, Marcus returns to Gracie who hasn't stopped staring at the wall as if she's fixated on a great movie.

"I brought you some ice cream," he says.

One of her shoulders shrugs. It stays tucked up by her ear like she's forgotten how to lower it.

"Here, before it melts."

He places in the cup in her cold hands.

"Go on, it's good."

Dipping the plastic spoon into the vanilla, he brings it to her lips. At first, he doesn't think she's going to respond, forever trapped, but then she opens her mouth enough for him to get the spoon in.

"Can you hold it yourself?"

She nods, her eyes darting from the wall, blaming him for what she did—murder.

She starts feeding herself ravenously. The ice cream

finished in seconds. The cup tossed to the floor. A belch follows.

"You were right that he was a bad man," Marcus says. "I know it must be scary to think about shooting a gun. To take a life. The pain you must be going through. We can talk about it if it'll make you feel better."

Her eyes dart to him again.

"He was a bad man, but he would've brought me home, right?"

He's caught off guard by her question, not expecting her to speak. The voice tired but commanding. More mature than it was a few hours ago, aging years in minutes.

"He worked for your grandfather, but so did I and I don't anymore. I can't say what his motives were. He could have taken you too."

"Like you did?"

"He might've brought you harm. I promise you I won't."

She gives a quiet laugh, looks down at her chained ankles.

"That's not harming you," he says. "I can't trust you won't run."

"See this bruise?" She points to a swollen ankle. "It hurts."

"I mean, Cagney could've *really* wanted to hurt you. Not a bruised ankle. He was capable of the unspeakable."

"Or he could have saved me?"

"Then why did you shoot him and not me?"

Her eyes swim with tears. "I don't know."

"You did the right thing. He's killed many, like your grandfather."

"Like you have as well?"

"Yes. Like me too. But I'm sorry now for what I've done. I'm trying to make up for it. I want your grandfather to shut down his organization. And you can help me. You already have. James Cagney was his number two guy. That seriously cripples the Card."

"Can we watch TV? I'm so bored here."

"Oh, okay. Sure."

Marcus turns on the TV, starts flipping through the channels. Wouldn't you know it, he comes across *Rebel Without a Cause* with his former alter-ego James Dean. It's the chicken-run drag race scene where James Dean jumps out of the car in time while his competitor isn't so lucky and goes careening off a cliff.

Marcus changes the channel to the News. A reporter is commenting on the James Cagney look-a-like washed up in the East River, believed to have kidnapped Gracie Stockton due to the eye patch that a witness described, yet there's no sign of where he was keeping the girl.

"You wanted everyone to think he took me?" Gracie asks.

Marcus lowers the volume. "I need your grandfather linked. Then I'll take you home. It shouldn't be long."

"I should be practicing my ballet."

She stands, elongating her spine. Wincing, she hops on the tips of her toes.

"Wanna see me practice? It's from 'Dance of the Blessed Spirits' from *Orpheus and Eurydice*."

"I don't want you to injure your ankle more."

"I've danced through worse."

With her arms, she makes a circle over her head.

She leans to the left, far enough that he thinks she'll topple over, but she keeps steady. She sweeps one arm across the floor, twirls around. The chains rattle along with her graceful movements creating a soundtrack to the dance. Then she explodes. Leaps and spins, landing with the force of a rocket on just a few toes. Still for a moment and then alive again. Her face reddened and stained with tears. She finishes in a tight ball while hugging her thin body so hard that her fists turn white. Then she stands and gives a dramatic bow.

He doesn't realize but he's crying harder than her. He claps, not having seen an element of beauty like this in so long. His days filtered by killings and blood, indistinguishable. And yet, a flower can emerge.

"This won't end well for you," she says.

Wiping his eyes, he manages a "What?"

"After I've been rescued. Because I will be. Because Papa Jay always gets what he wants. And he will kill you for this."

"Yes. I'm sure that's what he intends."

She scratches her temple. "You might as well give yourself up."

"I will if you're put in danger. I promise you that."

"...Thanks."

"But no matter what, if I die or not, the Card will die too."

"Tell yourself that if it helps. Whatever may help."

She kicks the cup of ice cream towards him.

"Could you get me some more?"

———

Out on the street towards the deli on Avenue C, he can't help but obsess over what Gracie said, this sooth-sayer in the form of the child. For forty years, Gable has weaseled his way out of surviving multiple attacks against him. How could Marcus believe he'd be the one to finally take the bastard down?

Nonsense, he thinks. *She's getting in your head. That's what Gable would do and it's bred in his grand-daughter to be the same. Cagney was a wrench in the plan that wound up being a boon. Even though the news hadn't reported it yet, the Desire Card had been found on Cagney and they were likely looking into what it meant.*

Marcus buys her Ben & Jerrys Cookie Dough Ice Cream because that's what he would've wanted as a kid. When he gets back to the house, the chains are still there but Gracie has gone.

18
GABLE

ONCE HE WITNESSES CAGNEY'S DEMISE ON THE news, Gable whisks Audrey Hepburn in his town car to New Jersey where the Card's base is located. His cell rings, but it's Vivien, and he doesn't have the patience to deal with her so he lets it go to voicemail. The Zeppelin album, *Houses of the Holy* cues up from the beginning with "The Song Remains the Same". *I had a dream, oh yeah, crazy dream uh-huh. Anything I wanted to know. Any place I needed to go.* Audrey weaves to the music, wide-eyed at the world passing by, since she hasn't left her apartment in months. She looks and points and giggles, describing everything along the way.

They reach the Jersey hideout somewhere in the middle of *Physical Graffiti.* During the ride, he called Sinatra, Gary Cooper and Mae West, luckily all around the Tri-state area and *en route* to the secure location. When he arrives at the drafty warehouse, Audrey complains of being cold so he goes into a coat closet and removes a fur on a hanger.

"I don't think she'd wear that," Audrey says.

"Who?"

"Hepburn. Me. I don't think I'd wear that."

"Improvise."

He has a few spare Gable masks in his office and puts one on because none of the operatives headed over have seen his real face, only Audrey. Nearly forgetting, he calls Brando and Astaire and tells them to rush over from the Bronx. They express concern for not being able to reach him for some time. They add that they left numerous messages. He tells them to just get their asses over here pronto.

While he and Audrey wait, she fixes his Gable mask since it looks askew.

"I haven't seen you wear it in a long time." she says. "You always come over to my place as yourself."

Staring at her through the holes in the masks' eyes, he says: "And who is that really?"

She smiles. "Jay Howell."

"Yes. But that's only a name. Who am I? Who are any of us?"

"Too philosophical for me. I'm gonna take a nap."

She lies down on the couch tucked in the corner. Her light snores filling the empty space. He'd do well to rest his eyes but he's aware he won't be able to sleep. He never fully sleeps. So he meditates instead. Dives into the deep recesses of his mind to conjure his next move. Olivier doesn't have too many operatives. Marlene Dietrich, likely his most formidable foe should she be sent to assassinate. Unless there are other operatives working under Olivier that Gable doesn't know about. When he emerges from his meditation, he tries Olivier's number but it goes straight to voicemail. Olivier must have found out that Delon has been killed. He probably expected an immediate response after Delon tried to off Gable. And then had already ordered a private jet to come for a sneak attack.

He could already be here.

"At the door," Gable hears someone say, as he opens his eyes. Audrey yawning. "They are at the door."

"Thank you."

She holds her hands out and he takes them so she can lift him to his feet. He hugs her because he needs a second of intimacy, smells her hair and the lavender shampoo she wears. Kisses her small lips, mask-to-mask. With it on, he cannot completely feel the sensation. Normally he doesn't mind, since he always kisses Audrey with her mask on. But at this moment, he desires her actual lips so he peels her mask off from her neck to her nose and does the same with his own. She's hesitant, not liking him to see her in that way, as he slides his tongue in her mouth. He then rolls the mask down over her chin, smooths it into her neck, and does the same with his own.

————

The posse of Sinatra, Gary Cooper and Mae West wait in the breakroom. Sinatra's blue eyes zeroing in. Cooper with his sheriff's hat like he stepped out of *High Noon*. Mae West giving a vampy pose, cigarette holder between her fingers, platinum blond hair curled in waves.

"To what do we owe this emergency in Jersey?" Mae West asks, and takes a puff.

"Where's the rest of us?" Gary Cooper asks, bowing his hat at Audrey.

"This is all of us," Gable says. "Cagney's been iced."

"By who?" Sinatra asks, making himself a drink at the small bar situated in the back.

"James Dean."

"You're saying Dean is still an issue?" Sinatra asks.

"He's always been an issue," Gable says.

Gary Cooper removes his gun from the holster, spins it around in his hand. "And you want us to take care of him?"

Cooper, while a newer hire, radiated the trustworthiness of the former screen legend. The all-American hero persona, that's why Gable keeps him on retainer.

"He is not the most pressing problem," Gable says. "I'm afraid Olivier has tried to kill me."

"War of the bosses?" Sinatra says, knocking back another drink.

"The two of us have been headed to this impasse."

"So call up the freelancers, right, before we can decide to take sides," Mae West says, brushing up against him.

Gable can tell Audrey doesn't like what she sees.

"Gable is your boss, Mae," Audrey says. "*He's* the one who hired you. You don't answer to Olivier."

There's a fire in Audrey that Gable has never witnessed before. Normally docile, the beast within has surfaced.

"Freelancers usually go where the money is," Sinatra says.

"I'm telling you that's here."

Gable nods to Audrey who goes over to open a safe under a desk. She removes stacks of cash.

"Enough for you all?" Gable asks, as each count their money.

"Looks like this should take care of things on my end," Cooper says.

Sinatra's counting slow.

"And you, Sinatra?"

"What does this job entail?" Sinatra asks.

Sinatra, the oldest freelancer at the Card, hired over a decade ago. The choosiest of all the operatives. The regulars doing whatever Gable asks, the freelancers rarely saying no since the money was always fair. Sinatra taking jobs Gable thought he'd turn down and refusing ones deemed too easy. It was never about the cash like the rest of them, an element of thrill required too.

"Complete elimination of the international office," Gable says, and Audrey's ears perk up. "That's how we'll have to rebuild. And I'll offer this. Whoever is able to destroy Olivier will get a promotion as the figurehead."

"What if that's not something we want?" Mae West asks, between puffs. "Lot of responsibility to lead the international office. I like the gig I got going now."

"What is it you desire then, Mae West?"

"Hmm. Good question, love. What does your girl say?"

"Who me?" Audrey asks.

"Gable's got another girl?" Mae asks. "You able to satisfy the Boss?"

Under his mask, Gable smiles at the two women fighting over him.

"I satisfy him fine."

"I'd guess he needs someone with a bit more meat

on their bones." Mae West runs a finger up Gable's arm. "I'd be afraid to break her in two."

"Ladies," Gable says, wrapping his arms around them both. "Let's focus on the task at hand. Olivier. On a platter."

"So what's the plan, partner?" Cooper asks.

"I can guarantee he's headed to the States to ice me. I also imagine out of desperation he might contact you all."

"Didn't you contact us out of desperation?" Sinatra says, swirling the liquor in his glass.

"You three are some of my best."

"Because all your regulars are dead," Sinatra says.

"Got some truth serum in ya, don't ya?" Gable asks. "You don't want the money, don't take it."

"No, I do. I'm just bustin' balls. Isn't that what Sinatra would do?"

Gable eyes him carefully. "I'll need bodyguards first and foremost."

"We'll take a bullet for you," Cooper says.

"I'm not surprised from you, Cooper," Gable says.

"You can count on me," Mae West adds, rubbing up against him. "That is, if your girl's jealous eyes don't cut me too deep first."

"I'm not jealous," Audrey says.

"Sweetie, I can read it all over that pretend face of yours."

With a huff, Audrey joins Sinatra by the pop-up bar. Pours herself a drink she sucks back.

"And you, Sinatra?" Gable asks.

Sinatra's eyes the color of clear waters, not even wearing contacts. No physical scarring, one of the few like that in Gable's orbit. Wounds internal. Psychologically bruised. Parents who kept him in a cage until he was six-years-old. Then od'd one day right in front of him. Foster care full of sexual abuse shaping him into a war machine. In a shadowed back alley, a pair of blue eyes once tried to pick Gable up, a john that worked the west side who Gable first used for clients with closeted proclivities. Sinatra had no boundaries, but soon showed an even greater talent as a marksmen. Would've been upgraded to operative had he agreed. Gable always figured he remained as freelancer just to piss him off.

"I never did like that prick, Olivier, with his shitty British accent," Sinatra says.

"I think this calls for a toast," Mae West says, swaying over the bar and pouring drinks for them all. "Even you, Audrey," she says, handing her a glass too. "To the true leader of Card, now and forever."

They clink glasses, toss them back. Gable smashes his and the others follow suit, the shattering echoing throughout the chamber. Even when he's down and out, Gable will never lose the ability to regale a pack of soldiers. He'd always have troops fighting under him, following his orders, swearing allegiance, raging against any entity with the nerve to cross him.

He'll devour whoever might be foolish enough to try.

He steps back and observes his wild animals, as a plan begins to formulate, one so devastating that if Olivier had any inklings of what it entailed, he'd flee home to Brussels the first chance he had with his rat tail weaving between his quaking legs.

19

DETECTIVE MONICA BONNER

As Bonner and Ramirez drive to the Howell's apartment to question the family about the dead James Cagney look-a-like without any ID, and the Desire Card in the corpse's pocket, they get word that Gracie's father has been taken to Mount Sinai hospital after it appears he's been mugged and is in a coma.

"This case gets loonier every day," Ramirez says.

At Mount Sinai, Helene sits over Harrison's bed, face emptied into her hands. Harrison's hooked up to more tubes than Bonner can count. The boyfriend Peter holds Helene's hand tightly as if his sole role is comforter. Their son Brenton has been taken out of school, looking like he's been punched in the stomach. His grandmother Vivien places a veiny hand on his shoulder and gives a pat every-so-often.

"What happened?" Bonner asks a nearby doctor.

"Contusion," the doctor says. "Nasty hit to the head. We imagine it was a fall to the concrete. A witness called the police about a noise on her block but didn't see the attackers. She gave a statement to the police already."

"And he's in a coma?"

"Precisely. He may be aware of what's going on around him, he may not. Sometimes they come out of it. Sometimes it can take a while."

"You don't sound certain."

"It's not an exact science. Excuse me," he says, and disappears into the hallway. The nurse tending to Harrison gives her a look that says, *Doctors, what are ya gonna do with them?*

"I need to talk to the family if that's all right?" Bonner asks the nurse.

"Doctor Killog is a pessimist but we're gonna do everything we can to revive your father," she tells Brenton, who wipes his sleeve across his reddening eyes. "Go ahead, Detective, I'll give you some space," she says, and leaves into the hallway too.

"I'm not really up to answering any questions now," Helene says, and then her eyes widen as if she's had a revelation. "Are we cursed?"

"No, ma'am. I've found in life that horrible things tend to stack on top of one another like different sized plates."

Helene's eyes become empty, the pupils small and brown with red veins filling up the iris.

"That's all this past year has been."

"We're only tested with what we can handle," Ramirez says, and Helene murmurs under her breath that she does *not* want a lecture about God.

"How much of the news have you seen?" Bonner asks.

"Not much," Helene says. "This morning was a

whirlwind of police at my home and then I fainted when I found out about Harrison."

"We put some food in her and she's doing better," Peter says.

"I forgot to eat yesterday," Helene says. "My mind isn't working properly."

"So, there's been a break in the case. We haven't found Gracie yet but a woman saw her being carried out of Central Park by a man wearing an eye patch. Then a man with an eye patch washed up in the East River this morning."

"Do you know if it's the same person?" Vivien asks, her slender hand covering her gaping mouth.

"We don't. This man had no ID. But, and this might sound ridiculous... He had the face of James Cagney."

"James Cagney the movie star?" Vivien asks.

"What are you saying?" Helene chimes in.

"We don't know yet. Although it appears as if the man had plastic surgery to resemble James Cagney's face."

"I don't understand what this has to do with Gracie," Helene says.

"We don't either...yet. But it's a lead and because of its unusual aspect it's a good one. A doctor had to do this surgery...somewhere. It can help us discover who this man was and if he has any ties to Gracie."

Helene whispers into Peter's ear.

"Of course," he says, standing. "Milk and sugar?"

"I don't care," Helene says. "Take Brenton please."

"I'm ok, Mom."

"No, honey, this is adult business. Go with Peter. Get a snack."

Peter offers his hand to Brenton, which the boy rejects, but he follows him out of the room.

"Helly, do you want me to...?" Vivien asks.

"No, mom, stay."

Vivien takes Peter's seat. "If this man kidnapped Gracie," Vivien begins, "and he's dead? What does that mean for her?"

Bonner sighs. "We don't know, ma'am. Speculation rarely helps in these instances. We have to work with the facts. Now I have to ask again in light of what happened to your husband. Is there anyone who might want to harm your family?"

"I should've said something before," Helene wails. "In the chaos of it all, I don't know, maybe I was trying to deny it to myself."

"Helly, what is it?"

"Ms. Howell, this is your daughter's life, anything that could be of help–"

"Last year, when Harrison had his health issues related to his liver..." She gulps a deep breath as tears spill. "I...I had *nothing* to do with this. It's part of why we've divorced. He contacted this...organization. They were called the Desire Card."

Bonner and Ramirez exchange *holy shit* looks.

"You've heard of them?" Helene asks.

"Please continue, Ms. Howell."

"They fulfill wishes. They were going to get him a liver from someone. He was in India and was scammed by a former friend."

"Who was this?"

"Nagesh Patel, we went to college together. But he's dead. At least, that's what Harrison said."

"He worked for the Desire Card?"

"No, I don't know. How I took it, Harrison contacted the Card after it didn't work out in India. But there were complications and he owed them money."

"Did he ever describe these people?"

"No. He paid them off. This was well over a year ago. And there's been no issues since. Really, I wasn't trying to keep anything from you. And it's not that I forgot. My mind, I've been taking meds since yesterday..."

"It's all right, Ms. Howell, this is very helpful right now."

"Mom, I didn't tell you either. I was ashamed."

"Darling," Vivien says, drawing Helene closer to her in a light embrace.

"Mrs. Howell," Bonner says, addressing Vivien this time. "Does any of this ring a bell in any way?"

Vivien purses her lips, appearing as if she wants to say more but something holds her back.

"If you know *anything*. This is your granddaughter."

"Not that I..."

"Or your husband, ma'am?" Ramirez adds. "Where is he?"

"Away on business," she says, clinging to a strand of pearls around her neck. "I'm often not apprised of his whereabouts. He's a very important man."

"What does he do?"

"He's a developer. In fact, he recently completed building the tallest casino in Macau. That's a province of China."

"Yes, I've heard of it," Bonner says, already disliking this woman's condescendence.

"Can we reach him?"

"I can give you his number."

"Please."

Vivien taps her phone and shows Bonner and Ramirez who put it in their cells.

"Anything else?" Ramirez asks.

Helene shakes her head. "I can't believe I didn't mention. I...you have to believe I'd do anything to get my daughter back."

"We know, ma'am," Bonner says, patting the woman's hand that's soaked in sweat. "Do not beat yourself up."

"If my stupidity hurt the investigation..."

Ramirez catches Bonner's eyes as a sign to leave.

"You'll also be in touch if you think of anything?" she asks Vivien.

"Yes, yes, I promise," Vivien says, but she won't look at either of them. The lady full of secrets.

"We'll keep you posted on anything from our end too," Ramirez says.

In the hallway, Ramirez squeezes Bonner's arm. "I don't trust the grandmother."

"Neither do I," Bonner says. "She knows something."

"And Ms. Howell? What do you think of her?"

"I believe her. When she told us about the Desire Card, it was like it had dawned on her. It felt real."

"This Desire Card definitely put the father in a coma."

"One hundred percent. But why him?"

"They have the girl. They have to. There are too many linking pieces."

"I don't think it's as cut and dry as we think," Bonner says. "An organization like that. We don't know how widespread they are. The ties they have. Those they've wronged. Ms. Howell said the husband paid back what he owed. What more could they want?"

"It might be like the mob," Ramirez says, raising one suspicious eyebrow. "Once you're in, you're fucked."

————

In the car back to the precinct, Ramirez drives while Bonner reads the papers covering the story of dead James Cagney.

"Any tidbits from the press?" Ramirez asks.

"Worthless," Bonner says. She has a sip of coffee, welcoming the burn. Clumsy as usual, she spills some on the front page of the *Daily News*. She uses the later pages to mop up the coffee when she sees an article about a dead man found in Greenwich, Connecticut on the side of the road, no ID on him just like Cagney, dressed in a retro suit and fedora like he'd stepped out of the 1960s.

"Ramirez, look at this."

Ramirez glances over as the car weaves to another lane.

"No, pull over!"

Finding a spot, Bonner shows him the article.

"No shit."

"Do you recognize the face in the picture?"

"Nope."

"An old movie star?"

"That's not my wheelhouse."

"My mom would know. She got me into them after my dad left. Like these old movie idols could be my pseudo-father."

Bonner pulls out her phone and brings up the *News* story. Forwarding it to her mom, she types:

Hey mom,

I owe you a phone call, but really quick—I'm involved in a case and this dead man in Connecticut might be connected. Does he resemble anyone to you? Like an old movie star? I say this because another man possibly involved with case had surgery to look like James Cagney. Call me if the face rings a bell.

Love, Monica

She hits send.

"There's no way to even predict what's gonna happen next," Bonner says.

Ramirez puts the car in drive. "Nope. This shit has gotten me hooked. My question is, who's gonna play me in the TV movie?"

20

HARRISON

On a beach Harrison has been to before: sand in toes, caress of waves, *merengue* music from a tent nearby. *This isn't real*, he tells himself. *But it's not a dream either.* There's an absurdity to dreams as an adult that keeps them removed from reality. This, however, blurs the lines. He's not in the world as we think of it but some alternate version only the subconscious can conjure, as if the mind had access to a possible future and wanted to sway the body in that direction.

She ascends from the tent as he remembers her. They'd only met a few times but it had such a lasting impact. Her large mouth crammed with teeth, crinkly hair sweating in the sun, coconut oil rubbed into elbows and knees, those silver star decals glinting on her fingernails.

"Naelle," he says. In this world, he cannot control the outcome. She holds the power as she should.

She walks with a Corona and a lime wedge. Placing the lime down the bottle's shaft and creating a suction with her thumb while the beer bubbles. Shading her eyes from the eternal sun, she takes a cool sip and he's thirsty for it, for her, for youth, for consciousness: all essentials that seem so far away.

Catching a glimpse of him by the shore, she makes her way over. Her body wrapped in a colorful sarong that he realizes is the Dominican Republic flag.

"Hey you," she says, sitting down. Her lips painted ruby red, plump and kissable. He recalls their time in the London Hotel before his body collapsed. How she tasted like hope.

"I'm sorry for leaving you on the beach when we last saw each other," he says, because it pained him to do so. But he had no choice. "I didn't want to put you in danger."

"In any *more* danger," she corrects him.

"Yes, I'm aware it's because of me that you almost had your liver removed."

It sounded ludicrous to hear out loud. He couldn't help but laugh. She does as well and that breaks the ice a little.

"How have you been?" he asks.

"With that?" She traces a silver star fingernail over the scar. "Oh, I'm fine. And you?"

"The liver transplant was successful."

"Yes," she says. "I can tell. But...?"

"Everything else about my life is falling apart again."

She swigs some more Corona. "That seems to be common with you."

"Yes, bad luck seems to follow."

"Your daughter?"

"She's been taken."

"By the Desire Card?"

"Someone in their orbit."

She shields her eyes from the sun again. It blazes on fire, the sand hotter under his feet than before.

"We're all in their orbit," she says. "Who runs the world? Greed. We're all responsible for the Card's growth."

He's crying now. Big fat globs of tears. "I've been so guilty."

"As are those men who put you in this coma," she says, resting the bottle against her forehead.

"Coma?"

"Sweetie, you know that's where you are. This is a hallucination."

His Adam's apple feels heavy in his throat. "You are?"

"This version of me."

"Then why are you here?"

She swats at a mosquito, wipes it bloody off her shoulder. "They are about to come out and feed."

"But if this isn't real?"

"I didn't say that. Hallucinations are real. They are happening."

"Will I wake?"

"That's what we're aiming for."

"We?"

"The universe." She smiles, upending his melancholy. All he needs is that smile to sustain. "Do you want your daughter back?"

"Of course."

"Then you need to tell the police who's responsible."

"The Desire Card?"

The words like a knife cutting into his tongue.

"*Gable?*" he continues.

She shakes his head. "Not Gable. Jay Howell. Strip away who he wants people to perceive him as. Show his true face."

The waves kick up a mask by his feet—Gable with his eyes hollowed out.

"That's all he is," Naelle says, shooing it away. "A mask."

"But he didn't take Gracie."

"No." She purses her lips. "But he's the key to getting her back. Whoever has her only wants revenge. Think of them more as an ally than a foe."

"But I'm stuck in this coma?"

She picks up a flat rock, flicks her wrist and watches it skip. "That can be a hallucination too."

"What do you mean?"

"Will yourself to wake up."

"It's as simple as that?"

"No, it's near impossible. But the impossible has been defeated by many. I was cut open on a table, hands reaching for my liver, leaving me for dead. And yet that didn't become my reality."

"Why?"

She throws up her hands. "Who knows the answer? It wasn't my time."

"What about me?"

"I can only give you the tools to work with. I can't revive you or nothin'."

"I think about you," he says, inching closer. "A lot. When my days are empty. You give me the power to push forward."

She takes his hand, entwining her fingers. "Sweetie,

that's why I'm here now. You want to kiss me, don't you?"

"More than anything."

"All right. Because you've come so far."

She kisses him, tasting of sand, and lipstick, and warm breath. It lasts seconds but seems limitless. She stops only because the mosquitoes start to feed.

"Ow," he says, slapping a few on the back of his neck.

"They have come to keep you frozen," she says, standing and waving her arms to direct them away.

A large bug stings his leg, drawing blood. "Damnit."

"Go in the water," she says.

Covered in mosquitoes, he fights his way toward the waves. The mosquitoes tug at him to remain ashore but his flings his body into the ocean, relishing its cooling embrace. He dunks his head under and when he comes up to surface, she is gone.

"Naelle? *Naelle*?"

There's no tent, no *merengue* music. Even the beach has vanished. He wades in darkness, a far-off spot of the universe. For a moment, it's as if he's been blinded, just a surrounding black void. And then, a star. It twinkles deliciously, forming into a silver star on the back of a giant fingernail. The finger beckons so he follows, swimming through the thick darkness until it can scoop him up and bring him closer to home.

He hasn't arrived yet, but he's getting there, getting there.

21

GRACIE

GRACIE DANCED TO LOOSEN HER CHAINS. WHILE the man with the one eye watched, she dragged the chains against the floor until they had worn down. Once he left the basement apartment to get her ice cream, she was able to able to wedge one foot out since she's so thin. For the other foot, she had to pull and pull but eventually she won the fight. Filled with adrenaline, she dashed for the door, flung it open, and was hit by a cool breeze. The apartment led to a back alleyway, a place her mom would've warned her to *never* go down but now she had no choice. Shivering and in socks, she tried to avoid stepping on anything harmful. A rat rattling in a garbage can made her scream. She wanted to run but her legs soon gave way from being inactive for days. So she hid behind the garbage can and waited until the man with one eye returned.

————

Gone no longer than five minutes, the man with one eye turns down the alleyway with a brown baggie in hand full of her ice cream. Free from captivity, Gracie's able to study him without being afraid. His one eye has closed over, looking like a scar she had from when she took cupcakes out of the oven and burned her wrist. The wound puffed up releasing puss, the skin soft like the underside of their cat Chauncey when he was a kitten. The man's other eye beamed ice blue. She'd never seen such a blue eye before and it gave him an alien quality. Broad shoulders and muscles that her fat daddy never had. This has been the longest she's ever been away from her parents. She's gotten used to being gone from one at a time since the divorce, and doesn't miss them so much that she wants to break down in tears. She certainly doesn't miss her brother yet, but if she had to say what upset her the most, it would have to be not going to ballet class. This realization stings: ballet more important than her family. But honestly, that's how it's always been. The amount of time she put into dancing far outweighs any spent with her family. This stings a little, like a mosquito bite, but she's impressed with what she's been able to accomplish without them.

The gun.

The memory had been lodged in the back of her brain, returning with vengeance. Not only had she never shot a gun before, she's certainly never shot *some-one*. She can barely recall what happened afterwards. A numbness took over her body as the man with one eye rolled the dead guy up in the carpet and left the apartment. She went through the "Dance of the Blessed

Spirits" over and over as a way to cope. When he returned, she was in the middle of a phantom cabriole.

The dead man that had burst into the apartment said he worked for Papa Jay, but so did the man with one eye. It hurt her head to think about who she should believe. But the dead man looked so much like a villain from the movie she used to watch with Papa Jay, so she had no choice but to fire at him. It would've been harder to turn the gun on the man with one eye because as much as she hated him for what he did to her she was also starting to like him too.

Now he comes back out of the apartment frantic, her name on his lips. He's creeping down the alleyway, his ear trained for any sound. She goes entirely still. In ballet, perfect concentration is required and she's better at this than all the other girls in her class. She can dive into the recesses of her mind and escape to somewhere else. Finally, the man with one eye pivots and leaves the alleyway.

She punches her legs to wake up and physically has to hold one at a time to get them to move. The steps are slow but at least she's in transit. She spins out of the alleyway onto the avenue. The sun is high so it must be early afternoon, she learned that in science class. There's very few people on the street and she wonders where she is until she looks up and sees the sign that says Avenue D. She's never heard of Avenue D before but knows that alphabet city exists downtown so if she can head west she can get to 1st Avenue.

She passes by a bum on the street and goes to speak.

"I've been..."

"Give me a dollar."

"Taken," she whispers. She wants to scream but her voice stays trapped. She doesn't have any money and shows him there's nothing in her pockets. He blows a raspberry and she hates the downtown where the bums are mean unlike the nice ones by her home uptown that sing songs for money even though most aren't really good singers.

She sees a deli up ahead and physically moves her legs to tell the owner what's happened, but down the block she spies the man with one eye. His ice blue eye zeroes in on her and he picks up speed. She's afraid her legs won't work to run away, but somehow, they overcome their paralysis and she darts farther from the deli. To her left runs the FDR a few blocks away with cars zooming past. Up ahead, cars are going through a green light so she zips across the intersection towards the FDR. A car almost hits her and she yelps but it's more of a tired yelp rather than out of fear. She just wants to go to sleep but knows she cannot. A bike flies past and she makes it to the other side of the street where she disappears into a courtyard of similar red brick buildings.

An old lady is pushing a shopping cart that's keeping her upright. She runs to the old lady. "Help, help, help," she pleads, but she can't catch her breath, and the old lady looks confused and brushes her aside.

"I'm being chased..."

She can hear him enter the courtyard between the red brick buildings, his feet heavy against the pavement.

"Him!" she says, pointing but the old lady doesn't care and mumbles something about her dog and shuffles along. Someone else is sleeping on a bench covered in a tarp. She runs past them feeling the man with one eye close behind, her little legs carrying her as far as they can. The man with one eye reaches out, twisting the back of her shirt in his fist. She yanks away and he loses his grip.

"Fuck," she hears him saying without swiveling around.

The zooming cars along the highway are closer now. She can smell the exhaust. Their horns clouding the air. She waves her arms in a dramatic fashion but none of them stop since they're going too fast. And then, he grabs her from behind. She fights back as much as she can, kicking and clawing, her fingernails cutting through flesh. He winces but gets a good hold, lifting her up and squeezing, marching her from the highway and the cars that don't care to stop.

Soon they reach the streets. Nothing left in her to yell anymore, her voice shattered. There was an excitement when she was running from him, as if it were a game, but it's not a game anymore. She'll return to her chamber and he'll find a new way to lock in her chains. There will be no other chance to ever flee.

"I'm sorry," he tells her over and over and she knows that he means this and has been put in a situation he does not like. She understands it's because of her grandfather who did terrible things and now she's paying for his mistakes. She wants to say to the man with one eye that it's okay because other than chaining her to the floor and the few cuts she got on her face when he first pulled her into the bush in Central Park he hasn't hurt her. She knows he does not intend to hurt her and this gives her the power.

When they get back to the apartment, he holds her

down on the couch and takes out a cord to tie up her feet.

"I don't want to do this," he says.

She growls in response because she imagines that's what she should do.

"I promise you you'll go home soon if you're patient. We can watch TV, eat ice cream, whatever it is you want to do. But you can't try to run again. Because then this will all be for nothing."

He finishes tying the cords so her ankles touch.

"Your ice cream has melted some but is still okay to eat."

She debates telling him to go fuck himself but her body needs nourishment so she nods. He removes the ice cream from the baggie and gives her a spoon.

"Chocolate chocolate chip okay?"

She gives a tiny shrug. "I guess."

"Are you hurt?"

"No."

"I don't want to hurt you."

"I know!"

"Please don't run away again."

"Fine!"

"Do you want to watch TV?"

"No."

"Let's find something good."

He turns it on and flips through the channels landing on a cartoon she used to watch that she's too old for now but it calms her to see because she was once small and had no worries about men with one eye, and grandfathers who may have done bad things, and other men she killed. A million lives have passed since then and she can never return so she watches this baby's show through hardened eyes.

She glances back up at the man with one eye.

If she's killed before, she certainly can do it again.

She continues eating her ice cream, the chocolate cool as it slides down her throat.

22

BRENTON

BRENTON HATES HOSPITALS. LAST YEAR WHEN HIS dad had a liver transplant, he spent three weeks at one. Everyone old and sick. Nurses telling him his dad was gonna be okay, but he heard doctors saying there was a chance a body can reject a new liver. And now his dad back here with an even worse problem. Mom's been a mess since Gracie went missing. He tries to be there for her, but it's like she's a different person. Usually he can make a joke and get her to smile. Nothing seems to be working.

"I'm going to take this back to your mom," Peter says, indicating the coffee. He hands Brenton two dollar bills. "Get whatever you want from the vending machine. Give your mom a sec after talking to the police."

Brenton accepts the money without saying thank you. While he doesn't dislike Peter, the guy's hero act gets annoying. Swooping in and saving his mom like Brenton couldn't be there for her. Peter always asking how she was doing and wanting he and Gracie to talk about their feelings too and blah, blah, blah. He wished Peter would get his own family.

Decides on Cheez-Its because they're his favorite. Any crappy day made better with Cheez-Its. Getting two bags, he rips one open and licks the salt off each cracker before biting in like he used to do as a child. The sogginess of the chalky cheese being the ultimate goal. In the waiting area, people are crying. A family nearby must have gotten bad news. He cried yesterday for Gracie, but doesn't have any tears in him at the moment. It's as if all the water has been drained from his ducts.

His grandmother, who dubbed herself Gran Vi, steps into the waiting area. She spies him and her eyes go judgy at the wet stack of orange crackers in his hand. She basically has only a few expressions: judgy eyes, frowns, and a slight look of surprise. He's seen her smile maybe twice.

"I needed a break," she says, fiddling with her diamond earring. Always sparkling.

"Is mom okay?"

"She's dealing with a lot."

Her hand on his shoulder is enough contact. She smells of too much perfume. Why do old ladies always have to douse themselves? Wanting to ask, his mouth starts to move but his brain says *nope*.

Gran Vi directs him over to a couch. He places his stack of Cheez-Its on a side table and wipes off the nuclear orange crumbs.

"James Cagney was an actor, right?" Brenton asks, because it's been bothering him since the detective mentioned the dead man with the eye patch had the same face.

"Yes, well, before your time. In fact, before mine too. I was a child when he was a star."

"I know. From black and white movies. Like Papa Jay and I watched."

"Oh yes, Jay used to do that with you and Gracie. I don't understand the appeal of films. Sitting there trying to be invested while some made-up *story* plays out. Waste of time. When I was young, we listened to the radio. Daddy had a television but I preferred the radio since I had to do the work and listen rather than just stare gobsmacked."

No one asked you, Brenton wanted to say. Usually with Gran Vi, he nodded and let her continue her spiel.

"I was born at the end of World War II and people didn't have time for trifles. My father was a bond salesman so it was it good time for all that, but even as a child, it was books and radio. I never really even saw a film until I met your grandfather. He'd take me to all these old movies and I went along because that's what you did as a girl back then. So I feigned interest and when I got pregnant with your mother, well, that was it for films. I was far too busy tending to her and then your uncle Chip to deal with *stories*."

"*White Heat*," Brenton says.

"What's that?"

"The James Cagney movie I'd watch with Papa Jay. We saw it more than once. He told us it was one of his favorites. It's about a criminal who's the leader of a gang. The scene at the end when the cops shoot him up and the gas tank explodes is pretty cool."

Gran Vi makes a terrible face.

"I can't believe he showed you that. How old were you?"

"I dunno like ten, Gracie probably five."

"You know your Papa Jay, he does as he pleases."

"And Papa Jay would wanna watch the end scene over and over. Like, he'd rewind it and watch it again. I wonder what he would think about a man with that actor's face washing up in the East River?"

"The fact that you know of any of these sordid details. Your mother really needs to put a leash on your internet activity."

"Really, Gran Vi? The cop said it all."

"Oh right, you're right."

"Are you okay, Gran Vi?"

Her face had gone white. She had a very pale complexion to begin with always declaring that "sun was her enemy." She wore big hats and sunglasses that often hid her from any rays, but now it seemed like she'd eaten something bad and is about to barf.

"Gran Vi?"

"I thought of something," she says, as if she's entered another world. "Your... Papa Jay... At the Faceless Children's Gala. He wore a Gable mask."

"Who?"

"Clark Gable."

She jerks her head, tiny eyes boring into Brenton, lips pursed so much it seems painful. Shaking her fist, she wobbles to her feet.

"I just need... My blood sugar."

Brenton offers her Cheez-Its and it looks like she's about to slap the bag out of his hands and then slap him too, but she hoards the Cheez-Its in her armpit and nibbles on a cracker like a squirrel.

"I'm headed back to Dad," Brenton says, ready to be away from her.

Gran Vi doesn't respond, munching and staring out the window with a slightly surprised look on her still ghost-white face.

23

AUDREY HEPBURN

AFTER BRANDO AND ASTAIRE ARRIVE AT THE headquarters in New Jersey, Gable goes over his plan for Olivier—iced without hesitation. Sparing Olivier means falling into a trap. Olivier will try to talk his way out of it, offer the world, but every operative must remain fixated on the mission to kill. All the man's haunts need to be staked out. The Core Club with his Blackstone Group Associates, Metropolitan Club if he wants to be formal, Soho House if he desires to be seen, so that's probably out, Union Club if he's looking for a men's only night since women aren't allowed, the Century Association if he's in the mood to hobnob with creative types. He'll be at these places since he'll need to make the most of his stateside trip and shore up new clients while attempting to overthrow Gable.

"I want him tortured," Gable says. "But a shot between the eyes will also do in a pinch."

His operatives all agree.

"Do we have to stay here?" Audrey asks. "It's so drafty."

"This is the worst place for me to be," Gable says. "He'll surely come here. I want him surprised."

She convinces him to go back to her apartment in the sky. A bodyguard needs to be brought along. Sinatra and Gary Cooper duke it out over who will "watch the Boss," since there's a bonus for whoever gets tasked with the job. Sinatra wins out and drives them in a SUV back to the city.

At Audrey's apartment, Sinatra stands guard at the front door in the shared hallway. Once the door closes, Audrey has him all to herself.

While he washes up in the bathroom, she places a call through the tiny receiver in one of her earrings. She doesn't need to say anything. The call is enough.

He steps out through the steam as Jay, the mask deflating on the sink. A towel wrapped around his waist. Another slung over his shoulder. He smells of musk, some cologne from a far-off place that costs as much as a person's rent. There's a sexiness to him she can't deny. A masculine quality that most younger men no longer have. He comes from long-gone era and she's equally disgusted and titillated.

"Come here," he says, arms wrapped around her. Only two men have touched her since the accident— Gable and... *If Gable only knew who else he'd snap her neck*. The deceptive thought more titilating than anything else.

"How did it feel to be outside?" he asks.

It has been a while, but the world seems to have stayed the same, moving on without her. The last time she left had not been with Gable. She'd been whisked away in the middle of night so Gable would never find out. She was taken to the top of Belvedere Castle where a picnic awaited. All of her favorite foods. It was summer and hot out and they were able to strip nude. He was being funny and put a row of caviar along his penis for her to lick off. He did things like that. They made love, and while drunk off Champagne which made her loopy, she told the moon she wanted his child. But then when she skipped her period and learned she was pregnant she got scared. Somehow Gable would know it wasn't his child. And he'd ice her for her deceit. She told the father who agreed that Gable could never know and had it taken care of: a doctor sent to her apartment to carry out the abortion. She wept for this perfect baby she never got to meet. She hasn't seen the father since, too afraid she'd wind up pregnant again.

Things shifted between she and Gable afterwards. She knew it was just nerves, but she couldn't get over lying to him. At night, in bed, it was as if he could smell her treachery. The nightmares she had of him trying to ice her in various ways. They bled into reality until it started to seem like she was losing her mind.

And then out of the blue, a pair of earrings delivered to her door. Assuming they were from Gable, she put them on wondering if this meant the two of them were in a better place, or if he was buttering her up before he stabbed.

She heard a buzzing sound coming from one of the earrings. Clasping it between her index finger and thumb, she squeezed.

"Audrey," she heard, and the tears welled. His voice of silk. The European accent. "This way he'll never know," he says.

"I miss you." She sounded like a foolish teenage girl

but she didn't care. She missed him deep in her loins, the tantric ways he could make love for hours. The one time he showed her his true face.

She thought it might ruin the desire she had for this matinee idol. His real face a poor substitution for the mask. But there were no scars or burns like most of them accrued. He had the face of a movie star: prominent chin, bedroom eyes, a nose that announced his presence, everything perfectly symmetrical. He didn't need a mask and yet he chose one, this beautiful human. The night they made love atop Belvedere Castle, he asked to remove her mask too. She had done it before with Gable. And while Gable wasn't grossed out by her scars, he viewed them as something he was able to hide. But that night, she was looked at in a way she hadn't been since before the accident. Not as Audrey Hepburn. Not a façade. Just a girl who grew up on a farm, and milked the cows, and fed the horses hay, and collected the chicken's eggs, and counted the stars at night since there was nothing else to do. She hadn't flown headfirst through a dashboard window yet. She hadn't learned how cruel people were, and that even worse, she could be the cruelest of them all.

The first time she killed for Gable was the first time she came alive. The mark, a candidate running against a senator trying to be reelected. The senator paid a handsome sum to ice the competition and Gable thought Audrey ready. She'd lost all her drive when her face was chewed up by the broken glass, but with the mask on she felt invincible. She picked the candidate up at a swanky bar even though he was married. It was late enough at night that all his lackeys had scattered. In his hotel room, he was a drunk and sloppy lover, trying to make her do things she didn't want. This made it easier to put a pillow over his face and not let up.

When she finished, Gable came down from Connecticut to celebrate. He popped a bottle of Crystal and poured it over the two of them in a hotel bathtub. He licked up every bubble from their skin. Once they toweled off, he told her the head of the international office was in town. A man named Olivier, after the great actor Laurence Olivier. They would have drinks in the lounge.

He dressed her in clothes Audrey Hepburn would wear. Each of them with their masks. Olivier was smoking a cigarette in a booth. Her knees knocked together as she and Gable slid across from him. Olivier took her hand and left a kiss and she almost orgasmed right there because Gable hadn't gotten her off even though she told him she did.

"Tonight was your first?" Olivier asked.

She tucked a strand of hair behind her ear. "Yes."

"Big accomplishment."

"It was a huge windfall," Gable added, flipping the hair she tucked back in front of her face. "Client is prominent. One of our biggest payouts yet."

"Were you scared?" Olivier asked.

She laughed her Audrey Hepburn laugh. "No, I was ready."

After that, she requested any international missions that would put her near Olivier's orbit. She told Gable she wanted to see the world. This was long before she almost got killed and he was scared to let her out of his cage. The stateside and international office worked closer those days. Whatever bad blood that existed between the bosses had been smoothed over for the sake of the company. She never questioned what caused the rift and Gable had no inkling of her affair with Olivier. In Europe, they were free to walk the streets hand-in-hand without worry Gable might see. They took his private yacht to Capri and booked the Bellevue Suite at the Tiberio Palace Hotel, they gambled at the famous Casino of Monte Carlo, vacationed with celebrities and royalty in Sveti Stefan, left footprints along the Page de Pampelonne. Once he told her he could leave the Card and escape with her to whatever tiny nook she desired; but she knew it was futile. Like Gable, his quest for greed trumped all else. He would not be fulfilled if he left it behind.

And then, a mark almost killed her, and Gable got nervous. Ending her international travels and keeping her locked in the apartment in the sky. She had the brief encounter when Olivier took her atop Belvedere Castle, but after the pregnancy scare, had not seen him since.

At least, the earrings kept them in contact. Without it, she would've torn out her hair.

Now as Gable drapes over her in bed, the earring gives a silent buzz with Olivier on the other line. She doesn't know if he's still in Brussels or has made it to New York. It's best for her not to know. Gable removes his towel flopping naked over her, hard as stone from those pills he takes. She's knows she'll be in for a long night. Waiting to ice him until he's inside of her while Olivier whispers *Cherie,* and her whole body buzzes. There is no time like the present. And tucked inside her pillow case is a Lakeside Browning 1919 gun, a rare commodity that shoots .22lr. Gable slides her panties down, fingers her a little and then presses himself inside, his eyeballs receding to the top of his skull. She bucks along, easing the gun between them, the cock echoing as his own cock finally goes limp.

A tear spills from her eye.

"Audrey?"

"Get out of me," she says.

He worms out of her, still lying on top with the butt of the gun pressed into his chest.

"Olivier?" he asks, as if he's not surprised.

She nods.

"Since when?"

"Since always really."

She wants to say she's in love, like she never was with him. She was thankful for her rehabilitation but she never lost herself with Gable, or even Jay Howell. Both nothing more than her Boss.

"I'm sorry."

"*Don't.*"

He's gritting his teeth in that scary way he does. She knows his mind is spinning for any possible ways out of this. If she doesn't fire now, she should already expect to be iced.

"What did he promise you?" he asks.

"It's not about that. It's not always about what someone can do for you. Life doesn't always equal desires that can be fulfilled."

She's getting angry because it's easier than admitting she actually cares, which she does, not in the way she feels for Olivier, but for the father-figure she's about to destroy.

"That's where you're wrong, Audrey. You desired him and he seduced you."

"It's not like that!"

"Olivier set you up from the start. Every move of his calculated."

"You don't know, Jay."

His eyes cut into her through the mask and she goes cold.

"Don't speak my actual name. Don't you *ever* speak my name again."

"You don't know what we have," she says, melancholy. "It's love."

Gable laughs. "You are a fool."

"I have been. Locked inside here for years."

"Oh, how we bite the hand that feeds us."

"Fuck you." She's crying now, snot swinging from her nostrils.

"Is Olivier listening? Watching?"

Silence eats the air between them. Gable tilts his ear toward a buzzing sound, traveling up her body to an earring the size of a ladybug that slightly vibrates.

"My spidey senses," he says, pinching the communication device between his forefinger and thumb.

"Please, Gable, make this easy and let me fire."

In the time it takes her to say this, he manages to get hold of her gun. She'd been paying attention to the earring and let her focus lapse. He directs her off the bed with the tiny gun, pointing it at her heart.

"Foolish child."

The snot streams all over her mouth and she's bawling.

"Stop it. Get hold of yourself."

"Don't... ice me."

"It's inevitable, Audrey. How can I let you live after this? I'll always have to watch my back."

He stands naked before her. Caresses her wet cheek.

"Is he hearing this right now?" Gable asks, and she nods. "I want to know who else is working for him. Another mole like yourself?"

"I...I—"

He fires a bullet that lodges in her shoulder. She lets out a scream that's silenced by Gable clamping his hand over her mouth.

"Tell me and I'll make this as painless as possible, Audrey."

The earring crackles, which only makes Gable's grin go wider.

"Okay," she says. "Okay, there is a mole. But I don't know who. Olivier thought it would be better if I didn't know."

He studies her masked face.

"I believe you," he says, and she lets out a deep sigh. "But I'm still going to kill you."

He sticks the gun inside of her mouth and she starts to choke.

"I loved you, Audrey. In my own way, I did and I think you know that. Because it isn't easy for me. You were my calm during the storms. And I thank you for that. But this is where we part ways."

He fires, the bullet shooting out of the back of her head. A face barely recognizable as a face anymore. He removes her ear that has fallen off, places his lips to the earring.

"Did you hear that you son-of-a-motherfuckin' bitch? Her brains are dangling from my fingers. Did you love her like I did? Because you caused this. That's the horror you'll have to live with. Until I ice the fuck out of you too."

He crushes the earring in his fist until it crackles no more.

24

DETECTIVE MONICA BONNER

SURFING THE WEB FOR ANY KIND OF INFO ON THE Desire Card but only an erotic card game comes up in the searches. An organization like this would certainly not advertise. Its slogan bats around in Detective Bonner's head: *Any wish fulfilled for the right price.* She imagines CEOs and celebrities, high government officials, billionaires requesting their services. Someone out there knows something.

Bonner's cell rings with her mother on the other line.

"Monica? Is this a good time?"

Her mother always hesitant, overly polite, never wanting to interfere. Part of the reason Bonner's dad left, at least that's what she assumes. Her mother never stuck up for herself so Bonner swore to live her life in the opposite way.

"Yeah, Mom, did you get my email?"

She's aware of how tired her voice sounds. Maybe three hours of sleep at most over the past forty-eight hours. Rotating rounds of coffee and Red Bulls. Stomach in knots.

"Yes, I did. But you don't sound so good."

"It's the case—wearing on me."

"You'll be no good to anyone if you don't stay healthy," her mother says in her chipper tone, which only masks her utter sadness.

"I know. I'm running entirely on caffeine. How are you?"

"Oh me? Oh, well, fine, dear. My back has been acting up. You know how it is? Hills and valleys."

"Did you get that mattress the doctor recommended?"

"Oh, too expensive. I'll make do."

She wants to tell her mother: *What else do you have to spend your money on*? But that will start an argument. The case more important than any petty squabbles.

"Did the dead man in the article remind you of any old actors?" Bonner asks, getting to the point like she would during any interrogation.

"It took me a sec, but it did!"

This wakes up Bonner. She grabs a pen and pad.

"There's a French actor Alain Delon. Still alive I believe, probably in his eighties. Very handsome. I mean, I always thought so. Probably most famous, well, at least in the States, for *Purple Noon*, or *The Swimming Pool*, that's a very erotic thriller. *Is Paris Burning?*"

"Is that a question?"

"No, it's a film."

Bonner doesn't recall any of the titles.

"But when I saw the fedora he wore, it made me

think of my favorite of his—*Le Samourai*, about a lonely assassin who's recognized and needs an alibi."

"The Samurai?" Bonner asks, plugging it in to Google and seeing the character come up on the monitor looking exactly like the dead man found in the newspaper. "Holy fuck."

"Really, Monica?" her mom says.

"Mom, this is the second dead man found recently that resembles an old movie star."

"Do you know who these men actually are?"

"No match yet. But forensics are working on it."

She avoids telling her that the fingerprints on James Cagney had been seared off, no word on the other guy, but she doesn't want to freak out her mom too much.

"You always said there are no coincidences in your line of work."

"This is a huge help, Mom."

"Oh, good," her mom chirps. "I do have to say something. Do you have a sec?"

Bonner doesn't but after the lead her mom has given, she owes it to her.

"Sure, Mom."

"It's just...well, Jim stopped by the other day. And he's not in a good place. Said you two talked and he mentioned getting back together."

"You don't have to deal with him, Mom."

"Well, sweetie, you don't just cut off family like that. And Jim is family. Even though you two have split. I'm in mourning too, and you're across the country, and Jim is...well, comforting."

"Do you see each other a lot?"

"He comes by to check on me—with my back and

all. Does some household chores. He's a good man. Your father wasn't half the man Jim is."

"Why do you...? Mom, what does Dad have to do with anything?"

"Just an observation. And we talk about... well, we talk about Kellan. Because it's hard for me to talk to you about him, so...so that's that. Jim's become a shoulder of sorts."

Bonner had successfully not thought about Kellan all day, since she left the shrine. This is exactly why she doesn't call her mom more.

"Honey, did I upset you?"

"This case..." is all Bonner can say.

"There will always be a case."

"A little girl was taken." Bonner is squeezing the cell in her fist. "Somehow these dead men with masks are related. She was...is nine years old."

Bonner knows her mom is thinking that Kellan was nine when he died. She doesn't need her to say why this case is becoming an obsession. She already knows.

"Terrible. Just...I have no words. You find this girl, honey."

"I will."

"He'd be proud," her mom says, her voice going soft as if she's afraid of Bonner's reaction. "He was always so proud of his mom."

Bonner breathes in to keep the tears from letting loose.

"Mom, I need to go."

"Please don't be mad about Jim."

"I'm not."

"We're all trying to handle our grief any way we can."

"It's good if you two can be there for each other, but we're not getting back together."

"You say that now–"

"I said it long before Kellan died. You didn't want to listen when I brought it up. Because...because you felt that any man was better than none. Because Dad fucked you up really bad when he left."

"Oh...oh well, I guess he did."

"He's an asshole, Mom. And Jim isn't, but that doesn't mean Jim is right for me to be with anymore. I gotta go."

"Okay, sweetie, well, keep me updated with your case. And stay safe. Always stay safe."

"Bye, Mom," Bonner says, but her mom has already hung up and Bonner knows she upset her. She'll tell herself not to be honest but somehow the truth sneaks out. Her mom will wedge a tissue in her sleeve and cry for a bit. But Bonner can't worry about that now.

Reading the newspaper article instead, her eyes zero in on Greenwich, Connecticut where the Alain Delon lookalike's body was found. She had recently heard Greenwich mentioned. Probably one of the wealthiest areas in Connecticut, let alone the country. Multimillion dollar homes. She grabs her notepad and flips back a few pages to when she first interviewed Gracie's family. The grandparents, Jay and Vivien, had driven in from Connecticut. She turns the page and sees exactly where in Connecticut she'd written —*Greenwich*.

"Ramirez!" she yells, but Ramirez isn't at his desk.

She books it to the hallway and finds him at the coffee vending machine waiting for his cup to fill.

"Bonner, what's the good word?" he asks, stirring in some creamer.

"Are you about ready for this case to open up even more?"

One of eyebrows raises in an umbrella-shape.

"Not only was the dead man found in Connecticut also wearing a mask from an old movie star, but he was found in Greenwich."

"So?"

"And where do you think Gracie's grandparents live?"

The second eyebrow raises.

"Holy cannoli fuckoli," he says.

25

SIR LAURENCE OLIVIER

"AUDREY'S NOT DEAD," OLIVIER TELLS HIMSELF over and over. To provoke this all-out war, Gable has probably fired a few bullets away from Audrey and covered her mouth to block her screams. Olivier remains on the line. He hears the slam of a door through the crackle of the device in Audrey's earring. Gable could've taken her out of the room, but there are no rooms in her apartment since it's a studio. The only door being the bathroom and a bathroom door doesn't have the same kind of heft as a front door so its slam wouldn't be as loud.

"But how could Gable kill someone he loved?" Olivier asks the wind blowing through a crack in a window. Nighttime in Brussels, the streets below alive with lewd behavior. The shades are drawn and he spies a man lifting up a woman's dress and burying himself in the tent she's created. Her face resembles that of Audrey Hepburn, smiling all the way to her earlobes. He lights a cigarette, and when he looks again, she's nothing but a poor imitation. When a death occurs, you mourn for the life that's been taken but don't get to miss the person yet. He can already feel her absence and that he will have many dark nights of despair ahead.

Everything on his desk gets knocked over in an impulsive sweep. Monitor crashing to the floor with a lightning bolt crack. Papers spiraling through the air. Gable won this round because he obviously loved Audrey less; that was Olivier's mistake.

Death to Gable would not be a cruel enough punishment. Only torture could bring justice. Fingernails ripped off one by one. Waterboarding. Teeth pulled out and collected in a bowl for him to see. That travesty of a face doused with lighter fuel, a match lit under his chin.

He'd seen the papers with Alain Delon's body. He had a feeling Gable would be triumphant but wanted Delon to be a scary threat. At any time now, an assassin could emerge to ice the Boss. Gable doesn't need to know that Olivier only has a few remaining operatives as well.

A knock at the door. Marlene Dietrich pops inside dressed out of the film *Morocco*: top hat, bow tie and tails. She does a nightly performance at the German club around the corner. That's how he met her.

It'd been a day where he had to bloody his own hands, a rare occurrence since usually his operatives took care of the messes. But this operative, a poor man's William Holden sent over from the American office who never really fit in, was pegged to ice a police officer who owed a lot of money to a local mob. The officer was squirrely and escaped so Olivier grabbed a pistol from his desk and showed up at the officer's place. Bullet to the brain and an axe brought along to chop up the parts and toss them in a garbage bag in the Woulwe stream along with any bloodied clothes. Dressed in the officer's plain clothes, Olivier wandered into a club down the street from his base because he wasn't ready to go and deal with the silence. He had killed before back in the 1970s during the Card's inception, but it had been decades since he'd taken a life. Settling in with a brandy cordial, Marlene Dietrich came on stage introducing herself as Amy Jolly, and performed "Give Me the Man Who Does Things" in French. She paid extra attention to his table as if the song was just for him. Afterwards, he waited in the alleyway for her.

"*You have quite the voice,*" he said, in French, figuring that was her nationality.

"*I'm German,*" she replied, in German.

"*Germany sure makes them beautiful,*" he said, in German, and offered one of his cigarettes.

"England sure makes them adept at corny one-liners," she said, in English, because his accent was obvious.

But she accepted his cigarette. And they went to a local café and ate Matentaart, round sweet pastry cakes. The owner was beholden to the Card and remained discreet. Until sun-up, Olivier learned her story. Orphaned as a child, fighting for food in the streets of Hamburg, a full life of pain before she reached the age of eighteen. Followed a boy to Belgium who wound up being a psychopath. Sleeping on couches and singing at the club for small tips.

"What if I said I had a more lucrative opportunity?" he asked, and her bedroom eyes told him she was ready for some type of change.

While Gable likes them physically scarred, that was

never Olivier's modus operandi. All he cares about is if they're committed.

Back in his office, he decides to rip the Band-Aid off with the news.

"Audrey Hepburn is dead," he tells Dietrich.

She leans against the doorframe and gasps. "Sweet thing. Too pure for this business if you ask me."

She lights a cigarette, the glow outlining her face in the dark.

"How was she iced?"

"Gable," he says. An enveloping rage taking over as the name spews from his mouth.

"But they were...?"

"*She and I* were together."

"I knew. A woman can tell these things. You lit up when you spoke of her in a way you never do."

"That's in the past now."

"I've worked for you fifteen years." She places a hand on his cheek. "You're allowed to be emotional."

"I'm never allowed. That's why she's dead."

"Are you ready for a war with Gable? A true war? No guarantee any of us will survive."

"Can I count on you to have my back?"

She gives his cheek a playful slap. "I've chosen sides long ago. Who else do we have?"

"No one. Delon is dead, Omar Sharif and Garbo a while ago. Only the mole in the States is left."

"My former co-star from *Morocco*."

Olivier taps his nose with a very Gable-like gesture. "Precisely."

"Between Garbo and Hepburn, I'm the only one of your female operatives you've never lain with."

She blinks her eyes and he can't tell if she's simply making a statement or truly longing for him.

"It's why you're the only one left alive."

She finishes the cigarette and crashes it into ashtray shaped like a movie camera.

"I'd give me more credit than just that. Hepburn was American, more concerned about painting her lipstick on right than an icing. No, I shouldn't speak ill of the dead."

"I'd ask you not to."

"The horror I faced as a child can't compare. Men having their way with me on the streets for a *deutsche mark*. Fighting a dog over a hunk of bread."

"There's no need to compare tragedies. You all have faced adversity."

"I'm a survivor is what I'm saying. And together we will take Gable down. What is the plan?"

"Private jet to New York, and then wait for our mole to give us Gable's location."

Dietrich removes her mask, having a hard time since it's adhered to her face like an alien appendage.

"What if we arrive, not as Olivier and Dietrich, like he expects? I've never worked for him directly so he doesn't know my true face."

"He knows mine."

Olivier stares at her without the mask. Even when they first met she was done up to look so much like Marlene Dietrich during her song. Her real eyes not as seductive, the mouth less of a frown. As if he's speaking to a stranger.

"True," she says, picking away at the leftover tape attached to her cheeks. "But how many years has it been since he's seen your true self?"

"Quite some time."

"Precisely."

She steps closer, gestures as if she'll remove the mask for him.

"You want to see my actual face?" he asks.

"No point in any secrets between us. I'm all you have left."

The words sting, a bitter taste on the back of his throat. The power Dietrich now holds. Without her, he doesn't stand a chance at domination.

"Come on, Olivier," she says, scraping at his neck with a fingernail to find the groove where the mask begins. "Or what is your real name?"

"Stop it," he says, but it's too soft for her to really hear.

"Let's be free for once," she says, starting to peel.

He's too tired to fight, too mournful to care. He imagines she's Audrey Hepburn because the last time he saw her on that night atop Belvedere Castle they peeled off each other's illusions and made love as who they used to be. And even though he spends every waking minute trying to get away from that man, sometimes it feels like home to return.

"My name is actually Oliver," he says. "It's as if I was destined to become what I did."

"I'm Evchen, at least that's what I think I was named. Or it's what's the street urchins decided to call me."

She finishes peeling off his mask and studies his face, possibly even more handsome than Sir Laurence Olivier.

"Why would you want to cover a mug like that up?"

"Like you, I'm a swirl of storms inside. Without the mask, I pity whoever gets in my way."

Evchen smiles, rare for him to see since she hardly does as Dietrich.

"Perfect then for this mission, *Chefchen*," she says.

He leaves the office with her, hesitant because it's been some time since he's stepped outside as his former self. Her hand on the small of his back leading him forward. *Can he love again?* he wonders.

If he succeeds in revenge, he believes he can.

26
CHIP

Chip had been living in Macau for upwards of a year following what he liked to refer as "Incident #1". He'd been at his favorite club *Chic Kink* in New York on the prowl. He'd done a tab of Molly and was flying, talking to a yummy boy who couldn't have been older than nineteen and had gotten in with a fake ID, when Chip suggested they'd go back to his hotel to do some crystal. He was living in New Canaan, not too far from his parents and his PR firm in Greenwich. But once a week he came into the city to let what little he had left of his hair down. The twink blinked in response to the hotel/drug suggestion, which Chip took as a definitive yes, and the two got royally fucked up at the Le Parker Meridian. This had likely been the kid's first time on hard drugs because halfway through a teeth-ridden blowjob, the twink freaked out and started biting down. Oh no, Chip would *not* get his dick bitten off by someone who hadn't even been alive before Britney Spears' first single dropped. So he proceeded to slap him around until he was able to loosen his dick from the boy's jaws of death. Before he knew it, he was wailing on the boy. He scuttled back in horror, the poor kid's faced bruised and some fresh wounds opening up and bleeding on the sheets. Chip booked it right out of there, the stupidest thing he could've done, since the kid went down to the front desk and had the police called. Chip never returned but they found him the next morning back at his home in New Canaan, along with some crystalized evidence, and arrested him.

Of course, Jay called the best lawyer he had on retainer. Chip's sentence got reduced, but he'd be damned if he'd spend any time in jail. He'd seen enough *Orange Is the New Black* episodes to know that he was too high maintenance to be locked in a cell. How would he get his special creams? What about his lactose allergy? And his reiki sessions? While the thought of being rammed in the shower by some thug named Rico did sound promising, more importantly, crystal would be hard to come by, and he was not about to go through withdrawal in any place but Malibu.

So, Macau. Jay had to be there for the casino he was building. While Chip was in hiding, his father would work on swaying the judge to clear the sentence. At that time, Chip understood his father knew a lot of very high-up people due to his business dealings over the years, but he had no idea the kind of business that Jay actually did.

And then along came "Incident #2". Crystal was tough to come by in Macau, but if he was going to stay there until he was free to return to the States, he'd find a way to get fucked up since he always did. He was at Club Destination, the only gay spot in Macau, a province that frowned on homosexuality. Club Destination became his prime destination, which usually consisted of local go-go boys that were fine for a fling, and certainly flexible, but not really his type. He liked the elusive; the straight-acting men who no one would suspect. A thrill in attaining the unattainable. Well, in walked a prize. Military-types are easy to spot and this one came with a buzz cut, a penetrating stare, and an eye-patch. Swoon. Eye Patch seemed to like Chip right away so they went back to Chip's hotel, however the guy had all these questions about Chip's father. Chip had already started to get fucked up on crystal and this man proceeded to tie him up. It had been months since he had properly gotten his rocks off. Just when he thought his military man would descend on top of him with a kiss, he started brutally whipping Chip. The guy demanded information about his father and wanted to know about something he called a Desire Card. It made no sense to Chip, and he feared for his life, especially when the guy took out a gun and put a pillow over Chip's face. Chip thought about what his life amounted to and decided he had not done nearly enough in forty-one years to justify it all coming to an end. His PR firm was a joke that only stayed afloat from funding through his father, he'd never had a lasting relationship relying on ten-minute pleasures from men who likely forgot his name when they walked out the door (if they even knew it in the first place). His family could barely stand him. His sister Helene kept him at a stick's-length from her children, who he found trite and boring anyway. His mother treated him as a pariah and his father always let his disappointment be known. Jay had wanted a football star for a son, a "chip" off the old block, which was where his name originated from. At the age of four,

Chip was trading his G.I. Joes for Barbies. Jay knew he had a lost cause.

Even when Jay was in town for his casino, he spared no time to see his son, so it flummoxes Chip months later when he receives a call on the secure phone Jay gave to him.

"Dad?" he asks in disbelief, answering the phone with hesitancy. If his father is calling, it cannot be good.

"I need you to come home."

The voice gruff and abrupt. His father never had time to mess around, but obviously even less time at the moment.

A tingling sensation courses through Chip's arms. "The judge threw out my case?"

"What? Oh, right. No. Well, he will don't worry. This is more important."

"But what if I'm seen...?"

"Goddamnit, Chip, listen to me. I'm in a crisis. Shut up for once in your life and just open your ears!"

Jay had never spoken in this way before. He'd certainly yelled at Chip plenty of times, but his tone had always been laced with anger, not fear.

"Ok, daddy," Chip said, feeling small.

"My company... We have a shortage of employees right now, and I need you to help out."

He couldn't help but laugh. "What? Me?"

"The fact I'm contacting you about this means I am really in a bind. The question of loyalty has arisen. And family, my son... I couldn't think of anyone who would be more loyal."

Tears squeeze out of Chip's eyes. Jay had never offered any kind words. Chip was referred to as a nuisance if he was lucky, and as a regret most days.

"Is this for...the Desire Card?"

The line goes silent for long enough for Chip to wonder if Jay had hung up, but he can hear a faint whistling of air. "Dad?"

"How do you know about the Desire Card?"

"I-I never told you this." Chip sticks his tongue in the gap where he lost a tooth due to the military man's whipping. "I picked up this man..."

"Oh, Jesus—"

"Wait, Dad, now I need you to listen."

The line goes silent again, and Chip's neck gets prickly and his stomach flips. He bites his tongue for speaking to his father in this way. He can picture Jay's face getting red and boiling.

"I'm listening," Jay says, gritting his teeth so loud that Chip can hear.

"This was right before you left. I-I didn't want to bother you. Anyway, he beat me up pretty bad and wanted information about you. His name was Marcus."

"James Dean."

"James Dean?"

"I'll...explain when you get into town. But yes, I apologize for that. He was a rogue employee that has caused a lot of damage."

"I meant to tell you, but you said to only be in touch if you contacted me. It—it had been months and I never heard from you so I figured you were too busy. And..."

"It's all right, Chip. You've told me now. Can you make a flight out today?"

Chip wipes his dripping nose. "Yes, of course, Daddy."

"It means a lot to me that I can count on you. Are you willing...? We will talk more in detail, but as I said, I need someone loyal who is okay with toeing the line."

"Like how?"

"Immorally. And, well, Chip, I know you have...*suspect* morals. I can't think of anyone who'd be better at this position."

Chipper PR, his joke of a company, had folded long ago. No other job prospects on the horizon. And he finds life in Macau dull as hell. How much can he walk around Taipa Village and look at the old historical buildings and eat almond cookies and beef jerky along the Rua do Cunha? Or lose a ton of money at the MGM Cotai, a futuristic casino with vertical gardens and thousands of LED screens showing landscapes from all over the world? There are churches and gardens that are supposed to be beautiful and a respite from all the gambling and glitz, but how many times can someone walk through a garden and look at an old ruined church without wanting to poke their eyeballs out? And besides, his crystal is running low.

"Of course, Daddy. Of course, I'll come. Anything you need."

"Chip, my boy," Jay says, and Chip's heart booms. "Make sure to be on a plane by tonight. I'll leave a voice mail as to where I'll be staying. I'm in flux."

Click.

"Daddy? Dad?"

He flips on his computer and sees there's a flight to New York departing at nine, which he can make if he throws everything in his suitcase and leaves now.

27

GARY COOPER

Lined up by Gable with Mae West, Sinatra, and Brando and Astaire at the headquarters, Gary Cooper hears the Boss barking about a "mole in our midst". Gable has brought out James Dean, but it's clearly not the James Dean that Gary Cooper once knew. This one puffier, flabbier, less assured—a new hire. The old Jimmy Dean made of ice. They had commiserated about what led them to the Card, those war-torn Iraqi skies of their wasted youth. To speak about their pasts verboten, but Gary Cooper didn't care, and neither did Dean. Both of them rogues.

Being lined up like this brings back memories of the other side of a firing squad when they tried to break insurgents to spill about hidden IEDs and wound up killing them all anyway, even if they talked. He'd been a good kid from Helena, Montana just like the actor Gary Cooper. The army wasn't in his family. In fact, his Pop cried when he broke the news of enlisting. His mother had passed when he was a child and his Pop tended to four boys on their cattle farm, all but him wanting to follow in the old man's footsteps. But when he heard of Weapons of Mass Destruction, he swore his patriotic duty would be to fight Saddam. He never met the real James Dean, had no idea what he actually looked like due to never removing their masks in each other's company, but they had a few missions together in the early days.

"I took you all in when no one else gave a flying fuck," Gable says, ranting now to his troops at the head-quarters. Gary Cooper had never seen him on edge like this, a fury in the man's eyes that resembled fireballs. "You came across a hidden IED, Cooper," Gable continues, thrusting a finger in Gary Cooper's face. "Blew up your hands and turned your face into soup. And who gave you new hands?"

"You did," Gary Cooper says. But Gable never aired any of their "laundries" before. Cooper looks down at his robotic hands and clenches his fists.

"You're damn right I did," Gable says, and proceeds to tell all the other operatives' stories. Gary Cooper shuts them out because he's taken back to when he picked up the IED disguised as something innocuous. The *tick, tick, tick* before the boom. A flash of white light and then his cheeks melting in his hands that had turned into nothing more than skeletal appendages.

He glances around at the line-up: Mae West trying not to cry. He can hear her quiet sniffles. Her past must've just been revealed. Brando and Astaire remaining stoic, leaning on each other like they usually do. He wonders what it must be like to have a true confidant at the Card. Being a freelancer keeps him from that. He'd gotten to know James Dean somewhat but oftentimes he rolled solo. The Card had been a way to banish his war demons, but even more so, his Pop's cattle farm was in danger of going under. Half the money he made from missions went to Montana. His Pop thought he worked in security detail, naïve as to how much the Card paid. The bills piled up even worse for his Pop, and Cooper had gone to Gable's office to ask for a raise.

"A raise?" Gable asked, looking out of his high-rise windows at the hundreds of ants below.

"It's my Pop's—"

"I'm going to stop you there because everyone has a sob story. You wouldn't be a part of the Card if you didn't. Sick family member, home being taken away. I've heard it all. How could I possibly give all my soldiers everything they wanted?"

"It wouldn't be much—"

Gable held up his hand. "It wouldn't be fair to give you more than another freelancer. What if they were to find out?"

"I would never say."

"Never is such an impossible word. I'm aware that my operatives talk. I strongly dissuade it, but I am not in control when you're not on the clock. And to pay you more would bump you up to a regular. You have not expressed interest—"

"I would consider."

"Let me rephrase that—I have not considered. There's a certain *elan* to my regular operatives that you do not possess with your aw-shucks nature. I'm saying you do not have the *cojones* I require."

"And you know this how?"

Gable's laugh ate up the room. He walked over to his majestic wet bar, poured a hefty glass of Laphroaig.

"The fact you've come to me with your weak sauce pity party."

So, when another opportunity presented itself, Gary Cooper jumped. How he'd been specifically screened as a turncoat, he had no clue. Certainly risky to inquire about going against the Boss. Cooper initially thought it a test so didn't offer any outright commitment. He let the offer dangle. And weeks later, when Gable didn't let on that he'd orchestrated this maneuver, Cooper met Olivier in a Kosovar bar in East Berlin after an assignment. Olivier promised to pay all the debts his Pop owed on the cattle ranch.

"Are we talking an icing?" Cooper asked, his hat tipped low over his eyes, the lights dim and the air clouded with smoke so Olivier had to lean in close to speak.

"Maybe someday, but for now I require intel the most. A *maulwurf*."

"Come again."

"A mole, my friend. Sorry, I've been in Germany for too long. My arteries hardening from all the *wurst*. It's the worst. Back to Brussels soon."

So for the past year, Cooper gave Olivier any info he requested. The relationship Gable had with Audrey Hepburn being a prominent request.

"James Dean, I think it's time to brand," Cooper hears Gable say.

James Dean picks up a hot poker propped against the wall that glows orange. He presses the hot poker against Brando's palm and makes him grip down.

"He's not the mole!" Astaire screams.

Brando collapses into a ball of whimpers.

"Are you?" Gable asks, directing James Dean to do

the same to Astaire until both operatives are writhing around on the floor.

Sinatra sees his fate next and speaks up. "What would I gain from working with Olivier? He's a fuck of all fucks. I never did understand how he held so much power in your organization."

"Is that what you think I want to hear?" Gable asks, indicating for James Dean to brand Sinatra.

"I'm going to tell you a story," Sinatra says, catching Gary Cooper's eye in a strange way through each other's masks.

What's he up to? Cooper thinks.

"The mole would be one of the freelancers," Sinatra says. "Brando and Astaire would never turn. They worship your feet. Look, you branded them and they offered nothing. They'd be willing to have their whole bodies charred to prove their loyalties."

The two wounded operatives look up from their shared miseries and mumble in agreement.

"And Mae West, now I've worked missions with her before and she's as loyal as they come. How do I know this? We were approached."

"By Olivier?"

Sinatra taps his nose with Gable-like gesture to get into further graces with the Boss.

"It wasn't by Olivier himself. He used his minions Dietrich and Alain Delon. They expressed frustration with you, Gable. See if we wanted to play along."

"It's true," Mae West says, shuffling over to Gable and running a finger up his arm. "And so, we played along to see how serious they were. Sure enough, I get a call from Olivier on my secure line."

"Did he want me iced?" Gable roars.

"No, just intel. Said he'd give us whatever we desired. I told him you had promised that already and I don't like to complicate things. I'd stay Switzerland in your war."

"Why didn't you tell me this?"

"Partly out of fear," Mae West says. "Didn't want to rock the foundation. Figured I could keep my eye on him for you. Both Sinatra and I decided this."

"We were paid by Olivier too, don't forget," Sinatra says. "If he's gone, our money is almost cut in half."

"So, you see our predicament?" Mae West says, sliding up to Gable now, tugging on the lapel of his sport coat.

"I have always said that the world revolves around money," Gable declares, and Mae West seems to exhale for the first time since they were all lined up. But Gable nods at James Dean who then grabs her arm and forces the hot poker in her grip. She lets out a dying squeal followed by a litany of sobs.

"And you?" Gable asks, nose-to-nose with Gary Cooper. "They've all been honest and forthcoming. Why haven't you?"

"I'm not the mole," Gary Cooper says, tilting his head so his hat covers his eyes.

"Nuh-uh," Gable says. "Lemme see those peepers."

Gable flings the hat across the room, ripping off some of Gary Cooper's fake air. A piece of real scalp peeks through: pink and gnarly. Gable takes Cooper's face in his hands, eyes locked.

"What do you think, James Dean?"

James Dean has finished branding Sinatra, who's howling on the floor with the other operatives.

"I won't kill you," Gable says to Cooper. "I will

brand the fuck out of you. And not your hands because they're not real." He glances down at Gary Cooper's crotch. "I believe that's one of the few old body parts of yours which actually still works. I won't hesitate. But if you confess, I'll use you against Olivier. You can get back in my good graces."

James Dean closes in, the hot poker dangerously close to Gary Cooper's dick.

"Choice is yours. I'm going to count down to three. One. Two–"

James Dean thrusts the hot poker forward. Gary Cooper scurries backward, facing out his palms in desperation.

"Okay, okay," he says. "It was me. Olivier paid off my Pop's debts against his cattle farm. You didn't want to listen."

Silence fills the room. Even the wounded operatives stop mewling. Everyone poised to see what will happen next.

"Thank you," Gable says. "For your honesty."

Gary Cooper grins under his mask, but it isn't visible.

Gable snaps his fingers.

A pistol is removed from James Dean's pocket and raised to Cooper's face.

"But you...?"

The trigger pulled, the sound like a truck backfiring. Gary Cooper's face exploding like it did in Iraq many years ago.

This time, James Dean finishing the job.

28

MARCUS EDMONTON

GRACIE HAD STOPPED TALKING TO HIM AGAIN. Having not left the apartment in over twenty-four hours, both were getting antsy. The girl had taken to counting the cracks in the ceiling. When Marcus tried to speak to her, she only counted louder. Depression sinks in between flipping between old black and white movies and the news. A man was killed in Greenwich, Connecticut who resembles a young version of the movie star Alain Delon. The police are seeing if there's a connection to Cagney who washed up in the East River. Without any fingerprints on the two, their real identities haven't been discovered. Marcus rubs his owns fingers that are *sans* fingerprints too.

"Fifty-nine, sixty," Gracie yells.

"No one can hear you if that's what you're attempting," he says. "The walls are soundproof."

She rises and drags her newly-fashioned chains over to him. Hopefully sturdier than the last ones.

"You said Papa Jay was responsible for killing someone you loved?"

Taken aback, he stammers. The track lights catching his eye and leaving floaties in his vision.

"Yes, he did."

She sits cross-legged, resting her chin in her palms. "I'm like, bored, so tell me about it."

He'd never had a chance at love. Met Annie when he was so young before he was shipped to Iraq. Came back bitter with a missing eye and took eight years to contact her again. All that time, they could've been together.

"What was her name?"

"Annie Duluth."

"What'd she look like?"

It's hard when you lose someone and you only have memories to reconstruct their face every time. He doesn't have any pictures.

"Blonde hair..." He gets choked up. "Really pretty and sweet. Southern accent. She was from Kentucky."

"Were you gonna get married?"

"Maybe in some other life."

"What did my Papa Jay do?"

"Do you really want to know?"

Gracie thinks for a second and then nods.

"He had the man you killed kill her. All because she was connected to me."

She sniffs. "That's really sad. Do you want a hug?"

"Huh? A hug?"

"You look like you could use one."

He studies this girl. She looks sweet with her doe eyes and tiny mouth, her batted lashes. But she'd tricked him before with her dance and then escaped. She does have the same DNA as Gable.

"I'm okay."

"I mean..." She sniffs again. "I can use a hug."

Tucking her head to the side, ready to burst into a load of tears, he doesn't have the heart to say no. The last time he'd been hugged was from Annie. Before her, he couldn't even remember. What others found commonplace is extraordinary to him.

Since his parents died so young, he doesn't recall their affection, only from his Gramps who raised him, stingy because he was a man from a different era who never liked to show emotion.

So he embraces her. Such a tiny body like hugging a bird. All bones. She tucks her chin on his shoulder, murmurs "thank you" over and over. And then, a searing pain to the side of his neck. He unravels from her and sees the blood leaking. She's laughing, actually laughing, but crying as well, a bloody nail in her fist that she must've found.

"Goddamnit it!"

He rushes to the bathroom, shutting the door on her screams. Turns on the faucet, washes the stinging wound with cold water. Opening up the medicine cabinet, he finds peroxide and an adhesive bandage. Rips it open with his teeth and sticks it over the gaping hole in his neck.

Staring into the mirror, he tells it to "get your shit together, soldier. J.D.—Marcus—*Marcus*, this will be your final mission. Don't fall apart."

Flashes of Siniyah explode in fragments around the bathroom. A dead baby he cradled in his arms. An insurgent stabbing his eye and leaving that part of him in Iraq.

He rips the mirror off and smashes it on the floor. Has a moment where he wants to pick up one the shards and end it all: this unlucky life, this never-ending purgatory.

But he heads out and finds Gracie sobbing with the bloody nail held as a threat.

"Don't come near me," she wails.

"You're a fighter." He presses the bandage harder against the wound, since it starts to feel as if blood is leaking out. "I'll need a tetanus shot."

"You deserve it."

"Yes, yes I do. Can we make a truce? Can I have the nail before you hurt yourself?"

"I wanna go home!"

"I know, I fuckin' know. This isn't fair. None of this is fair. This isn't what I wanted for myself. I wanted a little girl like you, a family. Just a job after the military, any old job. And little league games, and family dinners, shit, whatever it is that normal people do."

She lunges at him with the nail. Grabbing her arm, he twists it around until she lets go of the nail so he lets go of her too. She rubs her arm.

"That hurt."

"Good. It should have. 'Cause you really hurt me too."

"I hate you and your one eye."

"I hate me and my one eye most days too."

"Whatever you have planned, it won't work out like you think it will, mister. What I know of my Papa Jay is he always gets what he wants."

"He did. But all kingdoms topple eventually."

She holds her arms out. "Can I wash off all your stupid blood?"

"C'mere." He lifts her up and brings her to the kitchen sink. Turns on lukewarm water and squeezes some dish soap into her hands. Once she's all cleaned up, he brings her back to her corner.

"I'm like a dog," she says. "You've chained me to the floor. I pee in a bucket. I'm cold."

"Here."

He takes off his shirt and puts it over her. It's so large it swims.

"Is that better?"

"It's not worse." She touches her tongue to her nose. "You should go to a hospital and get that looked at."

"Was that your plan?"

She nods.

"Clever girl." He thinks for a moment. "What if I give you a time limit for this? I'll bring you home if this doesn't go my way after a certain time."

Tapping her chin for a second, she responds: "I'm listening."

"Two more days. Let me try to contact your grandfather again. I hate to tell you this but he never came to get you personally."

"He had his reasons."

"I'm sure he did."

"Can you take off these cords and chains then?" she asks, her voice sweet and innocent.

"You haven't proved to me I can trust you."

"I know."

"So I can't."

"I know."

"This is what's called an impasse."

"I've heard of that word. I've had very good schooling."

"I couldn't even go to a hospital if I wanted. I have

no ID. I don't exist. None of your grandfather's employees exist anymore. He makes sure of that."

"I'm sorry you don't exist. That can't be easy."

"It isn't."

"I'm sorry I stabbed you with a nail."

He manages to laugh. "I am too. It went in far. You had that all planned?"

She nods.

"Impressive."

She smiles.

"I hate to say this but your grandfather would be very proud."

29
JAMES DEAN

After killing Gary Cooper, James Dean retires to a large room off the side filled with hospital beds. He sits down and notices a streak of blood by his foot that hasn't been cleaned. Having never killed someone before, he's surprised to not feel empathy for the life he'd taken. He was a natural, the same thought echoed by Gable. His body alive with tingles from the notion that he's finally found his calling.

His cell vibrates. His mother. He lets it go to voice-mail. Having not spoken to her in some time, she can certainly wait a little longer. Touching the mask, he's surprised at its authenticity. He turns to his left towards a mirror and James Dean stares back. Certainly a fatter James Dean, but the face an exact duplicate.

"Why the masks?" he had asked Gable when he returned from overseas, as his new identity was handed over.

"I'm about rebirth," Gable had said. "Who you were before you put on the mask doesn't have to exist. You can keep whichever parts you desire and extinguish the rest."

James Dean tried to see the man behind the Gable mask, but even the voice had changed. More of a robotic tone, as if no human heart beat in these reprogrammed bodies.

"And why the old movie stars?"

He recalled black and white movies playing in the background throughout his childhood. *Gone with the Wind*, a favorite. The dramatic score rising after he was sent to sleep. Sneaking out and watching from a back hallway, a swelling in his nether region every time Clark Gable would appear. Picturing himself kissing that thin mustache.

"A chance to align with greatness," Gable replied, clearly having rehearsed this answer. "We are mere mortals, but matinee idols live forever. They are ideals of perfection. Why would you want to become anyone else?"

"And you see me as James Dean?" he asked, passing the mask between his hands.

"As you know, we've had an opening in the James Dean department. Be a shame to let it go to waste."

He had put on the mask and it contoured his face perfectly, as if it'd been meant for him all along.

Now, he touches his new features, wondering how he's lived this long without them.

The sound of footsteps. Gable entering the large room and standing over him.

"I wanted to check in on you," Gable says.

"I'm fine."

"You did very well."

"Really?"

His real voice hitting high octaves, but the mask releasing it as a robotic bass.

"Exceptionally."

A hand is placed on his shoulder, the muscle kneaded. He can't recall the last time he was treated this way.

"Thank you."

Tears leak from his eyes, but the James Dean mask keeps them hidden.

"What happened to all of them?" he asks. "Your employees? The ones I've branded."

"Ah, not to worry. They don't hold a grudge against you. They understand completely."

"How is that so?"

"Because they believe in what I've strived to achieve. This world I've built for them. It means more than a little branding. Brando and Astaire are taking care of Gary Cooper's body. Chop it up, scatter it around..."

"You say that as if it's the most normal thing."

"Does that make you uncomfortable?"

"No. I don't know what it says about me that it doesn't."

"Chip off the old block," Gable says, fake punching him in the jaw as a sign of affection.

"And Mae West and Sinatra?"

"Mae West has been sent off to find the location of the man we formerly knew as James Dean. And Sinatra, he's been tasked as my bodyguard. He's right at the door."

"Mother called."

He shows Gable his cell as proof.

"I need to make a trip back to our house," Gable says. "I'm afraid the police might be connecting some dots based on the dead bodies of Cagney and Delon. You need to help me remove any evidence that links me to those crimes. And keep your mother distracted while I do it."

"Does she...?"

"Know? No. Well, I will say your mother is very good at pretending unsavory things in her life aren't occurring. So, she might. But she's convinced herself otherwise."

"All those years, though..."

"You didn't have any idea, did you?"

James Dean shakes his head.

"See? Neither did your sister. Or the extended family. I'm a genius at keeping what needs to be hidden, hidden. But we've reached a roadblock, James Dean."

"It's still odd to hear you call me that."

"Get used to it. Because if you were to strut around outside as yourself, you'd be in handcuffs by dusk."

"True."

"However, with that mask, you're entirely innocent of all your transgressions."

"What's the roadblock you've found yourself in?"

"I didn't tell you this, but Gracie was taken by O.G. James Dean. That set off a ripple effect of vicious, vicious occurrences, culminating in where we are at now. But this is far from the finale. Only the gods can know how this will all wrap up. But I will be triumphant."

"How can you be certain?"

"Because I always have been. I like to say it'll be the cockroaches and me at the end of it all."

"Thank you for finally believing in me."

James Dean stands and goes in for a hug. It's herky-jerky at first, James Dean unsure about how much to commit. And Gable, far from the affectionate type, baffled by this alien exchange. Their masks touching cheek-to-cheek, if but for a moment, and then Gable pulls away.

"All right, enough of that. We're sitting ducks if we wait around here. Olivier is aware of this headquarters thanks to Gary Cooper. We'll make a pit stop at the Greenwich home and then head to the secret safe house that none of my operatives know about."

"I'm the first?"

"Yes, Jimmy Dean."

They head out of the large room with hospital beds. Outside, Sinatra had propped up his arm on a table wrapping up his wound. Gable goes to a safe in the corner and removes a tiny baggie. He opens it to reveal a handful of diamonds.

"For your service," he tells Sinatra. "And for your future loyalty. Can I be certain I have it?"

Sinatra inspects the diamonds.

"Worth about a hundred thousand from the right buyer."

Sinatra stuffs the baggie in his pocket. "You have it, Gable."

"Good. So, we're off."

Gable heads to the front door. Sinatra glares at James Dean. His blue eyes slicing through any confidence James Dean just gained. The branding hasn't been forgiven, especially if Sinatra knew that the new

James Dean had gotten the job because he was the Boss's son.

James Dean keeps a hand on the gun in the inside pocket of his jacket.

Finger on the trigger just in case.

Finger on the trigger from now on.

30

EVCHEN & OLIVER

Somewhere over the Atlantic, Evchen and Oliver fell in lust. Love being hard, since both had closed themselves off. From the time she was a child on the streets, Evchen swore off men as nothing more than business associates. And after Audrey's likely death, Oliver wondered if he'd ever love again. But on a private jet sharing a bottle of Armand de Brignac Brut, their Dietrich and Olivier masks in suitcases, they find it easy to get swept up in the idea of a warm body.

Afterwards, they cocoon in a throw on a reclining lounge chair. Because of his advanced age, Evchen is astonished at Oliver's fitness. Pecs and a stomach with a little paunch but hard as wood. His other wood a surprise for a man even half his age.

"It's pills from Madagascar," he says. "Contact of Gable's since the 1980s."

"You two have had some history."

"Enough stories for a book." He kisses her shoulder.

"Was there always animosity?"

"You know how they say never to mix business with friends?"

Evchen perks up and looks to the front of the cabin.

He turns her face back towards him. "I've told the stewardess not to bother us for the rest of the trip."

"Is she employed by the Card?" Evchen asks.

"No, we utilize a lot of different companies that are hired for their levels of discreetness. They don't know what the Card does, per se, just that we're important enough to keep their lips sealed."

She runs her fingers through her hair. Something Audrey never could do with her short bob. Oliver has to stop comparing the two.

"All these years and I never knew all the ins and outs," she says.

"Would you like to know some of our secrets?"

She leans on an elbow to prop her head up in her palm. Traces his nipple. "Do tell."

"What would you like to know?"

"How the Card began."

"Ah, our immoral origins. I don't think we have enough time on our flight for that story."

"It was just you and Gable at the start?"

He shakes out a cigarette pack from his coat and pops one in his mouth. A silver Zippo engraved *Sir Laurence* lights the cherry.

"Yes, Gable would like to think he came up with the idea, but it was me. And we weren't in the hit man business at the onset. For that, I will credit Gable. We simply wanted to fulfill the wishes of the rich. And get rich off of it ourselves."

She touches his chin, runs a fingernail across a scar.

"How did you get that?"

"My first dust-up with Gable before I was sent to start up the international office. He wore his college ring back then, cut straight through my chin when he landed a left hook."

"It gives you character."

"It's covered by the mask so often, I rarely think about it. Anyway, we were successful, not like we are now, but enough for two guys with expensive tastes. We had a small team of operatives then. They weren't quite *operatives*, but we did have them wear masks. Cheap knock-off in comparisons to the works of art we currently use, but it helped us maintain a veil of secrecy. And our clients got a kick out of it. This was the late seventies so we were closer to the primes of a lot of these stars. Fans saw them age, some had passed on, so I imagine it was treat to witness a star in their youngest form while delivering a feather of a Hula bird, or a crystal piano, or a rare Ferrari. You're a millennial so it's hard to imagine, but this was long before you could go on the Internet and with the click of a button get anything you desire. Wishes were more sacrosanct back then."

"I'm not so young that I don't remember life before the Internet."

"We filled a void." He shifts and wraps his arms around her, drawing her close. "Clients with a lot of money but not a clue they desired some elusive object they never even thought about before. We'd put the bug in their heads."

She reaches down and starts jerking him off, the pills making him hard in an instant.

"What changed?"

"Gable, for one. I would've been content with facilitating moral wishes. The psychopath you're jerking off now grew out of necessity. I was not born this way. But we began to get offers. Objects are nice, no one would argue with a Ferrari, but the truly rich want power. They want to be able to get rid of those standing in their way. And this became a lot more lucrative than our cut for locating a hard-to-find Ferraris."

"But you had to keep offering those Ferraris. To remain semi-legit in most of the client's eyes."

"Precisely. The average celebrity or CEO we work with doesn't have morbid designs. Or if they do, they'd never realistically have those wishes facilitated. So on paper, our business appears *kosher*. We do our taxes. Gable is very good at keeping us free from scrutiny. We've rarely had any trouble with the government. We pay off the right people. We have many of them as clients. And most think all they're turning a blind eye to is the acquisition of these wishes, not dead bodies."

"And yet, you don't tell any of your operatives all this?"

"We like to keep our *Card* close to our chest."

She playfully slaps him on the cheek. "Not funny."

"I thought it was very *punny*."

"As far as the immoral acts," she says, looking out of the window as the plane sails through a cloud. "I look at it as a job. A job I'm very good at."

"And all those you've killed?" he asks, kissing her breast.

"Unlucky. Does that sound heartless?"

"I'd say practical."

"You know I didn't come from much. I don't owe the world anything. I've been kicked at since I was a fetus."

"I came from a lot but I don't owe the world anything either. Survival is paramount, all else superfluous."

She tugs on her lip with her fang tooth. "Were you thinking of her when you were fucking me? Audrey Hepburn?"

"Do you want me to lie?"

"That answers my question."

"The wound is still fresh but it doesn't make what we did any less lovely."

"It wasn't just a one time bang?"

"Evchen," he says, and it takes her a second because it's been so long since she's been referred to by her actual name.

"Oliver," she whispers. Hearing the slight change in his own name takes him back to carefree days of youth. Before Gable. Before he'd ever seen blood other than from a scrape. The amount he's seen now could fill the ocean they're flying over.

"What will you do when you take over the Card?" she asks.

"You mean, will I return to it to the way it once was?"

He can't tell which answer would please her the most. He can only be honest.

"No. Because this is the only kind of Card I know how to run. My only experience for the last thirty-odd years has been with death."

"Good," she says, giving an eerie smile, one that tells him the two of them are not like most people. Even though he was not evil from the start, that villainous rage beat inside of him, as does with her.

"Let them judge us at the end," he says. "God or the

devil or whoever tips the scale. I'm banking on the fact that there's nothing and we spend eternity in the dirt until we become dirt as well. So we should live our lives answering to no one or nothing."

"Amen."

She kisses the coarse white fur on his chest resembling a cross. Travels down further until his dick is in her mouth.

"No, no, it's your turn." He flips her over and buries his face in her bush. "Let this old dog make you go wild."

She points her toes in the air, as he spells Audrey Hepburn's name with his tongue, but it feels amazing and she doesn't care. She's wanted him from afar for too long and has reached the apex of her power in this organization. If they're successful with icing Gable, she'll be more than a station agent: his number two, never to be replaced.

And if they fail, it'll be a hell of way to close out this strange and unusual trip that has been her life.

31

DETECTIVE MONICA BONNER

SURPRISE THE HOWELLS UP IN GREENWICH, Connecticut. Traffic horrendous getting out of the city. Bomb threat in Times Square clogging everything up. Even the horn doesn't help. So Bonner rolls up the window to block out the clamor and turns off the radio.

"You don't like Cardi B?" Ramirez asks.

"I don't know who that is. My musical knowledge stopped at the Backstreet Boys when I was twelve."

"What a time to stop."

"Fuck you. Twelve-year-old me would've murdered you for saying that." She leans on the horn again.

"It won't do anything."

"Okay, we have time to kill and I'm antsy. Let's go over facts about the Stockton case."

Ramirez strokes his finely-tuned goatee. "Fact: the little girl was seen taken out of Central Park by a man with an eye patch."

"Fact," Bonner continues. "The man with the eye patch's body washed up in the East River. No fingerprints. All his teeth were fake so no ID. Except if you count the James Cagney mask."

"Shit, yeah I saw that about the teeth too. Really fucking weird."

"Fact: A second body wearing an Alain Delon mask was found murdered in Greenwich, Connecticut. No fingerprints and all fake teeth as well."

"Fact: The girl's grandparents live up in Greenwich, Connecticut."

"Fact: Something called the Desire Card connects this all."

Ramirez keeps rubbing his goatee like he's trying to rub it off. "*Any wish fulfilled for the right price,*" he says, repeating the mantra. "Like a corporate genie in a bottle?"

"I'm guessing these wishes are not of the legal variety."

"No, what would be the point then?"

"This company gets you unattainable wishes. But two of their own turn up dead."

"Rival corporation?"

"I'm thinking more of a disgruntled employee."

"And the little girl? How does she fit into all of this?"

"Haven't worked that one out. But someone in her family is connected to the Desire Card. Fact: the father was mugged and in a coma. The wife said he contacted them for a desire, but paid his dues?"

"Or maybe someone in the family works for the Desire Card too?" Ramirez offers.

Bonner slams on the brakes, almost hitting the car in front of them. A swarm of tourists squeeze through the narrow distance between bumpers.

"Where do all these people come from?" Bonner asks.

"I swear, New York would be ten times better with half the population."

"I hate people. I mean, I love the people I love, but in general, people, no thanks."

"Spoken like a true New Yorker." Ramirez turns the radio back on, finds a station playing samba music. "I wonder what I'd wish for if I could have anything."

"If money wasn't a factor?"

"Maybe my own private island for me and the missus? A vacation spot only for us."

"That sounds lovely."

"You have anyone you'd like to get a private island with, Bonner?"

She shows her bare ring finger. "We're in the process of getting divorced."

"Ah, I'm sorry. I didn't know."

"Really? I thought I was wearing a sign."

"What happened, if you don't mind me asking?"

"I do. But it'll be a thousand hours until we get out of here. So, he—Jim—was a good man, treated me right. Blah, blah, blah. Put up with my cop shit."

"Let me tell you that ain't easy. The missus, she was sent from above."

"Jim wasn't. And I don't believe in God anyway."

Ramirez's eyebrows fly to the top of his forehead.

"I have reasons, though. My son..." A lady with a fanny pack runs past the car. Bonner slams on the horn and makes her jump. "My son died, Ramirez."

She watches the same expression that everyone gives upon hearing the news. The inability to know what to say next, a stammering of words, a few tossed "sorrys." People feel like they need to say something meaningful and find a way to contain this awful grief. But it's not anyone's job.

"Man, Bonner, I am so sorry. I don't know what to say."

"You don't have to say anything. I mean, everyone always tries..."

"I lost..." He shuts his eyes tight, opens them in fear. "She was stillborn. Little girl. No complications beforehand. It was our first, but then we had–"

"Kellan was my only child. I...I couldn't have another. It was cancer. It was a month in the hospital. So fast. I wouldn't have the strength to go through anything like that again."

Ramirez reaches over and hugs her with his meaty arms. Normally, she'd reject this. Receiving any affection foreign, she's learned how to battle it alone. Jim needed constant support. He wanted to continue making love through it all while she didn't even want to be touched. His hand on her shoulder made her want to scrub for hours. And to have him inside of her while Kellan fought for his life hooked up to machines? Monstrous. And afterward, when Jim desperately yelled that he needed to be held, she turned her cheek, finding him repulsive, wanting to become a monk and live in silence until her end of days. If she didn't leave him, she would have destroyed him completely.

"Thank you," she says, wiping her nose on Ramirez's sleeve and then they both lightly laugh at the yellow glob of snot clinging to his watch.

"Jesus, Bonner, allergies much?"

"I'm okay, Ramirez," she says, because some days she believes she will be. In fact, this morning she didn't spend time at Kellan's shrine. She was too busy searching for any information on the Desire Card.

"I know it's empty words. But if you ever need... anything. To talk, or vent, or just fucking scream, I'm your man."

"You're my man, Ramirez."

Her cell rings.

"Fuck, who's calling me...?"

She fishes it from her pocket and frowns at the unrecognizable number.

"Hello?"

"Hello, can I speak to Detective Monica Bonner?"

"Speaking."

"Yes, Detective, this is the head nurse at Mount Sinai where a Mr. Harrison Stockton is in our care. You said to contact you with any updates."

"What's happening?"

"He woke up, Detective. A few hours ago. He's out of sorts but..."

"We're on our way." She hangs up and tosses the cell to the side. "Get the siren."

"What's going on?"

"The father just fucking woke up is what!"

Ramirez bumbles with the siren but manages to roll down the window and place it on top of the car. Bonner sticks her head out.

"Out of the way," she screams, and then keeps screaming. Letting out all her frustration, her throat raw.

The mass of people surrounding the car obey. They see the urgency in the spiraling red lights and her brutal appeals.

32
VIVIEN

THE HOUSE IN GREENWICH, VIVIEN'S GREATEST accomplishment. An eight bedroom, over sixteen thousand square foot Elizabethan Tudor built in 1927 with English oak linen-panel walls, a forty foot ceiling vaulted living room, a sumptuous master suite where she had Calcutta gold installed in the bathroom, a hi-end movie theater (that she personally never used), a double chef's kitchen, a landscape that housed flower gardens, a boxwood maze, and a spring-fed lake with a dock, flagstone terraces that overlooked a lighted tennis court, pool, and life-size chess set along with a stable and horse paddock.

In lieu of a job, the house became her profession until it was finished and charities took over as an obsession. When she'd come home, she'd dip into the calming aura of her English Park setting once owned by a famed movie star of the fifties, part of the reason Jay had selected it over other mansions in the exclusive enclave.

But when she returns from the hospital, shaken and scattered, the house seems less of a home and more like a menacing castle used in horror films as a backdrop for terror.

All who enter will perish.

The fact that Jay's company could be related to unsavory dealings not surprising. Her husband had a flair for being slick, one of the reasons she fell in love. In a time of safe boys with their hair parted just right and their careers in dentistry, or law, or finance, she chose the unlikely path with potential for even greater rewards. Any shadiness that may occur she chalked up to financial loopholes which Jay was adept at maneuvering, nothing involving—*she couldn't even think the word*—murder.

On her way back, she had tried his cell twice after calling her son Chip as well, only to have both go to voicemail. Often Jay didn't answer her calls during the workday. The second time she left a vague message about Harrison, but stressed that Jay *should* call her back. The two had an agreement long ago to treat each other with respect, even during times they hated one another.

Sure enough, no one's home. Not bothering to turn on the alarm, she whisks into his office at the end of the hallway on the first floor. A powerful scent of bourbon and musk hits her upon entering, but it doesn't mean Jay's been here recently. The windows kept shut and a decanter left open, providing the aroma. Not having been here in a while, she inspects his office like a curious maid, opening drawers and peering behind bookshelves and a desk where she almost knocks over a ship in a bottle. He'd built it himself when they moved in to their first place, a painstaking process of many hours. She remembers calling him to bed wearing negligible negligee, and yet, he didn't return to their bedroom until dawn. *I married a diligent man,* she'd thought, because in the mornings he made up for not pleasing her during the night.

Sweeping her foot under the desk, she hears a clanging sound. Crouching down on her arthritic knees, she spies a safe hidden in the back. Tries the combination of Jay's birthday, her birthday, Helene's birthday, Chip's birthday—*yeah right*—even the grandkids. Pulling out her phone, she looks up Clark Gable's: February 1st 1901. She tries 02-01-19-01, her heart nearly stopping when it opens.

Jay and Harrison were talking about a *Card* in hushed tones and Jay appeared upset.

The man who possibly kidnapped her grand-daughter washed up in the East River wearing a James Cagney mask.

The news also spoke of another man in a movie star mask killed nearby her home.

Jay ran a multibillion-dollar company and she never knew exactly what he did. She could shut the safe and play ignorant. Be happy with her twenty million-dollar home and never leave for fear of what fate lurked outdoors. The wife of a monster just as monstrous for turning a blind eye.

Inside the safe, she feels something rubbery along with a stack of cards. She removes the cards first, old business stock yellowing from age. *The Desire Card. Any wish fulfilled for the right price.* No phone number. No way to contact. Her shaking hands take out the rubbery objects: two masks, more like from well-made Halloween costumes as opposed to what James Cagney wore. The first, obviously Clark Gable, the thin mustache giving him away. The second mask recogniz-able, although since she isn't a film buff, she can't quite place the face. Both masks fraying from age, the color diminishing, the rubber getting soft and malleable.

"Vivien," she hears, the voice deep and robotic, one she's not heard before. But she knows it's her husband even before she spins around.

———

Three men stand between Vivien and the door: Clark Gable, Frank Sinatra, and a portly James Dean. She eyes the masks in her hands, poor imitations compared to the ones on their faces. She's never seen anything so lifelike, so real, as if they'd been born as these idols and not mere mortals.

"I'm going to need you to hand me those," Gable says.

She takes a step, then hesitates, unwilling to let go of the masks as if they're keeping her tethered to a semblance of sanity. The masks' eyes swirl due to her touch of vertigo. Gable descends toward her.

"Vivien," he says.

She can hear a hint of his real voice, even though it's been digitally altered.

"Mom?" James Dean asks, and Gable gives James Dean a biting glance. She wonders if she's imagined it.

"W-what's going on?" she asks, in tears. She hasn't cried in some time, not when she found out that Gracie was taken. The word *monster* rumbles through her skull again.

"This is all easily explained," Gable says.

"Jay, is that you?"

Gable places a finger over her lips, warning her to be silent.

"What have you gotten mixed up in?" she asks.

"All can be explained, but not now. There is no time."

"What have you done?"

"Give me the masks and the cards."

"No, no, I refuse." She clutches them close to her chest as if they're her babies.

"Vivien!"

"Forty years of duplicity."

"You don't know what you're talking about."

"There is a man in the East River wearing a mask for a face just like you are. And he took Gracie!"

"That's not entirely true. He was trying to rescue her."

"What?"

"A rogue employee of mine has her. Someone who wanted revenge. Do you understand?"

"I understand *nothing*."

"They killed Cagney too. They're after me next."

"These masks—what do you mean? What have you been doing?"

He holds out his palms as an attempt to ease. "A way for us to remain stealth, that is all."

"That is not all. Don't take me for a foolish woman. You have for too long. And your son-in-law? Are you responsible for him being in a coma too?"

Gable looks at Sinatra, who turns to Dean.

"I'm getting out of here," Vivien says, attempting to rush through their blockade.

"Sinatra," Gable says, as an order.

Sinatra grabs her arm, loosens the masks from her

grip, and swipes the cards. She slaps him across the face.

"Vivien, you need to calm down."

She lets out a shrill cry, a dog's whistle that shatters their eardrums.

"Listen," James Dean says. "Just listen."

She spits in his face and gives a triumphant huff.

"Subdue her," Gable says.

"*What*?" she says. "What does that mean?"

Sinatra pulls a cloth from his pocket. She can smell the chemicals before it's even placed over her mouth. Her feet go light, the floor turning to air. Collapses in Gable's arms like a slain bride.

"I loved you," she says, eating her tears, as the fuzziness consumes her vision.

He doesn't answer back. She fights unconsciousness for as long as she can before she gives in to dreams, waiting for him to say it too.

33

GABLE

A SHORT DRIVE OVER TO BEDFORD HILLS, TWENTY minutes from Greenwich. Gable and James Dean have taken off their masks and enter a horse farm owned by a man named Rune, derived from the Old Norse word rún, meaning secret. Rune waits in a cowboy hat and chaps, his snow-white beard eating up most of his face except for tiny black eyes. He waves them through a gate, shoos away a few rambling horses, and pulls a lever causing a hole in the grass the size of a car to lift upwards, allowing them to descend.

"Secret, secret headquarters?" Chip asks, fixing his stark white hair in the rearview.

"What do you have a date to go to, dollface?" Jay says, rotating the mirror so it's in line with his vision.

Down below, they reach a huge dank garage with a few SUVs and a stockpile of guns and ammo.

"This is my apocalypse bunker," Jay says. They exit the vehicle and go through a door into a room set up like a 1970s den. Wet bar, wooden walls spanning three quarters except for a walled mirror on one end, shag carpet, and a burnt orange recliner. A fire is already cooking. They warm their hands.

"What happens next?" Chip asks. "And by the way, you're in desperate need of an interior design overhaul here. I have a guy."

"You think I care about fucking ottomans right now?"

"No, I-I don't know what else to say. Is mom going to be...?"

"She's fine. It's a mild sedative. Sinatra is monitoring her."

"I mean, like marriage-wise. Is it over between you two?"

"That's up to her. She's not entirely innocent in all of this."

The respect Gable felt towards Chip waning. Able to handle the kid for an hour tops before Chip begins to nag. How it's always been.

"There's a bathroom with a shower if you want to freshen up," he says, hoping Chip catches the hint so he can be alone with his thoughts.

"Ok."

Jay points to a door hidden in the wooden walls and Chip slips inside. He pours himself a glass of Scotch from the wet bar, sits down on the recliner across the roaring fire. He throws in the business cards, eliminating all evidence in case the bunker is found. The masks harder to fully destroy. There's the newer Gable and James Dean masks. Chucking them in as the flames eat at the eyes before they melt entirely. All that's left are his original mask and the one of Errol Flynn.

Foolish of him to hang onto the Errol Flynn mask all this time. No one wearing it since 1980, belonging to his star protégé, a lanky kid named Jake Barnum. One of the first to join the organization when it was just Jay, Oliver, and a few others feeling their way through the madness. Oliver, a business associate on a formerly failed venture, a man with a flair for luxury and decadence in the form of narcotics. They'd been introduced by his Yale classmate Douglas Sanford, the coxswain on his rowing team, whose father and Oliver's father invested in some Belgium properties together. He could barely remember much of the first year he knew Oliver due to all they ingested, hence the failure of their initial company, which matched rare wines with collectors. This led to the idea of the Desire Card after one collector whined that he desired a certain wine no one had been able to find. They were driving back from the client's house in Sagaponack to New York City where the two shared a two bedroom that overlooked Gramercy Park, a rotating door filled with various nightly women when he wanted a break from Vivien and the kids. Lines of cocaine spread out on the dashboard helped birth a gem.

"What if we set up a company that facilitated people's desires? Not just wine."

"I'm listening," Oliver said, but truth be told, he was snorting a massive line and rubbing the residue into his gums.

"You and I, we come from money."

"I'm not arguing with you on that," Oliver said, in his accent that swayed from French, to German, to flat Midwestern.

"But we don't have the kind of money some people in the city do. Or like the client we just left. He'll pay us anything if we find him that bottle. But we're thinking too small."

"What else do people want?"

Oliver had turned on the radio, *Cold as Ice* by Foreigner. He sang along in his off-key falsetto.

"Whatever they want," Jay roared. "It doesn't fucking matter. The rich want anything they don't have. We charge outrageous finder fees and laugh while we cash the checks."

"Should we have a card?"

"The Desire Card," Jay says, his eyes aglow, a tingling down his spine. Time froze on that highway, and all that existed was a light that clicked on in his mind. He saw his glorious future in flashing lights (which turned out to be a car almost hitting them because they were swerving into an incoming lane), but still, it was revelatory. He knew he was destined to leave a mark in this life. His father was a corporate lawyer before he passed. Made money, but it was his clients who really got wealthy. Jay would have it be the other way around. Ever since, he and Oliver would forever argue about which one of them came up with the Desire Card, where in reality it was a merging of two great minds.

He goes to fling the old masks into the fire, but realizes he never said a proper goodbye to Jake Barnum, who signified the very moment when the Card shook off any morals that slowly were diminishing over its first years. Drugs and guns easy to look away from, a corpse on the other hand became a wasp's sting on his medial temporal lobe—at least the first corpse of one of his own. After a while it gets easier to place coins over a stiff's eyes. But Jake—innocent Jake—tow-headed with his flesh-colored beard and freckles along his nose. A kid brother who needed money for surgeries leading Jake down this perilous road, which Jay exploited. An early time of lavish parties and celebrations before spilled blood dampened pleasures. Of Marilyn Monroe and Bette Davis, of Gregory Peck and Katherine Hepburn, and Spencer Tracey who was iced not long ago. His small team of upstarts, and a son in Jake. Listening now to Chip singing a Lady Gaga song in the shower, he'd known since Chip was little that he'd never connect with his actual son, so Jake filled that void.

The day he handed over the Errol Flynn mask into Jake's bloodied hands, a proud one. The boy never thought himself capable of greatness. Came from abject poverty without a hope of rising, but Jay saw talent, exceptionalism. All his operatives part of his collection, but Jake the one he showed-off and shined the most.

He places his fingers through Errol's eyes. Justified for his actions—what he tells himself when sleepless nights used to drag into mornings. How many ships in a bottle can he perfect? Everything he'd done to accelerate the Card, no second-guessing. But although the voices through the masks were made to sound robotic, he wasn't made entirely of metal. Over the years he hardened more, but back in 1980 a conscience still rattled around. After Jake—it was banished to the neverworlds.

The shower cuts off and Chip steps out with a towel wrapped around his chest like a lady.

"What?" Chip asks. With his whitened hair and turkey neck, Jay is astonished how old his son looks.

"Who's that?" Chip asks, nodding at the Errol Flynn mask with his double chin.

"A great man," Jay says, and when Chip shrugs his shoulders, Jay snipes: "Errol Flynn. *Robin Hood. Scaramouche.* A hero of that time."

"Why isn't he in the fire like the rest? Doesn't it behoove you to burn every last shred of your Card?"

Choking up, Jay can hear his voice cracking before he even speaks.

"I've never been ready to let him go."

Chip screws up his face. "I've never thought you were one for sentiment."

"You don't fucking know me, Chip. Okay? Can you compute that? You know an image I created, but it was never the full picture. Just the surface, not the guts."

Chip crosses his arms in a huff. "I could say the same about me."

"Go back in the bathroom and give me a second."

He points to the steamy door until Chip finally concedes and disappears back into the wooden wall.

Across from Jay, the mirror penetrates. He's heaving, trying to catch his breath, fighting the tears back. It's been forty years, but at that moment, only seconds. Destroy someone you considered your child and no one afterwards as difficult to extinguish. The rest of them objects in the way.

He tosses the Errol Flynn mask into the fire, but can't watch it burn. It doesn't melt right away, as if it knows it's power. A semblance of the face exists each time he looks back, each time he closes his eyes.

34

HARRISON

WAITING IN A STERILE WHITE ROOM, NOTHING TO differentiate the ceiling or floor from the walls. Harrison does not know how long he's been here, only that he misses the beach where he last saw Naelle. Normal not a word to describe their relationship. Began as a hooker and a client through the Desire Card, then she almost unwillingly became a donor for a liver transplant until he stopped the procedure halfway and they fled. Gave her enough money to fly back to the Dominican Republic to be with her mother and daughter and he considered staying too. But the fact that the Card would always be watching him made it necessary to keep her at a safe distance.

She returns in his subconscious. He's unaware it's not reality. Comas not like dreams, the hallucinations authentic. So when he met her on this imagined beach and she warned that he must unmask Gable to the world, he listened to her wise affirmation. Now the beach has gone, a lost memory. As he stands in the white room, he's certain he's waiting for something but doesn't know what.

The lights get brighter, careening off the walls like the sun has cast its glow. The ceiling melts away to reveal the cottage cheese ceiling of his hospital room along with fluorescent lights stabbing his eyes, and Helene in a chair clutching a cup of coffee as if it's her lifeline.

The next hours are fuzzy at best. He tries to speak but they tell him not to. The room filled with boisterous activity. Doctors and nurses spinning around. An incessant beeping of machines. A sip of water feels like a thousand daggers in his throat. He goes under and worries about reentering the white room, but only tumbles into dreamland, hovering at the edge of wakefulness. It's daytime, but then instantly it's dark. A doctor peers over the bed, checking his vitals.

"You gave everyone quite a scare," the doctor says. Harrison focuses on the doctor's silver nail polish.

"Naelle?"

"What's that?" the doctor asks, waving over Helene whose hand is warm as she grasps his. She's speaking but he drifts away again back to the beach where he and Naelle are hand-in-hand and he's told her something that's made her laugh. It's a private joke between them, and he's happy they can share this. They watch the sunset as she places her head on his shoulder, her curls clinging to his chest. The sun is nuclear, the sky a spread of reds and oranges, purples and pinks. The world is beautiful. And even though he knows it's not real, he wants to hold onto this mirage for as long as he can.

"You know what you need to do," she says, admonishing him with her finger.

"Yes," he says, seeing a Clark Gable mask wash up along the shore like it did the first time he sought her out in Punta Cana. As the waves fling it in his lap, tiny crabs emerge from the eyes.

"Will there ever be a chance for us?" he asks, with the deepest sigh of his tumultuous life.

"Who knows? I told you before I don't believe in fate."

"I've been trying to be a better person. The kind of work I've been doing in non-profits, and to be there for my kids. I'll tell the police who Jay Howell is."

"That's a start."

She kisses him on the cheek, then rises and wraps a sarong around her body since the air is getting chill. The sun has now set, the sky a shade of ink. Hard to distinguish it from the waters. The dream has ended for good. He's aware of this in his burning heart.

———

Detectives Bonner and Ramirez arrive after the doctors give the okay to speak with Harrison, since his daughter's case is of utmost importance. His mind foggy but he clearly remembers that Gracie remains missing. Brenton is on his way over from after school, and Helene and her new boyfriend Peter tend to his side.

Detective Bonner, all business, tucks her short hair behind her ears and sits down introducing herself and her connection to his daughter. She asks if he knows his name, the year, the president, and the names of his children and ex-wife. His brain has retained all the truly important things.

"Short term memories are more difficult," the doctor tells the detective, as if Harrison isn't in the room. Helene reiterates that anything he recalls could help find Gracie.

"Do you know who attacked you?"

His mouth is dry and he indicates for water, which the doctor cautions to take in sips even though he wants to chug.

"Not specifically, but yes...I do. I was hit from behind, and I fell down against the curb. But I saw them."

"How many of them, Mr. Stockton?" Bonner asks.

"Two."

"Can you describe what they look like?"

"This may sound crazy but Marlon Brando and Fred Astaire."

He'd encountered Brando and Astaire before when he sought a liver from the Card. After realizing Naelle had been drugged to be the donor, he knocked those operatives out to help her escape. It had to be sweet revenge for them to finally return the favor.

"They were wearing masks?" Bonner asks.

"Yes, it's this org..." He stops as the beginnings of a migraine surface. He knows it will creep up, but he must push through.

"These are the same people who harassed him before," Helene says, while Peter strokes her hand. "Tell them everything, Harrison."

He swallows, taking a moment to piece together the whole story—the past year and change of his life.

"I needed a liver," he says, wincing at the thought of

what he did. "The Desire Card is an organization that promises 'any wish fulfilled for the right price'. You have to understand how difficult it is to get a liver off the Organ Transplant Network. I...didn't have time."

He starts to cry, but he's so dehydrated that the tears barely release.

"Mr. Stockton, whatever you've illegally done does not matter if it can get your daughter back," Bonner says. "We'll handle it once she's safe."

"She's all that matters."

Bonner pats his hand, and he finds her touch soothing. "Now continue."

"They had a donor, an unwilling one. I-I went along with it. But when I saw the donor, I knew her."

"You didn't tell me this," Helene says, uncoiling from Peter's embrace.

"Ms. Howell, not now, okay?" Bonner waves Helene away, who's stunned at first and then obeys.

"I knew her...Naelle," Harrison continues. "I don't know her last name. God, I never learned her last name. What kind of piece of shit am I?"

"Focus, Mr. Stockton," Bonner says, shaking him. "I'm sorry. Go on."

"They were gonna cut out her liver. I couldn't let it happen so I saved her... I knocked them out, stuck them with tranquilizers..."

He sees Helene gasp and cover her mouth.

"Anyway, I wasn't going to pay them for the procedure. And so, they targeted me. I put Naelle on a plane to the Dominican Republic where her mother and daughter lived. But they caught up with me in Central Park, hit me over the head with the butt of a gun, and took the money back. I thought it was over."

"It was over," Helene says. "You didn't tell me about them contacting you again."

"It's because of who runs the organization."

"I can't believe you, Harrison. Every time I don't think you could sink any lower—"

Helene moves towards the bed so Bonner stands between them.

"Ms. Howell, I'm going to have you leave this room if you can't contain yourself. No one is arguing that your ex-husband isn't a son-of-a-bitch. You have every right to be mad."

"I do."

"You do. But your daughter is all my partner and I care about."

"Come here," Ramirez says, directing Helene away from potentially lunging at Harrison. Ramirez has his arm around her, holding her close.

"You don't understand the Card," Harrison says. "They get victims in their web, and once you are, y-you don't have a chance to get out. You'll always owe them."

"How big is this organization?" Bonner asks.

"Big, international too. I overheard that. There's...." He searches for the word and finally locates it through the fog. "There's a hierarchy, but a Boss at the top of it all. I'm so sorry, Helene."

He wonders if she already knows who he's going to say runs the Card. If she's suspected all along. She shakes her head, as if warning him not to decimate her life anymore.

"I wanted to keep you in the dark," he says.

"Mr. Stockton, who's the Boss?" Bonner asks.

As the name readies to fly off his tongue, he has an overwhelming sense of relief. There are no more secrets, his soul excavated. A faint sound of *merengue* music floats from the overhead speakers, a trickle of his coma that remains. And Naelle, sashaying away in her sarong on her powerful legs, disappearing into the crystal waters because she wasn't his and never will be.

"Jay Howell," he says, and then in case of confusion, he repeats the name over and over, until there could be no question.

35

MARCUS EDMONTON

THE WOUND ON MARCUS'S NECK PROVING problematic. Bandages stop the blood flow but not enough to close up the cut. Stitches required. He can either get the equipment he needs to do it himself, or he knows a guy because the Card employs a bevy of subcontractors that work for them with the promise of keeping silent. He has a little cash left from the money he made in Washington with Abram's crew so he heads to East 10th St., the basement apartment of a man named Stitches, given the moniker for precisely what he's hired to do.

Kismet that he's practically around the corner so he doesn't have far to travel. Also, Gracie, having forgone another meal, has curled up in the corner like a napping cat. A blustery wind hits him upon exiting. With one hand clamped over his wound, he jogs a few blocks and rings Stitches' buzzer four times before the guy finally opens the door.

"Yes?" Stitches asks, and Marcus realizes that he's

not wearing his James Dean mask so Stitches can't recognize him.

"It's James Dean," he says, thinking of a way to give proof. A quote from one of Dean's movies, but he's drawing a blank because it's been a while since he thought of himself as Dean.

Stitches steps back into the darkness of the apartment, but leaves the door open as an indication for Marcus to enter.

The inside reeks of shut windows. Various candles situated on tabletops and sills flicker, most of the wicks about to be snuffed. Stitches wears a bathrobe and slippers like an old man, yet he's likely the same age as Marcus.

"Something happened to your mask?" Stitches asks, in his nasal twang. Marcus knew his story once, or at least a variation. From down South, missed out on graduating medical school to a technical error, swept up by the Card when there were no other options.

"The mask? Yeah, I need a new one."

Stitches carefully observes. Marcus unsure if Stitches would even care whether he was lying. The guy worked for the Card, but in an ancillary role. It wasn't about loyalty.

"Lemme see your neck," Stitches says, waving him over to a portion of the back room set up like a doctor's office. Stitches places tiny glasses on the tip of his nose. He peels off the bandage, makes a face, slaps on gloves and proceeds to stitch Marcus up. "Wound looks to be from the rusty nail variety."

"You would be correct."

Stitches stabs him in the shoulder with a tetanus shot.

"Just to be safe." Stitches blinks through the tiny glasses. "You know, I haven't heard from the Card in some time."

"None of the operatives needed to be stitched up recently I guess."

"Or there are no operatives to stitch up."

Marcus has to be careful. He can't trust anyone completely and definitely not Stitches. Although if he feigns ignorance, Stitches could realize everything's a lie.

"I've seen the news," Stitches says, lining up his medical instruments. "Looks like Cagney's been iced, Delon too."

Marcus eyes the front door, ready to escape. "I'm in as much of the dark about that as you."

"Gable can't be pleased."

"No, he is not."

"Rival gang?"

"Something like that."

"Or a client exacting revenge?" Stitches picks up a scalpel and cleans it with a cloth. "I know, I know, none of my business. But you can't fault me for being curious."

"I need to go, Stitches."

"Us subcontractors so out of the loop. Even more than the freelancers. At least they get masks."

"What do I owe you for the services?"

"Let's say two thousand."

Marcus pulls a stack of cash from his pocket.

"We all talk, ya-know?" Stitches says, fanning himself with his newfound bills.

Marcus is already lunging for the door. "Who's that?"

"The freelancers and the subcontractors. I mean, never with the operatives. Stitch 'em up and keep my lips sealed. You're the first of their actual faces I've seen. Not what I pictured."

"What did you picture?"

"Your missing eye—that void. I never knew."

"There's a lot we don't know about each other."

"Yes, yes there is. Anyway, the freelancers are my only *entre* to your world. Mae West, do you know her?"

"Not really. We haven't done any missions together."

"She's a doll. A real firecracker. Born to wear that mask."

"Stitches, I don't need to remind you that this stays between us."

Stitches fans his face with the bills again. "This is rather light."

"I don't have much more—"

"I wasn't implying."

"Yes, you were."

"Fine, I am. Like I said, it's been a while since an operative has passed through my door. Rent's due."

"And blackmail's on the table."

"What an ugly word."

"How much?"

"'Nother grand should cover it. I'll even throw in a beautiful pill to dull the pain."

Marcus digs into his stack knowing he has no other choice. He hands over practically all that's left.

"Pleasure doing business with you." Stitches picks up a small capsule bottle and takes out a light blue pill. "This'll keep you covered for about six hours. Make you rest your...eyes, I mean, *eye*, as well. You look like you need it."

Marcus swipes the pill and then backs Stitches into a corner. "You keep silent, you hear?"

Stitches mimes zipping his lips.

On his way out the door, Marcus chomps down the pill, its chalky tang remaining on his tongue.

———

When Marcus returns, Gracie still naps so he lies on the couch to rest his eyes and instantly he's asleep. From the chemical assistance, he hasn't slept this hard since he went against the Card and became its number one target. He's on a beach in Matagi Island where a volcano erupted many years ago and left the sand white and hot. He used to keep a postcard of this very place tacked up in his bedroom. It was where he and Annie were going to meet after they escaped the Card for good. He walks up and down the shore waiting for her arrival but in the pit of his stomach he knows she's long dead. Upon Gable's orders, Cagney put a bullet in her brain while she blew him a final kiss.

But then a miracle occurs and she's bringing him over a Corona with one for herself. Even in this dreamland, he's aware that she's nothing more than a mirage. Yet the beer tastes so crisp and refreshing, and the lemony smell of her perfume circles, and the way she says "J.D., you and me in paradise" as if it's a song, not Marcus—he was still J.D. to her—the last time he had a shred of hope.

"J.D., this revenge... Is it worth it?"

"What else do I have?" he asks, draining the beer. "You're gone."

She moves her blonde nest of hair from her face, puts it in a side-ponytail.

"Go to Matagi Island anyway," she says, shielding her eyes from the sun. "Do what you planned without me."

"And Gable?"

She frowns at his name: this man who made her deceive, responsible for her demise.

"Who said it's your job to play judge, jury and executioner?" she asks, in her Kentucky twang. Like when he first met her before he shipped off to Iraq. Before life got its claws in.

"He has to pay," Marcus says, because nothing else will give him meaning.

"That's just revenge talking. He'll get his."

The void where his eye once was throbs.

"But *I* have to be the one to do it."

"It can't be more important than this."

She indicates the island with a sweep of a tan arm. A volcano in the distance that once spewed lava over the entire beach. She's already fading.

"It's all that matters," he says.

"Well then, J.D., be ready for an endgame you may not like."

She leans in close, kissing his missing eye, and then vanishes into the air.

The last sip of his beer chalky as he comes to with bits of the light blue pill stuck in his molars.

36

DETECTIVE MONICA BONNER

SPEEDING UP TO GREENWICH, CONNECTICUT WITH Ramirez at the wheel, Bonner's not ready to involve the FBI. Then the media get involved, and Jay Howell gets tipped off and runs. While she's not expecting to find Jay at his house—his daughter said he's been unreachable—his wife was certain to be there. She called it into her chief, who listened to her sworn statement from Harrison and would begin the process of obtaining a warrant. He was sending backup to the Howells' house from local law enforcement. Depending on what went down, the FBI would be called in next.

"Man, the daughter turned white as soap when she heard about her father," Ramirez says.

"Imagine, you think you know someone and then —wham."

"How do you think the granddaughter is connected to all this?"

"Got to be someone involved with the Card who wasn't happy with their agreement. As much as we might want to bring Jay Howell down, we may need him to help find Gracie Stockton first."

Make a right turn to reach your destination, the GPS tells them.

"Looks like local police haven't arrived yet," Ramirez says, observing the enclave.

"We don't have time to wait."

They park the car in the driveway behind two other cars. Bonner wants to scope the house first before knocking on the door.

"You see any lights?" Ramirez asks, peering in a window.

"Yeah," she says. "But that doesn't mean anyone's home. Giant house like this probably has timers. Let's go around the back."

She takes the safety off her gun as they walk past the tennis court and the life-size chess set.

"Fucking rich people," Ramirez says, inspecting a knight piece.

A sprinkler turns on, bathing the back lawn with its spray. They're forced to weave around, hugging the façade. Bonner feels a gap in a window.

"Looks open to me," she says, opening it more.

Ramirez's eyebrow raises with his telling, *you know you shouldn't be doing that but I'm gonna let it slide because I was thinking the same thing.*

He helps her inside, since Bonner weighs one hundred twenty pounds at the most, long and lean. Ramirez, at a buck more with a midsection that has favored jelly donuts over the years, knows it'll be a tough fit.

"Give me a few minutes to search around," she says. "I'll radio you. Then go and ring the doorbell."

"I'm busting in if I hear anything suspicious."

"Hopefully, the local force will be here by then."

She leaves him lurking by the window, her gun pointed downward as she tiptoes through a room with a grand piano and modern art paintings bigger than her. The kind of money the Howells have unfathomable. There were times growing up when her mom worked two jobs and still the heat got turned off. Or they shared a can of salty soup for dinner. Or she wore the same pants every day for a week because they didn't have enough quarters for the laundromat.

She picks up a tiny golden statue of Robert E. Lee. "What an absolute dick."

Bending the head until it snaps off, she places the statue back on the mantle and keeps the head.

From the piano room, she enters a grand hallway and is greeted by a painting of the Howells dated 1988. Jay and Vivien look to be in their forties, their children surly teenagers. Jay's hair thick and black in a pompadour style like Elvis. She stares into his eyes and decides he looks as if he's hiding a delicious secret.

"You're about to be exposed, fucker," she whispers.

Down the hallway, a scraping sound echoes. Furniture being moved along a rug. Gun ready, she sidesteps toward the source, turning into what appears to be an office. Bookshelves lined with tomes, a ship in a bottle on a grand desk, and Vivien Howell bound and gagged in a chair she's desperately trying to inch toward the door.

Vivien's eyes go big as Bonner rushes inside. The woman has wet herself, the piss smell strong enough for Bonner to know she ate asparagus. She checks behind her in case someone's planning on sneaking up. Vivien squirms and attempts to scream through the cloth tied around her mouth, but Bonner places a finger to her lips.

"Is someone still here?" she mouths to Vivien, who nods. "Where?" Vivien shrugs her shoulders. "Don't make a sound while I take it off."

She undoes the cloth as Vivien gasps for air. A little overdramatically, but Bonner understands the woman has probably never been put in a perilous situation like this.

"Where is your husband?" Bonner asks.

"Gone," Vivien manages to say after taking big gulps of air.

"Who else is still in the house?"

As if on cue, "I Get a Kick Out of You," starts blasting. Both Bonner and Vivien jump in place. Bonner gets out her radio.

"Ramirez, I got Mrs. Howell tied up and the perpetrator in the house."

"I heard the music turn on."

"Back up here yet?"

"Negative, I'm gonna—"

The radio gets knocked out of her hands by the swift kick of Sinatra who stands in the doorway in a fedora and suit with a glass of bourbon in one hand and a pistol in the other. His eyes so blue as if it's they belong to an alien species.

"Pick up the radio," Sinatra says, indicating with the gun. "Tell whoever's outside that I will put a bullet in the old *hausfrau's* brain if I'm not let out of here alive."

"Ramirez," Bonner says.

"Yeah, what's going on?"

"There's a man in a Sinatra mask who will kill Mrs. Howell if we don't let him go."

"And you," Sinatra adds. "I'll kill you too. Don't forget to tell him that."

"Did you hear him?" Bonner asks. "He'll kill me too."

Vivien screams, thrashing her head from side to side.

"Mrs. Howell, please," Bonner says, but Vivien screams louder.

"Goddamnit." Sinatra whacks her across the face with his gun, which causes her to whimper.

"Shut the fuck up, you old bag. Now, Copper, I'm aiming to walk out of here."

"We're not after you," Bonner says. "We're looking for Gracie Stockton."

"So is Gable," Sinatra says.

"Gable? You mean Jay Howell?"

"If that's his actual name, yeah."

"Do you know who took her?"

"The operative formerly known as James Dean. Goes by Marcus Edmonton now."

"But Jay Howell doesn't know where he is?"

"That would be a *no.*"

"So what are you doing here?"

"Gable was worried about his identity being revealed." Sinatra takes a stinging sip of his bourbon. "Obviously justified. We came here to eliminate any evidence, and the wife got mixed up."

"They drugged me," Vivien cries.

"Minor sedative. But listen, Copper, I'm what's

called a Freelancer in the organization. Meaning I haven't pledged my full loyalty or anything. I work for the money, for the thrill, nothing more. So I'll let you be on your way if you let me be on mine."

"Do you know where Jay is now?"

"Secret headquarters."

"And where is that?"

"You ask a lot of questions for me having a gun on you."

Back in the day as an officer when Kellan was alive, Bonner wasn't nearly at gutsy. She had reasons to go home. Now she has nothing.

"Help us," she says. "You'll get immunity. You're not our target. Bigger fish, right?"

They hear a crash from down the hall.

"Is that your partner?" Sinatra asks.

"I don't—"

"C'mon." He grabs her by the arm. On the way out of the office, he kicks Vivien's chair until she tips over with a howl.

At the end of the hallway, Ramirez has hoisted himself through another open window and knocked over a large vase in the process. He leaps up on his feet, he and Sinatra pointing their guns at one another.

"Put down the gun," Ramirez yells.

"I'll fucking kill her, I will."

"Ramirez, don't put down the gun," Bonner yells back.

Sinatra fires off a shot hitting Ramirez in the shoulder. Ramirez spins around, his gun going off and the bullet hitting the painting of the Howells and landing right between the son's eyes. Sinatra fires again, hitting Ramirez lower down in the same arm he capped before.

Ramirez lets out a raging shriek that rattles Bonner's eardrums. She imagines Sinatra must be experiencing the same tinnitus too. Swiveling out of his grip, she knees Sinatra hard in the stomach as he doubles over and pulls her to the ground. They wrestle around, skidding across the marble floor. He's still holding the gun, trying to direct it toward her. She fights with everything she has inside of her, forcing him to fire a bullet that goes nowhere. He's heaving over her, spit flying, foaming at the mouth. She watches Ramirez getting to his feet, stopping the bleeding from his shoulder with one hand while the weak arm raises a pistol. He's inching their way, the click of his gun ready.

"Don't shoot him, we need him!" she cries.

Sinatra gets a whiff of this new development, taking his eyes off of her for a second too long. She knocks him off her, the gun scattering away. Sinatra scurries to his feet but it's too late, both of them with their guns trained on him.

Outside sirens blare and red and blue lights stream into the house.

"You're coming with us," Ramirez says, spitting a glob of blood.

"I won't go to prison," he says.

"You can talk to your lawyer about that. There could still be deals on the table. Although, after shooting my partner, the deal might not be as beneficial to you as it once was..."

Sinatra squeezes his eyes shut. "Can you light me a cigarette? In my front pocket."

He shifts until a pack of Camels emerges.

"Don't try anything funny," Bonner says, swiping

the pack and a Zippo too. Lighting it for him and placing it between his lips.

"How's your last cigarette as a free man?" Ramirez asks.

Sinatra puffs an O, studying its disintegration. Leaves them hanging without an answer.

37

GABLE

Dear Helly,

This was never a letter I wanted to write to you, but I imagine it would be harder to tell you in person. Likely, by the time you receive this, you will already have learned who I really am. I need you to know that it doesn't mean I love you any less. They may call me a sociopath, but if I'm truly proud of one thing I've done in this life, it's you. You and I always had a stronger bond than either of us had with your mother and brother, and I don't mean that as an insult to them. We're alike, you and I, in terms of our determination. Yet there is a humane quality to you that I never possessed. I believe you deserve to know where my callousness came from. I've never even told your mother this.

My own mother was a good woman, but she had problems. These days, they likely would've been able to balance out her medications better, but then, well, science hadn't caught up with her troubled mind. When my father died—and he tried to love her as well as he could—she lost it. He did everything for her, and in the absence of that, she dissolved. I'd just become a teenager at the time. I wasn't ready to be a man, but I had to step up. Feed her, dress her. Lucky my father did well for himself so we had help, but she could get violent and nonsensical. Oftentimes, our help would quit and I'd be left to pick up the pieces. This was my life before she died and I went off to Yale. But those years I cursed any other kids that were able to hang out and go on dates. All I could do was study. I played football, but that was really an escape more than anything else. And I paid for it when I'd get home too late and she'd defecate on the bed. The only thing that seemed to alleviate her suffering was watching old movies. There were times I don't know how much she was able to retain, but the black and white images put her in a state of calm. She wouldn't rant or rave. She was the mother I remembered as a small child.

"Gone with the Wind" was a favorite. I liked its length because it provided us with nearly four hours of peace when it was on. She was mesmerized with Clark Gable, since her name was Scarlett. She'd imagine the film was her own life, and Gable's relaxed tone as Rhett Butler put her in a wonderful stupor. So, I began to mimic it so much that I started to talk like him. She would eat when Gable ask her to, as opposed to when I or the maid did. She wouldn't throw fits. While she didn't return completely to the mother I'd grown up with, at least she was closer to becoming that woman. I could see with Clark Gable around she wanted to try.

I'd found a Halloween costume mask of Rhett

Butler, and when I put it on, the joy in her eyes was unrivaled. Really, Helly, she just lit up. So, I'd wear it around the house. And when her dementia really started to take hold, she'd refer to me as Gable. For the majority of high school that's who I was to her, and when she died it was difficult to give him up— this persona I'd gotten so used to. But the Desire Card, which the news outlets will condemn ad nauseum, didn't come from her. I tended to her because I loved her, not because it was the right thing to do. I've never done anything in my life simply because it was the right thing to do. The Card was a means to put a mark on this world. I'd devoted so much to her, I never had a chance to really grow into myself. And while my father was a successful litigator, that wasn't enough for me.

When the Card began, it wasn't as nefarious as it became. I wanted to provide a sense of wonder for my clients. We've spanned politicians, celebrities, CEOs, innovators: the pulse of society. Even for these people who touched greatness, there were elusive wishes they weren't able to obtain. That's where I came in. And I was good at it. We all were. Olivier and I and our band of merry genies. Precious diamonds. Rare furs. Ancient artifacts. Life became a game of pushing ourselves to see what we could procure. And we were paid handsomely. We entered the who's-who of elite society. Only those worthy enough obtained our Card, and we kept the worthy at a bare minimum. But of course, human beings as they are—vile, vengeful, rotten at the core—had greater designs for their ultimate desires. What was wearing a diamond compared to ruining a rival, or even—God forbid—

eliminating them entirely? Not all of our members had these diabolical wishes but enough did. There's a celebrity or two you'd be shocked to learn called in a debased favor. And these desires paid even more handsomely. You and your brother grew up wealthy. I did as well, but not with the kind of riches you were used to. That does something to a child. I'm not saying you were spoiled—well, your brother was spoiled, but you, dear Helly, never let money rule your world. Your mother did. Enough for her to look the other way in terms of what afforded her lavish lifestyle. I don't think she knew about all the killings, but she was aware of shady business dealings if it meant another jewel on her body. I imagine she will plead innocence, and I don't mean for you to condemn her, just to understand that she's not the fawn in the woods she'll make herself out to be. I digress. My love for her vanished some time ago. I was having an affair with one of my operatives who wore an Audrey Hepburn mask. She was a true love where your mother was a means to create a façade. There was love between us once, or at least, a youthful passion. But true love? Even she'd agree that never occurred. I suppose you had a similar marriage with Harrison, a bad egg I attempted to save you from when the relationship began. But I don't have time in this letter to waste on him.

About your daughter, for that I am sorry too. My hope is that she will be home with you soon and the whole endeavor will be thought of as a nightmare. My former operative James Dean, a.k.a. J.D. Storm, who is going by Marcus Edmonton now, has caused more trouble for the organization than one would have ever anticipated. He kidnapped Gracie to get back at me. He doesn't intend to hurt her. Not that he doesn't have a killer's blood coursing through him, but I can promise you her safety. And I never intended for her to get stuck in the middle of all of this.

So now comes the hardest part of this letter. I fear it is the last time you will hear from me, at least for a long while. I am fighting for my life from the international office wanting to ice me, and I'm certain the Card and myself are about to be exposed. I will be fleeing the country. Where to, I haven't decided. I've spent years in international business and have many places and saviors I can turn to— safety nets I've kept close with in case of an emergency. I likely will never be able to tell you where I am, but it may not be the last time you see me. I am stubborn, one of my best and worst qualities, and I have NEVER not gotten what I wanted. So I assume I will find a way to orbit back into your life, my darling, Helly.

Be good, do well, and don't be like me.

Your loving father,

Jay

———

AFTER READING OVER THE LETTER FOR ANY mistakes, there's more Gable wanted to say, but he knows he doesn't have the time. He leaves the spare room where Chip is napping into the giant garage stock-piled with SUVs and ammo. There's a bell attached to the ceiling that he rings and a few moments later, Rune appears through a trap door, shifting his cowboy hat over his black eyes as he hangs down headfirst.

"Make sure this is mailed to my daughter."

Rune tips his cowboy hat, swipes the letter, and disappears back into the trapdoor. It shuts closed and the loneliness that sweeps over Gable is overwhelming. His limbs burn and he can barely catch his breath.

The trapdoor reopens and Rune pops his head back down.

"You're on the news," is all he says, in his Swedish accent that has lessened over the years.

Gable returns to the spare room and turns on a television affixed to the wall. This wakes up Chip, who hugs a pillow and watches transfixed. They listen to a journalist on MSNBC exposing the Desire Card as a "sordid glorified hitman operation that also specializes in granting wishes for the wealthy and absurd." His face splattered across the screen and spoken of as the "ringleader." The journalist talks about two of its members that wound up dead in the past week and Jay Howell's granddaughter who somehow got "caught in the Desire Card's web too." It's explained that there isn't knowledge yet about how far the tentacles of the Card reach, but it's assumed that there are many powerful politicians and celebrities "mixed up." The meaning behind the masks uncertain, however the public is urged to be on the lookout for anyone resembling an old-time movie idol. And to contact the police if Clark Gable is spotted, since that's Jay Howell's disguise. In every photo they show of him, he looks pissed off, and Gable wonders if he has Resting Angry Face. They didn't wait to drag him through the mud. He should've known with this 24/7 news cycle they'd pounce on a story as juicy as this. The reporter interviews Detective Monica Bonner who was tasked as the lead officer on Gracie Stockton's case. She has short hair and a lean lizard-quality to her face. She looks into the camera dead serious and promises that Jay Howell, or Clark Gable, or however he identifies himself, is "about to get the reckoning he deserves."

Gable turns off the television.

"I have to make some calls, Chip."

"What the fuck are we gonna do?"

"Go into the garage while I figure it out."

"Do you have...?"

"Chip! Don't wear on my last nerve."

He gives Chip a little push until he's out of the door. He gets out his cell, debates who to call first and dials. The other line rings a few times before it's picked up.

"Speak of the devil," the voice says. "And on my secure line?"

"Sanford," Gable says, his old rowing buddy from Yale. A voice from the past but a good one, the few that remain.

"You're all over the TV. I've already contacted my lawyers."

"You're a little fish in the grand scheme of this all."

"I'm going to pretend not to be offended."

"You were one of our first investors back in '78. You and your father, and we were grateful for your support. The Card would've never reached such great heights without those early funds."

"Is this your way of making sure I'm implicated?"

"Like I said, small fish, Sanford. You chose to run a

legit financial firm while I dipped my toe in a lake of illegality. They won't be coming after you."

"My former employee Harrison Stockton is all over the News too."

"Dougie, I do not have the time or patience to worry about your fucking meager problems. You will be fine. You have not become Americas Most Wanted today so shut your fucking old lips and listen. The offshore money I have–"

"Oh, now you come around to what you want?"

"What do you think, I want to swap tales about our rowing days with the Bulldogs? My accounts are about to be frozen, but we've always kept those offshore in another name for desperate times. These are desperate times."

"And where do you plan to wind up?"

"I haven't decided. Somewhere fuck off the beaten path. I'm going to call my Do Not Break In Case of An Emergency Contact and see what they have to say. No one else will know."

"Your family...?"

"Already left in the dust."

"How cold."

"Would you expect me to be any different?"

"No, you always had ice in your veins. What allowed you to row so well through those frigid winter days on the water."

He pictures he and Dougie back then. Waking up at three at in the morning, their limbs stiff, and the quiet of the Mill River welcoming: eliminating his past, guiding him into a better present. Dougie with his tree-trunk legs and sweep of blond hair, ghostly pale, and kissed with freckles along his cheeks. They spoke of their plans once they'd graduate. "Titans of industry," as they referred to themselves. And Dougie was successful. Sanford & Co. one of the biggest financial firms on the Street for nearly fifty years. Began as his father's, but Dougie was the one who formed it into a great success. Gave a pittance of their savings to help fund the Desire Card, and Sanford & Co.'s top employees were allowed access. Most used it for carnal pleasures, blow, or trifling wishes like securing a grand yacht. Dougie insisted it would stay as "above the line" as possible. When Gable last saw Dougie at a function about a year ago, the man had lost all his hair after a promising bout of chemo, and the weight he dropped made him a percentage of the man he used to be. He could barely fill out his suit and his wife doted over him, fussing with his appearance, while he couldn't stomach the alcohol being passed around.

"But you beat it," Jay had said, squeezing his old friend's shoulder and feeling the shift of bones.

"May you never experience the fear of the end, Jay," Dougie had said.

"Won't we all someday?" Jay replied, swiping a beef tartare hors d'oeuvre off a waiter's plate.

"Hopefully not in the ghoulish rush like I did."

"I have a feeling mine will be full of fire."

"At least it'll be spoken about," Dougie said, shivering from the air conditioning in the room.

"For ages, they will. That I can guarantee."

Thinking about this, Gable clutches his cell that has gone slick against his ear with sweat.

"I hope you are well, Dougie," he says. "The cancer, did it come back?"

"Don't pretend you care."

"Have you ever known me to be polite?"

"No. And it hasn't. And yes, your offshore accounts are all set up. Under the name William Clark as you requested."

"And my fake passport should suffice?"

"Unquestionably."

"Then this is goodbye."

"It is," Dougie says. "Unless I'm implicated. Of course, then I'll spill everything, including the where-abouts of the accounts."

"That's fair, Dougie."

"Be well, old devil," Dougie says, and then hangs up before Gable can respond.

He goes through his contacts to make his final call. It rings a few times before a voice picks up that sounds like the person is chewing on glass.

"Yes?" the voice asks.

"Hello, I was wondering if The Doctor was in?"

38

THE DOCTOR

AFTER THE BLOODBATH IN KILLENROY, OREGON that splattered across the papers, The Doctor needed to lay low. Didn't help that a rat fuck named Abram had brought over a large amount of cocaine The Doctor had already started to sell and then wound up with a bullet in his guts on the side of the road. Abram was certainly linked to the bloodbath in the woods where three men were found dead with coke residue on them. This meant the coke was tainted and the DEA would follow a trail that led to its source—i.e. The Doctor.

Solution: no more selling, at least for a while. He got rid of his underlings who cut up drugs at his place *sans* clothes so he could be sure that none of his goods might be stolen. It also made them vulnerable while he wore his bathrobe and sat perched atop a throne with John Lennon sunglasses and A-Ha's "Take on Me" playing on loop in the background. He retained two tree-trunks posted by his front doors as bodyguards. If an upset client, or God-forbid the police came a-knocking, they'd have to get through his tanks first.

This was the first vacation he'd taken in some time. Massive amounts of cash hidden under floorboards, in pillow cases, and stuffed in mattresses, always so he could have the option of what to spend it on. He was a man of desires. Some blow, an occasional girl, his favorite song—any wish fulfilled. Went by the motto, "All that spirits desire, spirits attain". Desire meant the ability to have whatever you wanted with the snap of a finger. To never be stuck in a realm of *NEEDING* only *BEING*.

Laurita had slinked out of his cabin around noon, eyes dancing and licking her gums after they fucked off pills from Madagascar his old business associate had given to him. Pushing sixty and ingesting cocaine since his twenties had left The Doctor limp, but the pills only required a two-minute window until they kicked into action.

It was a good romp with Laurita, who wore white lipstick that she left evidence of on his dick. But minus the thrill of making deals and selling his product, he had nothing to do. He imagined this must be how retirees feel. Searching for ways to fill up their days. Questioning the regrets of their life. He was once an actual doctor before the malpractice suit. He even fucking ran drugs with Pablo Escobar! He'd lived a million lives in this short one, and this was far from his final act. So, he chopped up some lines and got to brainstorming.

During the third line, somewhere between lucidity and flight, his cell rings—the private cell, not the number given to clients, only a handful knowing the digits. He lowers "Take on Me" so he can hear.

"Yes." His hand twitches from the drugs, his voice all over the place.

"Hello, I was wondering if The Doctor was in?"

"Depends on the ailment," The Doctor says, deadpan.

"What isn't ailed right now?" Jay Howell says, deadpan too. Speaking to his confidant, he lets go of any Gable*isms*. The Doctor can sense desperation, a hint of sadness. He was always good at parsing out weak emotions to exploit. "Have you seen the news lately?"

"I try to avoid in case my mug becomes the local six o'clock."

The Doctor lights a Delicados *cigarro*, a brand from his youth. Keeping one behind his ear at all times for easy access, that's what Pablo used to say.

"Look at us," Jay says. "Two old fucks on the lam."

"And what criminalities have finally caught up with you?"

"Oh, the usual—murder and mayhem. But now I'm unmasked for the world to see."

The Doctor rubs his smooth chin, unable to grow a beard. His skin sags like a Shar-pei's with dirt tucked in the folds. His nose tingles and he fires a bloody booger toward the wall, watches it drip. His cabin empty, devoid of life, where days ago it had been filled with bustle. He exhales a long smoky sigh.

"My area's plastered with cops so I wouldn't recommend hiding out here if that's why you're calling. Bit of a gun parade in the woods a few months ago. I'm not responsible, but they're looking to point the finger The Doctor's way."

"No, Javier," Jay says, and The Doctor can hear him wince. "I apologize. I know how much you don't like to be named."

"Something we always had in common."

"The life of a criminal mastermind requires alter egos."

The Doctor sucks in half the *cigarro*, the smoke sticking to his lungs which he pictures look like chimneys. When he's dead and cut open, all he'll be are smoke and coke ether.

"So, why the phone call, Gable?" The Doctor asks.

"I need to be smuggled out of the country, preferably Mexico which is why I thought of you."

The Doctor taps the ashes in an astray with a picture of the lead singer from A-Ha. The song finishes in the background and starts automatically playing again.

Outside, it rains so hard you can't even see the water coming down. A product of living in Oregon. The Doctor damp at all times. Only during a few weeks in the summer does it feel like Mexican weather: where he was born and raised. But the smells cannot be duplicated. The forests a poor comparison to a sweet and spicy *elote* grilling on the street.

"That's funny," he says, snorting a fresh line and pinching his nose. "I've been contemplating a trip back to the homeland myself."

"Got any room in the back of a van?"

It had been a while since The Doctor was in Gable's orbit. But true friendships mean falling out of each other's lives and finding your way back together. He'd met Gable in the '70s as the guy was beginning his Desire empire. Those were the early Escobar days. He brokered the contact between the two. Jay (he wasn't completely Gable yet) had the means to get drugs across the border. Cocaine exploding in Miami where the Card had its satellite office purely for the cane. They reorbited back into each other's lives when a valet mixed up their white Ferrari Berlinetta Boxers. The Doctor had been sent up the waters to gauge the scene. Snowfall everywhere. Both he and Jay's noses crusted with white, a stripper on each arm. They stuffed into one of their Ferraris and Jay played this song, this religious experience, synth beats ramping up, *We're talking away, I don't know what, I'm to say*. The Doctor had never left Mexico before for more than a few days, and this glorious song signaled him shooting into the next stratosphere. He'd be more than Escobar's flunky. He'd use Escobar's *cocaina* and set up his own stateside gang. He'd find his American father who walked out on him and his Mexican mom and kill him. Had the *bastardo* stayed, who knows what path The Doctor would've gone down, but his mother had to work as a housemaid for a mean *mestizo* family who had three brats that pulled her hair and pissed all over the house to give her something to clean. They lived in a tiny house that rocked in heavy winds. He once caught *dengue* and almost died because they didn't have access to medicine. He shared a bed with two brothers and two sisters. He ran away from home because they kept giving him lice. Made his way to Guadalajara with his friend Diego who had a cousin in a drug cartel that controlled all illegal trade from the U.S. to Mexico. Began as a *halcon* for Pablo Escobar, the eyes and ears of the streets, reporting activities of the military and rival groups. Moved up to become a *sicario*, responsible for carrying out assassinations, kidnappings, thefts, extortions, operating protection rackets, and defending their *plaza* from rivals. Despite his young age, he was one of the best, silent but deadly.

The cartel suffered a major blow when the co-founder killed a DEA agent. Had to split up into sub-cartels that later became warring gangs. When Diego got shot, The Doctor was able to save his life. He'd done some reading on how to take out a bullet, since it was inevitable that he'd get hit. He had a come-to-Jesus moment. Leave bloody Mexico for the States and go legit. On a whim, he threw everything into getting a medical degree at the age of forty and opened up a side-practice until a malpractice suit forced him into bank-ruptcy. That was around the time Gable reorbited into his life once again. Gable needed an on-call doctor. Someone who could stitch his operatives up and stay quiet. Plus, The Doctor still had contacts from the Miami Days, able to get the best *yayo* for exclusive clients. Did this for a while until he heard from Diego who formed a new cartel with the need for guns. America needed coke and so The Doctor moved to a border town and helped trade guns for drugs for around a decade. Then, 9/11. Border measures put in place and it wasn't as easy to funnel guns for drugs. Diego needed out of Mexico so they set up shop as far away from the sun as they could imagine—Killenroy, Oregon, a redneck town that everyone drove past to get to better places. The local cops easily bought. The DEA and FBI with no clue where they escaped. The Doctor good at slipping into cracks, disappearing before your eyes. No competition so their empire seized the Northwest. If you did cocaine anywhere from Washington to Idaho and down to Colorado, it was The Doctor's goods. And Gable had a lot of high-paying clients out west where it had run dry before The Doctor's arrival. But Diego got greedy, as it happens when there's more than one boss—

something Gable always warned him. He also got sloppy. Did so much coke everyday he couldn't think straight. Liabilities are not something The Doctor could work with so he shot Diego in the head one night over a card game of *conquian*, like they used to play when they were teenagers. Problem solved—only one Boss now with the capital B. He shipped his family money and bought them a giant house with a pool and two house-cleaners for his mom.

But he hadn't been back since moving up here.

He could hit up his remaining contacts to look the other way as he'd cross the border. He could do a solid for Gable and get him across too.

"Let me ask you, Gable," he says, lighting another *cigarro*. "If I get you to Mexico, are you retiring? Because I've always been a man on the move. And this place doesn't suit me anymore. But I can't just put my feet up and die. *El Doctor* needs to be challenged. *Comprende?*"

"You're saying you'll take me across if we start up a new venture?"

The Doctor exhales twin smoke beams from his nostrils.

"Your Card may be toast in the States, but in Mexico, we can still leave a legacy."

"How fast can you be here?"

"I can be there in two days."

"I'm texting you the coordinates of where I am. It's also a bit down in the earth once you get there."

The Doctor receives the text. The die is cast. He stands up from his throne, shucking off his bathrobe, and does a final line while A-Ha sings, *I'll be gone, In a day or twooooooooooooooo.*

39
MAE WEST

Hand wrapped in gauze to hide the burns, Mae West doesn't blame Gable for the hot poker. She knew what she was getting into when she signed up for the Card. And she'd been the bearer of worse pain. An ex who used her face as a punching bag. Broke her nose, busted her eyes, split her lip, shattered her cheekbones. She met Gable through a plastic surgeon she couldn't afford. Gable paid for it all. Had the surgery with the real Mae West's "I'm No Angel" playing on a screen above her, the fantasy rise of a woman from the wrong side of the tracks—a role she was born to play. Bawdy, sexually independent, full of double *entendre*, Mae West was an inspiration. Mae West would never let a man hit her again.

Tipped off by the tracking device that Stitches placed in Marcus Edmonton, Mae takes the F train down to 2nd Avenue. She receives some looks, but no one identifies her as Mae West. Occasionally, a very old man has commented on their resemblance. But never anyone under the age of seventy. A lot of Gable's stars were becoming a product of cruel time. Maybe Bogart was recognizable, possibly James Dean, and Marilyn Monroe (who'd been spoken of as an early employee). Beyond that, most of the operatives can blend better into society now. That is, until the news picked up the Card as their top story.

Her hand throbs so much that she pays Stitches a visit. He gives her Silvadene cream for the burns and wraps it up well. Never asks who did it: either because he knows, or knows enough not to poke and prod. They speak on a surface level about the Card. What it means for their futures. She always liked Stitches, who was quiet like her real personality before the mask. A girl from Oklahoma that came to New York with enough money for a bus ticket. Parents had passed on and she couldn't picture herself getting married and popping out babies in the Sooner State. Met her ex while bartending. He was a jeweler and gave her watches, which she later learned were fake. He lived in a walk-up in the Bronx with a pit bull and had a bad case of gut-rot that he took out on her. Like Mae West would do, she knew how to push his buttons and often went to sleep with a puffy face from him railing on her.

One night she went to bed with a hammer under her pillow. He came home pickled and mean. Started kicking her out of bed. She hit the floor with a thud and the hammer in her hand. Swung it like a golf club right up into his chin and knocked him off his feet. He squirmed on the ground, and when she went for the final blow, he fought back. Turned her face into a pulp, and she could barely see out of both eyes. Swung hammer at what she hoped was him. Came into contact with his skull and was met with a splash of blood. That she could see.

The plastic surgeon had been a regular at her bar. He was sweet on her, and she had his number. Called him up in the middle of the night, and he said he knew someone who could help. An hour later, Marlon Brando and Fred Astaire showed up at her door. She watched them roll her ex's body up in plastic and throw him in the tub where they proceeded to chop him into pieces and place his parts in garbage bags. They even came with a cleaning kit to get out the blood stains in her rug and made her throw out her stained nightgown in one of the garbage bags too. In lieu of money, she was taken to their Boss, whose office was on a high floor in midtown where he offered her some good Scotch and a proposal. Recently, his organization was looking to hire freelancers since they were expanding. If she agreed to the position, he'd have the plastic surgeon work on her for free. How could she say no?

"Maybe it helped that I had already killed my ex," she says to Stitches. "So it wasn't hard to kill again...and again..."

"What's the order on Marcus Edmonton?"

"Tranquilized. Brando and Astaire will be outside the place he's staying at in a van. Gable wants to torture. And to bring back his granddaughter of course."

"You're all set," Stitches says. She admires his handiwork, her hand not throbbing for the first time since Gable made her hold a hot poker.

"Thank you."

"I'm closing up shop by the way," Stitches says. "You can tell that to Gable. I stick around and the fuzz will inevitably come looking. Once you walk out the door, I will be following."

"Any idea where you're going?" she asks, a little jealous. Not that she wanted to run away with him. He wouldn't beat her up, but that didn't mean he was her type. But the idea that he could flee without repercussions. He'd been planning this for some time.

Stitches wags his finger back and forth. "I'm not telling. No one can know. Not even myself. Headed to the airport and whatever flight is leaving when I get there is the one I'll be on. You should do the same."

"I have to bring Marcus to Gable," she says. "Just in case Gable gets out of this alive, it's not worth making an enemy."

"If you're smart, you'll drop off the mark and leave before Gable can lure you into another request. After all, what if some other part than your hand becomes his next target?"

She covers her mouth with her burned hand. Had she implied that Gable was to blame for the burn? No, Stitches had a way of honing in on the truth. Always had.

"I will," she says, but doesn't even believe her own words.

———

Down a back alleyway off Avenue D, the tracking device beeps the loudest. She pulls out a 9mm with a silencer and shoots at the locks. The door swings open. A shot whizzes past her arm, missing by only inches. The little girl screams. Out of the corner of her eye, Mae West can see the girl's chained to the ground. Mae does a somersault from her gymnastic days as a child and another bullet zips past. She shoves a tranquilizer syringe between her teeth and dives at Marcus Edmonton. The two roll around, bullets hitting the ceiling, but no blood shed. She moves the syringe around with her tongue until it's pointing forward, ready to stab. She throws her head back and jams it into his chest. He lets out an ogre's yell and she stammers back, fixing her blond curls. The girl is still screaming so Mae West pulls the syringe out of Marcus Edmonton and plunges it into the little girl's shoulder, whispering "sorry". The girl gives a side-eye as her eyelids flutter, meaning she doesn't accept Mae West's apology. Marcus Edmonton groans and tries to sit up, but flops back and hits his head as the roar of the van pulls up outside in the back alleyway. Brando and Astaire step inside, loosen the little girl's chains, and drag them both into the van. They whistle for Mae West to join and for a second she thinks of telling them no. But they wouldn't allow it; Gable's two most loyal soldiers. They were burned and don't care. They'd die for him and certainly kill her if she refused to go. So she gets in the back of the van with the two sleeping bodies, her mind racing for an endgame to this all that won't involve her tombstone.

"You only live once," she tells herself quietly, from one of Mae West's most famous quotes. "But if you do it right, once is enough."

40

SINATRA

Handcuffed to the desk as two vultures circle. Call themselves Detectives Bonner and O'Reilly. Switched off from playing good cop to bad cop; he'd been through this kind of charade before. They order him to remove his Sinatra mask. He doesn't comply. There's a trick to taking the mask off. Even if they try, they wouldn't be successful. This angers the cops and pleases him.

"We have you on a host of charges," Bonner says, clearly the one running the show. "Wounding a police officer..." She bites at the words, and Sinatra knows that was her original partner, not this O'Reilly who looks to be fresh out of cadet school. "That could be ten years in maximum security alone. Plus, assaulting Vivien Howell and breaking and entering. We can also tie you to the abduction of Gracie Stockton."

"How?"

"Your face alone gives it away. That is unless you give us a bigger prize."

"I want my lawyer."

Bonner slams the table in front of him. "All I want is that little girl. *Where* is Gable?"

Sinatra's grinning beneath the mask, but she can't see that. What's a few years in prison? He's done it before. Half of the nineties spent locked up for burglary and grand theft auto. There's no way they'd get the abduction charges to stick. And the Card retained a top-notch lawyer to weasel them out of jams. Except he'd used his one call and left a message with the receptionist and the lawyer hasn't called back yet.

"It's been hours and your lawyer hasn't responded," Bonner says, clearly enjoying this mindfuck. "I'm thinking after what's been on the news, he doesn't want to be associated with Jay Howell. Which means you'll be appointed one who won't be much help."

She nods at O'Reilly to get them coffees. The green cop slips out of the door, and Sinatra understands a deal is about to be brokered.

"Why don't you take off that mask?" she asks.

"Why don't you take it off for me?"

"What does it represent?"

"The world wants to know, don't they? I've heard all the pundits guessing. The masks are a way to be incognito."

"But why the movie stars specifically?"

"Do you like Frank Sinatra? Not many have been able to toe the line so successfully between acting and music. And his legacy. 'New York, New York' will be played for eternity. His unabashed style. He exuded a thrilling sense of danger. Cocky and tough, riddled with tension. You didn't want to cross him. They don't make 'em like him anymore."

"So, is that why you wanted to fill his shoes?"

"Not as cut and dry as that. I told you before I was a freelancer."

"What does that mean?"

"It means I work for the organization when I want to. I take the jobs that interest me. So, I'm not Sinatra all the time."

She grabs his hands, flips them over so she can see his palms.

"You still have your fingerprints."

"All the freelancers do. Something Gable only asks his regular operatives to remove. And not all comply. It's not a requirement."

"Neither James Cagney or Alain Delon had theirs."

Sinatra puffs out his cheeks. "Their prerogative."

"Sounds like they were all in with the Desire Card."

Sinatra wags his finger, bats his blue eyes. "I see where you're going with this. I'm not an integral part of the organization so I can give up its secrets, right?"

"Why not? If it could lessen your jail time?"

"Enlighten me on your offer."

"Tell us where Gable has fled and if we catch him, I'll make sure you receive nothing more than a slap on your wrist. With the public defender you'll likely get, could be a life sentence depending on your age."

Gable had never told Sinatra where the secret hideout was located. As a freelancer, he wouldn't be enough in the inner circle to be privy to that information. But once at the regular headquarters, he overheard Gable on the phone. The headquarters had giant rooms and acoustics that bounced around sound. Gable was talking to a man named Rune about a secret location. So Sinatra did some detective work. He found a man named Rune Gunnarsson who owned a horse farm in

Bedford Hills, NY. He staked out the man's place and once saw an older man pull up in a black car that resembled the kind Gable used for the Card. The man stepped out *sans* mask, but Sinatra knew it was Gable by the way he walked. He'd studied the Boss's movements for years. Rune roped a few horses into a pen and greeted Gable. He tugged on a pulley and the ground opened for Gable to get back in his car and drive down. Sinatra kept it all in mind for when he'd need to have something on Gable during desperate times.

"You know where he is," Bonner says, as if she's reading his mind. "I can tell."

"How?"

"By the way you're shifting in your seat. The nervous sweat on your upper lip."

"These lights are hot."

"Let me see your face," she says. "Let's start there."

Sinatra holds up his hands, acquiescing.

"You know when you go to the supermarket and there are those plastic bags for fruits and vegetables that are hard to open?" he says. "You have to squeeze the ends between your fingers to find the groove. The masks are like that."

Bonner touches his neck, searching for an opening. He's making the mask grin in an absurd way that evokes the Joker. She pinches the skin, works at it, eventually finds the groove. Starts peeling it back over his chin, his nose, and then his eyes until the masks recoils in her hand. Staring back is likely not what Bonner would expect. There are no burns or marks on Sinatra's real face. He's not like the rest of the operatives at the Card. There's no one he was running from when he joined, least of all himself. He's an ordinary older man. Wrinkles and sagging jowls. A large hooked nose. Tiny lips like two lines. You could pass him by the street and not look twice. He picks off the sticky bits that have stuck to his face.

"Now tell me where Gable is," Bonner says, and he can see that she's tired, that this case means more to her than others for reasons he cannot understand. Sinatra would go down swinging; he'd never let a copper beat him. But how much of him *was* Sinatra? He'd always kept a safe distance.

"You shot my partner," she says. "But I'll still find a way to get you off. I'll do whatever I can in my power to make it happen. This organization you're connected to, you have to realize how evil it is."

"It was a paycheck."

"Then it won't mean anything to give them up."

"If you catch Gable...you're right that it won't mean anything." She goes to speak, but he grits his teeth and she steps back as if she can see the animal he's able to become. "But if you don't, I'm dead."

"We can put you into witness protection."

He laughs. "You think that matters? Gable will have me hunted down in a matter of days, even hours."

"We'll get him."

"Why, because you've convinced yourself that? Gable doesn't go down. Don't you see? He's immortal, omnipresent. He's already plotted an escape. He may already be gone."

"Then it won't matter if you give up his location."

"His employees are a vast network. Some look like my mask, and others are completely normal. They may be a part of your police force. That other officer who was here..."

Bonner looks toward the door, which O'Reilly opens with his shoulder, two coffees clamped in his fists. Sinatra can sense her nervousness, a second guessing of everything she knew.

"O'Reilly, give us a second," she says, regaining her composure. O'Reilly leaves the coffees and slips out of the room again.

Silence eats at the foundations. An apparent stalemate. The detective's gears turning, pondering a way to reorder this.

"What do you want?" she asks.

"This mug," Sinatra says, pointing at his wrinkled face. "I need complete surgery so there wouldn't be a chance of recognizing who I was. Slice me up and make me new."

"I-I think that could be done."

"Full immunity. I so much as touch a prison and one of Gable's contacts could be waiting with a shiv."

"We get him and you get off, that'll be the deal. No negotiations."

"He's on a horse farm," Sinatra sighs, because he's old and tired and was going to give Gable up from the start but didn't want to make it easy for the cop. He doesn't owe Gable anything. He'd been paid for every bit of work he did except this last task, which landed him here. So Gable actually owes him, and he doubts he'll ever see that money anyway.

"A horse farm owned by a man named Rune Gunnarsson in Bedford Hills, New York," Sinatra says. "But you'll need to go below the earth to find Gable."

"If you're lying..."

"Sinatra was known for one thing above all else... honesty. He'd never mince words. He told you exactly what he thought. And if there's one thing I picked up from him, it's that. You go to Rune's horse farm, and you'll find Gable and likely his granddaughter too."

Bonner goes to leave but he grabs her arm awkwardly, since he's still in handcuffs.

"Now I want the best plastic surgeon you can find," Sinatra says. "Never break a promise."

41

GRACIE

WAKES BUT STILL IS HALF ASLEEP. HER MIND LIKE she's walking slowly through a fog. Similar to when the man with the eye patch took her. Back of her throat stuck like she'd gargled Elmer's glue. She fully comes to once they're taken out of the van by an older man with a cowboy hat who speaks in a funny accent. The ground opens and they're led down into an underground warehouse full of giant cars and guns. She's separated from the man who used to wear the eye patch and finds herself reaching out for him. Hating and missing him at the same time.

Through the fog she sees her Uncle Chip. She never liked him but at least he's a familiar face. Uncle Chip barely spent time with her or her brother. Her father always said he was high on drugs. She didn't like him because he had B.O. The lady with the blonde hair brings the man with the eye patch over to Uncle Chip who begins to slap him. Uncle Chip is smiling as he does this. He's yelling and talking so fast that it's hard to make out what he's saying. She's so exhausted and wants to sleep, but she's curious enough at what's going on to stay awake.

"Sweetie," the lady with blonde hair says. "Come see your grandpa."

"Papa Jay?" she manages to ask, having to pull out the words from deep within.

"Yes, hon, your Papa Jay."

The blonde lady takes her hand and leads her into a room where Papa Jay sits on an orange recliner.

"Gracie," he says standing. He holds his arms out waiting for her to come into his embrace. She's still so sleepy and doesn't want a hug from him. The lady nudges her and finally she shuffles into his arms. He has a tight grip and hugs as if he's about to go away and never see her again. "Are you okay?" he asks. He inspects her face, the cuts on her cheeks.

"No," she says, and starts crying because she doesn't know what to do.

"Whatever he did to you, I'm gonna make him pay."

He's still holding her tight and she wants to get out of his arms. They feel like the boa constrictor she saw on her school trip to the zoo.

"Tell me what hurts," Papa Jay says.

"My head," she says, not because it hurts but because it seems like it weighs a thousand pounds.

"Did he hit you?"

"No."

"Tell me what he did."

Her grandfather is grinding his teeth, and he has a weird look in his eyes like the villains in the cartoons she used to watch.

"He took me," she says.

"I know—"

"He took me because of *you*."

Papa Jay looks over at the blonde lady who eyes him back and the two have a full conversation without saying anything.

"He was a bad employee of mine," Papa Jay says, crouching down to her level. "He wanted to hurt me and that's why he took you."

She can't stop crying.

"Oh hon, lemme get you a Kleenex," the blonde lady says.

"I'm fine."

"You can blow your nose."

"I'm fine, you dumb cunt."

The lady jumps back, her mouth hanging low enough to fit a golf ball inside.

"Well," the blonde lady says, with her hands on her hips.

"Mae, maybe you should leave us alone," Papa Jay says.

"Yeah, Mae maybe you shouldn't be such a cunt," Gracie says.

The lady gives a huff and marches out of the room.

Papa Jay laughs. "You're a tough one."

"Fuck you," Gracie says, spinning around and crossing her arms so she won't have to look at him. "You've done really bad things and that's why he took me."

"Is that what he told you?"

"It's true."

"What some people think of as bad things, actually aren't. I've always done what's in the best interest of our family."

She needs to sit, possibly lie down. She pushes past him and curls up in the orange recliner.

"I just want to go home," she says.

"And you will." He stands over her with a hand on her back. "You'll see Mom, and Brenton, your dad too. Everyone's waiting for you."

"Then why am I here?"

"We need to make sure it's...safe before you go. That there's no one else who wants to take you."

She cranes her neck until she can see him. "Other employees who hate you?"

"Yes, exactly."

"Well, I can take care of myself." She swims through her clogged mind to find what she wants to say next. Stops at the memory she's been trying the hardest to forget. "I killed a man."

"*What*? Who?"

"He looked like the actor from the movie you would watch with us–"

"James Cagney?"

"Yeah, I guess so."

"And you were the one who killed him?"

"I shot him with a gun and he died."

She says this without any emotion behind it— scaring her the most about what she did. It happened and she should care, but she doesn't.

"I always knew..."

"Knew what?" she asks.

"That you were the one who had the most of me in you. That you could do the kind of immoral acts your mother or your brother couldn't. That you could replace me one day when I'm gone."

She yawns, a veil of darkness hovering close. Sleep coming.

His hand cups her head. "Why don't you rest? Then we'll get you back to Mom."

She wants to fight it and yell and scream and call him every curse word she knows. But sleep is too powerful. It tugs at her eyelids until it succeeds. She can hear him mumbling to himself before he leaves the room, the door clicking closed, and then she tumbles into a deep rest, her dreams fraught with demons wanting blood.

42

MARCUS EDMONTON

So many close calls with death that Marcus has managed to survive. Siniyah, Iraq where a knife took out his eye but left the rest of him standing. A flirtation afterwards with heroin and even setting up a noose to end it all, which came crashing down due to a loose pipe. All the countless operatives that he killed before they could to do him in. Bogart, Cary Grant, Garbo, Jimmy Stewart, Rita Hayworth; he was losing count of the rest. He should have iced Gable's son in Macau when he had the chance.

"Do you remember me?" Gable's son asks. "It's Chip. We went back to my hotel room where you proceeded to whip me. Do you see my face?" He points to the scars. "You did this. And my chest..." He opens his shirt to reveal an X in dried blood.

"I had to get to Gable," Marcus says.

"And where has that led you? When he comes out of that room, he's going to kill you. All you've worked to accomplish...it's over."

Marcus doesn't respond so Chip slaps him across the face again, his cheek stinging red.

"I saved this for you," Chip says, pulling out a partially burned mask from behind his back. It takes a second for Marcus to realize it's James Dean. Not his former mask, the hair-style a bit different.

"You're the new me," Marcus says, and he can't help but laugh.

Chip puts on the mask. It looks as if James Dean walked into a fire face-first. One of the eyes has melted along with a hole in his cheek. The hair singed. The neck blackened. A monstrosity.

He thinks of the times he became James Dean. During the initial days at the Card when it seemed new and fresh. When he wanted to try anything that could erase Iraq. He was a sniper who never got to meet his full potential. In war, death was inevitable so he treated the Card in the same way. He'd killed an innocent Iraqi boy and his mother in Siniyah. He didn't deserve the possibility of heaven. The odds had been against him from the start. Parents dead in a car accident before he turned two. An old grandfather who tried to raise him, but passed on before Marcus was sixteen. He tried to leave all of J.D. Storm behind and vanquished James Dean too. As Marcus Edmonton, he would begin again. But it was all the same. Death simply followed him. And now it was time to follow it.

Chip takes off his belt, winds it around his fist until it's ready to sting. Snaps it against Marcus's face. He can taste the blood dripping into his mouth, his vision turning red. Chip's sadistic laugh, a horrific spawn of his father. He'd beat Marcus within an inch of his life and let Gable have the last licks.

Another whip from the belt like a left hook. Marcus doubles over, holds his palms out in protest, but Chip keeps whipping. His blood splashes onto the James Dean mask. His energy low from being drugged but the adrenaline building. He charges at Chip, knocking the man's flabby body to the floor. They both go down hard. Chip lets out a squeal that would rival a little girl being scared, and he thinks of Gracie, who he used as a means for taking Gable down, but ultimately wasn't successful. It was a faulty plan from the start. One that unleashed waves of consequences. All the lives affected by his decision. But he told himself it was for the greater good. Exactly what he and every other operative had drilled into their heads during their time at the Desire Card. Making excuses to justify their immorality when they had already dipped a toe into the flames.

He fights Chip with every ounce of life left in him. He fights himself as the James Dean mask drips blood into his eyes. Others had been placed in this situation, fated to have James Dean be the last thing they ever saw. He'd never taken a moment in their shoes until that night in Marrakesh when he couldn't kill that mark in front of his boy. It had all been a game until then. Surreal, a skewed reality, an alternate universe he entered. If this was to be his end right now, he deserved every beating, every shred of pain, a long and torturous icing.

Chip has his hands around his neck, thunking Marcus's head into the solid ground.

"I'm gonna show my father, I'm gonna show my father..." Chip says, and Marcus understands that Chip has entered his own skewed reality where nothing else mattered but proving to Gable that the apple doesn't fall far from the tree. Gable had likely treated Chip growing up with contempt, ridiculed the boy. A bruised Marcus would mean that Gable had been wrong all along. That his son could be a part of whatever endgame Gable had planned.

Or Marcus's bloody face would be the last thing Chip would ever see.

Wrenching the belt from Chip's fist, Marcus wraps it around Chip's neck and cinches it closed. It happens so fast that Chip can't even process. Chip spits curses that land in Marcus's good eye, still slamming Marcus's head into the ground. Marcus closes the belt in a groove as Chip's neck turns purple under the mask. Now Chip realizes his fate. His eyes go soft—Marcus can tell even through the mask. He lessens his grip on Marcus's neck. Marcus pulls the belt tighter and notches it into another groove. A gasping sound utters from Chip, echoing in the lair like a snake's hiss. Out of instinct, Chip tries to remove the belt but Marcus is faster. He grabs Chip's hands, twists the man's fingers until he hears a few *snaps.* The hiss morphs into a fatal wail from Chip as he looks down at his fingers that are sticking out in abnormal directions. He holds them out, as if asking for absolution. Marcus grabs the belt and closes it even tighter, fully cutting off circulation. Chip writhes on the floor like a fish out of water until he comes to a dead stop.

Marcus, in his exhausted state, watches Chip's soul rise from his body and descend to the depths below— what he imagines his own will do. But it's not time yet. Chip's head tilts toward Marcus, no life issuing from the James Dean mask. Marcus can't help but visualize his own end—the man he used to be, this ghost's body he inhabits now. He wipes the blood off his face with his shirt and hears a rustling from above.

The ceiling opens and two hazy human blurs walk down. He zeroes in on their faces. Even though they are not wearing masks, Marcus recognizes that they will not be on his side.

Because no one is anymore.

43

RUNE

Pushing eighty, Rune has witnessed a lot in his long life. His father supplied steel and machine parts to Germany throughout World War II, since the Swedish government felt it was in no position to openly contest Germany at the time. To his father's credit, he stopped selling once Sweden began rescuing several thousand Jews from internment camps, but that was really because his father saw Germany was losing and didn't want to be on the wrong side of history. He remembers Nazi artifacts his father kept in a locked case in their basement. Not because his father believed in the cause, but because he assumed they might be of value someday. After the war ended, young Rune would sneak down into the basement with a stolen key and touch a silver Nazi pendant. Sometimes he would pin it to his shirt and ape the forbidden Heil Hitler salute.

What he retained most from those times was to follow the money at all costs. Money promised safety, everything else superfluous. When he migrated to the States in the seventies after Sweden's period of decline due to the oil embargos of 1973-74, and 1978-79, he surmised he didn't owe Sweden any loyalty until the country righted itself. He met Jay Howell at a Disco club. With his long blond hair, sideburns, and cowboy hat, Rune couldn't have looked more out of place. Jay had a table in the back chock full of scantily-clad women and pyramids of cocaine. He called Rune over, since Rune was sitting solo at the bar and looked glum. Rune had never tried cocaine, or any drug before, but after one toot, a chunk of his personality awakened that had been hidden for too long. He started speaking fast with his Swedish slang and everyone around the table laughed. Afterwards, he and Jay grabbed cocktails at the Odeon where he ate escargot and downed dirty martinis. Jay spoke of his new business venture, *his baby*, and asked what Rune considered his passion.

"Horses," Rune said, his lips sticking together from the escargot drenched in butter. "I want to own a horse farm."

Jay happened to have a contact in Bedford Hills, NY, an old timer looking to sell his horse farm. Rune realized that someone like Jay Howell seemed to know *everyone*. Always had a contact, or an *in*. He asked Rune if he had the kind of capital to buy the farm, and Rune explained about his father, who had recently passed, and left him his entire savings. All the money made off the Germans in World War II.

"Do you feel guilty about taking that money?" Jay asked.

Rune hadn't thought about it before. The money was rightfully his so why should he feel any guilt? He rationalized it as his father taking money away from the Nazi regime, but that was a stretch and Jay didn't buy it. So, he confessed. The world had gotten into a terrible war, lives were lost, but why shouldn't someone on the outside looking in be able to profit? Jay wholeheartedly agreed.

And so, the friendship began. The Card was in its infancy and hadn't descended into treacherous territory yet. Rune got his horse farm up and running. It wasn't until the early 90s that the two really crossed paths again thanks to Pablo Escobar. Well, thanks to massive amounts of cocaine that Jay—now fully known as Gable—was selling in the States after Escobar's death. Gable had divorced himself from Escobar's orbit, but not before pilfering enough blow to use it as mini mountains on which to ski. Rune had no idea how Gable was able to get the blow into the States without pissing off the Cali Cartel that dominated the market after the collapse of the Medellín Cartel, but what he knew of Gable was that the man had an inspiring way of making magic happen. Rune's horse farm became the base of distribution until they sold every last snort and made millions. Then Gable decided to make the horse farm his *safe house* if the heat ever got too much to bear and he had to flee. For the last twenty years and change, Rune has sat on his stacks on money and entertained Gable if he needed to hide away.

This time: different. He'd never been exposed to a fearful Gable before. Anytime the police came close to sniffing around the Card, Gable always found a way to pay off the right cop, or ice a cop that was in the wrong place at the wrong time. But due to what's been blasted across the news, there was no way out for Gable but to hide and run.

Rune had planned for this when he remodeled the horse farm. In addition to the basement facilities only accessible by pulling a specific lever camouflaged by a tree, a back entrance also existed that opened into the woods. Rune got hold of Brando and Astaire, two operatives he knew best since they'd been at the Card the longest and set them up by this back entrance to wait for The Doctor to drive up in the van. In the meantime, Rune kept watch for any fuzz or enemies that might come knocking.

He popped a long cigar between his gums and puffed away, a rifle slung over his shoulder, his cowboy hat tipped low. The horizon flirting with dusk. Sky a mix of purples and yellows, gassy and picturesque. Just forty miles from New York City, but the stars already stretching across the skyline even before night arrives. He cracks open a book of his favorite Swedish poet, Tomas Tranströmer, "The Half-Finished Heaven" being one of his best.

He pulls from a bottle of burn-wine and reads it out loud to his Australian Shepherd Tone, whose blue, blue eyes respond in delight.

> *Despondency breaks off its course*
> *Anguish breaks off its course*
> *The Vulture breaks off its flight*
> *The eager light streams out*
> *even the ghosts take a draught.*
> *And our paintings see daylight*
> *Our red beasts of the ice age studios*
> *Everything begins to look around*

We walk in the sun in hundreds
Each man is a half-open door
Leading to a room for everyone
The endless ground under us
The water is shining through the trees
The lake is a window into the earth

"Sometimes," Rune tells his dog Tone, "the best acceptance we can wish for, one that names the anguish we feel, will be when we return to the only place we can be certain of, 'the endless ground under us,' whether we like it or not."

Tone gives a clipped bark, and Rune follows the dog's blue eyes to the distance where a car has parked. The engine isn't running but it recently had been since Rune can still hear its hum. He lowers his rifle off his shoulder. Behind him, a clopping of horses stir in their pen. Tone barks again, spinning around. Rune points the rifle to his left where the horses have kicked up swells of dirt. A bit gets in his eye and he goes to rub it out when he feels his head being pulled back and a knife ripping across his throat. Tone starts barking even more madly until his cries turn into a whimper and then stop suddenly. Rune's throat exposed, blood spurting out at an alarming rate. Through cloudy vision, Rune watches a woman searching the surrounding area for the pulley that opens the earth to the basement below. How can she know of it? She does not wear a mask. His feet give out on him and he collapses into the dirt, his killer stepping over him. He squints to make out his assailant. A handsome older face, one he hasn't seen in years, hovers before him—Olivier without his mask, an integral part of the cocaine distribution operation in the nineties, grayer and with a faint touch of wrinkles, but mostly as if time had not held him in its grip.

"Night, night, old sir," Death tells him, and closes his eyes.

44

OLIVER

Walking down into the earth with Evchen and silencers in hand, Oliver spies a man missing an eye and covered with blood hunched over a dead body in a James Dean mask. He'd expected such a gruesome sight entering Gable's abyss, for the Boss brings forth doom wherever he goes. Not that Oliver's a saint; he'd never claim to be. But when judgement comes, his sins will pale in comparison. The ability to grant any wish, his genie in a Card—all he wanted was power, since there's no one more powerful than those able to supply. The rich, the politicians with their clout, the celebrities with their sway, the Card kept them hooked like a drug. He and Gable called themselves titans, but it was Gable who had his sights set on playing God. And to play God means to usher death.

Oliver set up shop as far away from Gable as possible, working in tandem, but out of sight. And the foreign office kept things relatively clean in Europe. The Card there had more *pedigree*. The hit jobs usually to clean up mistakes from the States. Very few of his

European clients of the unsavory sort. They were the politicians and celebrities he'd catered to at the Card's inception. The foreign office became embroiled more with the *who's-who* rather than those *who'll murder to get what they want.* The missions involving the unseemly took place far from Brussels so Oliver felt removed from it all. He thought of himself like an operator, patching phone calls together, but not responsible for what transpires over them.

"Hands in the air," he tells the man with the missing eye. His mind flips through a Rolodex of faces, both masked and clean. The old James Dean. He had to set up a mission in Marrakesh with him that went bust. Then who was the new James Dean dead on the floor?

"Where's Gable?" Evchen asks, following his lead.

Evchen helped ease the pain of Audrey Hepburn on Oliver's private jet. Their bodies stuck together, his nose in the musky pocket of her armpit. With his two ex-wives, he'd ended the relationship. Francine, a childhood sweetheart, too sweet to remain connected to him once the Card took over his life. The Card hadn't delved into dark territories yet, but Francine could tell it was headed in insalubrious directions. Marguaritte, his second, was more of the unsavory sort. Looked the other way as long as her pockets were lined and she could buy expensive hats. But he never wanted children and ultimately that was too much of a hurdle. She desperately wanted kids, even poked holes in his condoms. Little did she know, he was infertile. She packed up all her hat boxes in a fury when she found out, stormed from his Brussels pad. He'd met Audrey Hepburn soon after. Because of their busy schedule, seeing each other was a treat. He failed in other relationships because he lived with that spouse, never got any breathing room. Just like he did with Audrey, he would keep a distance from Evchen, similar to the way he dealt with the Card.

"Gable's in that room," the man with one eye says, pointing towards a door. "Mae West is in there too along with his granddaughter."

"Who's that?" Oliver asks, nudging the dead James Dean with his toe.

"Gable's son. I killed him. Gable doesn't know yet."

With the silencer still pointed at the man with one eye, Oliver signals Evchen to train her gun on the door. They can hear muffled voices coming through the crack.

"We want the same thing," the man with one eye says. "Gable out of the picture."

"While the outcome may be the same," Oliver says. "We want it for different reasons."

He lights one of his brand of cigarettes because it keeps him calm. Offers the man with one eye as well, who declines. Oliver shrugs.

"You left the Card," Oliver says. "You want it destroyed, that's been the word on the street. I just want it for myself. Evchen, how are you doing, baby?"

She hasn't taken her eyes off the door.

"Fine, baby," she says.

"Shoot at whoever walks out."

"Aye-aye."

The man with one eye starts to get up, but Oliver shakes his head. He wants him low to the ground and subservient.

"The Card will never end," Oliver says. "Our tentacles reach too far. Cut off the head as the cliché goes and a new one will appear."

"And that's you?"

"Of course." He puffs a perfect circle. "But I want to divorce us from this version of the Card. Too much pointless death. Yes, hit operations bring big money, but there's other ways of maintaining our omnipresence."

"I fear that no matter what, the Card brings bloodshed."

"You think you'd be more amenable to someone holding a gun to your face."

"I'm not making it out of this alive."

"So certain? But yet, you've wiggled out of situations just as dire."

"I had more fight in me then."

"What happened?"

"You reach a point..." The man with one eye takes a huge gulping breath. "I can barely recall life before the Card. Just snippets. Moments of childhood that weren't happy but in retrospect were wonderful. The horrors of a war in the desert. A love I lost due to Gable. There's not much I even want to remember."

"He fed off of you. Your pain. Your bygone innocence."

"Yes."

"I wouldn't be the same. There's no thumb of oppression over those under me. I did not collect the scarred. I'm not like him."

"Yet you still want the Card to continue?"

"You can't kill us all. You may have tried, and you succeeded greatly. But we've woven into the tapestry of your country. What is that movie, the one with Michael Douglas and Charlie Sheen. 'Greed is Good'. Is that

Wall Street? Greed is what allows us to excel, keeps us focused. We want to be better than whoever stands next to us. We want our lives to have meaning."

"But don't you see, we are meaningless?"

"You have given up. That is why you feel that way. I am seventy years young and just getting started. My third act will blow the others away."

"Oliver!" Evchen says, raising her voice because the doorknob is turning. Oliver has the gun pointed at the man with one eye, but he's got the door in his sights if need be. It swings open and Mae West steps out. Due to its heaviness, it swings shut behind her before she has a chance to scurry back.

"Hands," Evchen says.

"Damn," Mae West says, raising her arms high.

Evchen frisks Mae West with her free hand. Finds a gun and sticks it in her waistband.

"You're going to call Gable out here," Evchen says.

"You'll kill me anyway," Mae West says, scrunching her lips.

"Mae, you don't owe him anything," Oliver says.

"I don't," she says. "Lemme out of here and I'll give him up."

"I wanted to trust you before," Oliver says. "I came to you with a plan to oust Gable. And you chose your side."

She puts a hand on her hip in a teapot's pose. "That's before I saw what you were really capable of."

"We can't trust her," Evchen says, the gun shaking as the butt gets pressed into Mae West's skull.

"Evchen, I'm going to need for you to chill."

The sweat pouring from Evchen's face. It's hot down here and making everyone antsy, Oliver included.

But he wants as little bloodshed as possible, only Gable's.

"Mae, you may have made a wrong choice in choosing sides," he says. "But it doesn't have to be a fatal one. Call him outside, and with no funny moves. Tell him you need help with old James Dean."

"And you'll let me go?"

"I'm aiming to restart this Card. And I'll need operatives, freelancers," Oliver says. "But it'll be a better version. You won't have to do the debased things you did. But I need to know I can trust you."

She fixes her hair with one push of her curls. Eyes Evchen who still has the gun pressed into her temple.

"Tell the lady to ease up."

"Evchen," Oliver says.

"All right," Evchen says, stepping backwards but keeping the gun locked on her target.

"All right," Mae West says, creeping up to the door and giving it three solid knocks.

"Gable, honey," she says. "I need your help out here."

No answer.

"Gable, honey, can you hear me?"

A giant blast rips through the door and Mae West, sending her flying with a gaping fiery hole in her stomach. She singes on the ground, a lost cause. From the room, Gable gets up from leaning on one knee with a Panzerschreck hoisted over his shoulder, a rocket launcher developed by the Nazis that Rune must've left lying around. Gable knocks the door down, pivots right and launches another rocket at Evchen, whose face explodes upon impact before she can even scream. Oliver and the man with one eye both break in different directions, separately hiding behind two SUVs. Out of the side-view mirror, Oliver can see Gable standing over the body of his slain son. No tears emerge from his eyes, stoic as a statue. The side-view also shows Evchen dead beyond identification, a headless body twitching on the ground. He doesn't have time to mourn. He goes to shoot at Gable, but the man has disappeared, the faint patting of shoes all that's left of him. Oliver tries to trace Gable's location, the warehouse full of echoes. But then the sounds stop entirely. Each man still alive and trying not to exhale.

They will wait for each other to make the first mistake.

45

GABLE

GABLE STANDS OVER HIS DEAD SON. THE JAMES
Dean mask has deflated and sticks to Chip's face unnat-
urally. Part of him wants to remove it, to see his actual
son one last time, but he's not ready for the gruesome
reality. There's also two targets aiming to take him out:
Olivier with a gun and Marcus capable of toppling
armies. He can mourn, but only briefly, for he cannot
lose focus. That's what they want.

Still, he is human. And while he's adept at locking
emotions away, the gravity of losing a child eats away.
Flashes of Chip as a little boy, always singing and dancing. His son sought attention that Gable rarely gave. To
be honest, he was afraid of Chip because he didn't
know how to relate. It had nothing to do with Chip's
homosexuality. What bothered Gable more was Chip's
lack of drive. He simply floated. He spent the family's
money and didn't understand the concept of working
hard. Gable found that despicable. Most of their relationship was making up excuses for Chip's fecklessness.
And then, "The Incident". Gable having to hide Chip

in Macau during the biggest deal of his life. He regarded Chip as a nuisance. He can't ever recall saying "I love you."

Too late for that now. We make tough decisions in life and have to stand by them because regret is a wasted nag. Regret is for people who never soared. Who stuck to a boring existence and wished they had taken a chance. Gable took many chances.

At some point when he's fully escaped and hidden in some tiny *puebla* down in Mexico, he'll have a proper funeral for Chip. He owes him that much. And he owes it to himself, for he's not so far gone to the dark side that he doesn't understand he's responsible for Chip's death. But the kid had moxie at the end, a term he recalls his own father saying. Chip helped weed out the turncoat Gary Cooper and ice him. Who knows if Gable would've made it to the safe house without his son. His baby boy. Dead on the floor and covered by a James Dean mask.

A shot rings by Gable. Olivier holds a gun and has always been a sharp shooter. Gable hoists the Panzerschreck on his shoulder again, observes the large basement where flames lick at the ground and Mae West and Dietrich cook as if they'd be grilled. His granddaughter snoozing in the room after giving her another mild sedative. He listens. There's a snap coming from the direction of an SUV so he launches a final rocket. The SUV explodes with a brilliant show of fire and light. Anyone near it sure to be fried. He doesn't hear screams. He runs behind another SUV and takes an AK-47 off the wall. Checks the magazine for bullets, gets on one knee, and lets off a spree. The bullets dot a row of SUVs and he can hear the mice scurrying. An arm peeks out from behind a bumper and he fires again before it ducks away.

"Gotcha," he says, diving behind a closer SUV. Through the side-view mirror, an image of Olivier *sans* mask. He knows Olivier's whole game. Thinks he's morally better than Gable now. Doesn't want to be associated with the masks anymore. Olivier was so weak. He wanted it both ways. The oodles of money, but none of the blood. The argument after Errol Flynn was iced almost forty years ago when the Card truly began to slip, and Olivier got scared, and Gable saw the future.

"I want to be able to look at myself in the mirror," Olivier had said. He had a rudimentary Sir Laurence Olivier mask at the time, not nearly in the same leagues as their current masterpieces.

"What do you think the masks are for?" Gable asked. He had sharpened his own, definitely above the Halloween mask variety. He got looks on the street that actually thought he was Gable.

"We've crossed a line," Olivier said.

"We were always headed in that direction."

"*You* were always headed in that direction," Olivier said. "He was just a goddamn kid."

"He was gonna turn us in."

"We don't even know what the cops would've been able to prove."

"You loved him like a son," Olivier said. "I know you did. That's what scares me the most."

Now, the flames have made its way over to Chip's body, licking at his coat. If it had been Helene, Gable would've lost it. His sweet baby girl, what she must think of him now that she knows the truth. Or is she relieved? Because she knew the depths he could sink all along and still loved him anyway.

Another bullet clangs off the wall. Through the side-view, he can see Olivier on the move. He fires off another round, but slips and lands hard on his back. The bullets *pling* off the ceiling, useless. Groaning, he rolls around until he can prop himself up. No eyes on Olivier anymore through the side-view. But Marcus pops up at the other end of the basement. Gable balances on his elbow and fires off a round, bullets shattering glass. Fucking J.D. Storm. He definitely wouldn't be in this situation if not for that lowlife scum. Gracie wouldn't have been kidnapped. Most of his operatives still alive. Olivier wouldn't have had the balls to make a move. One son-of-a-bitch ruining it all.

He'd taken a liking to J.D. Storm, a war veteran who never had the opportunity to shine on the battlefield. Lost an eye a few weeks in. But the kid was the sharpest shooter he'd ever seen. Someone who Gable could mold. Jumped in line to operative status faster than anyone else ever had. Could've been a station agent if he hadn't caught morals. Gable was gonna put him right behind James Cagney, who was set to retire within the next five to ten years. And what did Storm throw it all away for? A stupid mark in Marrakesh because the mark's kid was there. A mark trying to build a taller casino than Gable who wound up getting iced anyway. And Gable had the guy's wife iced and their kids thrown from the top of the mark's unfinished casino out of spite. Meaning that Storm threw away a plush life with perks aplenty all because of his silly conscience. And a ton more people wound up dead anyway. Storm was too naive to predict the consequences. Changing his name to Marcus Edmonton won't bring back all the lives destroyed. It's like with the masks. Gable's underlings could strive to morph into these great idols, but it's all just a façade. Their faces still burned. Their scars palpable. The hurt within raging. Gable comes by with his Band-Aid, uses them for his own gain, and discards once they've served their purpose. But could they ever be absolved of the sins they committed? The hurt they caused? The abuse they suffered? He knew they couldn't because he'd never be able to fully transcend. But he'd given up making excuses long ago. The devil had resurfaced in his body and he was happy to be its host. Usher in the apocalypse.

The AK is out of rounds so he grabs a Glock from off the wall that he can aim better. Unfortunately, Marcus has moved out of sight. He'd save Marcus for last. Kill him slowly for what he did to Chip. Next to him lies a crisp Mae West who he decides to use as a shield. Props her charred body up and rushes forth toward where he thinks he hears mice scurrying. He's firing, firing, firing, raging, raging, raging, wanting blood to spill. A gasp echoes in the basement, the sound like a tire deflating. He checks the SUV in front of him but the tires are intact. Streaked across the black trim, a bloody handprint. A gun *clangs* to the ground. Olivier collapses soon after trying to hold in his spilling guts.

"You lost," Gable says, cocking the gun and poking Olivier in the nose.

All Olivier can do is to weep.

"Crying like a child, a weak little pussy," Gable says. "My business partner... You were never worthy."

"I...wanted..."

"I know, you had less evil designs for the Card. But that's not how this world works. I am the face, what people aspire to be."

"You're on your own island," Olivier manages to say, coughing up blood. "No one wants to be you."

"I will rebuild. I will get stronger. I will leave my enemies in the dust. I will rise. I will soar."

"Until death comes for you too, asshole."

"Only when I am ready," Gable says. "When I have done all I've set out to accomplish. My final act begins right now."

He fires the gun into Olivier's nose blowing the man's face off. Unrecognizable. What Olivier deserves for his treason.

A new mouse scurries. That of his slipperiest enemy: Marcus Edmonton. There are enough bullets left in the gun so even if Gable misses, he won't miss for long.

46

MARCUS EDMONTON

GABLE JUST SHOT THE OTHER LAST MAN STANDING in the nose, blew his face right off. Looks like in the cartoon when Elmer Fudd peers into the barrel of a rifle and his head bursts into smithereens. Now only Marcus and Gable remain. There are no more operatives Marcus can think of except for maybe Brando and Astaire and they aren't here. Both he and Gable will not make it out this basement alive, only one of them.

There's a gun on the wall Marcus grabs while Gable is busy wiping guts off his suit. He runs behind another SUV. Best to play defense, keep Gable in the distance until he can line up a perfect shot. The basement smells of blood and flesh. Multiple bodies lay charred. He swears to himself that he will not follow in their unfortunate footsteps.

This was war, no different than in Iraq. The clever enemy in sights. It hadn't turned out well for him there, but he's older now, sharper, with a lot less to lose. Back then, he'd fallen in love with Annie Duluth after only knowing her for a week. He dreamed of them together after he'd be shipped home. If he hadn't lost his eye, that might've been the case. Years later they weren't meant to be. She was in debt from very bad men. He doesn't blame her for making him fall for her again. She wanted the money from the coke he sold to The Doctor. But a shred of him believes she wanted him as well. Circumstances had fucked them both. Refused to allow either happiness. In another world, they made it to Matagi Island where a volcano had erupted a thousand years ago and left behind a beach of entirely white sand. They'd have a little bit of money to start over. They wouldn't have needed much. Soon she would start showing. A baby giving him purpose. Gable could've left him alone. This didn't have to end with so much death.

The final person to kill would be Gable. Then Marcus will disappear. Maybe Matagi Island, or simply somewhere quiet and beautiful where he can live out the rest of his days. Because he's seen enough brutality for many lifetimes. He looks down at a woman who Gable blew a hole through her head. Smoke billows from the body, twitching due to rigor mortis. He saw Gable use a different body as a shield. If he's to survive, he needs to do the same.

The body is hot to touch, but he fights the pain and holds her up. A shot whizzes by, ruffles her hair. It's not from an AK-47, meaning it might not be powerful enough to pass through her body and hit him. He has to go for it.

"Employing my strategy?" he hears Gable ask, the voice thundering through the basement.

"I learned from the best," Marcus yells back.

"Haven't you learned yet that I don't die? It'll be me and the cockroaches at the end."

"That's exactly how I'd describe you," Marcus says, getting off a shot but he can't see Gable. Due to the extreme echoes, it's hard to tell precisely where the voice is coming from.

"There are worse things than cockroaches," Gable says. "They are survivors. They burrow underground. They multiply."

"You have no one left. You're wanted on the news. This is the end."

"It's only the end when I say it will be. As for you, I fear that will be very soon."

Marcus closes his eyes so he can absorb the sound in the basement. To his right, a soft patter of shoes against the ground. Gable has moved. He spins the dead body around and lurches toward the target. His own body still drained from the sedative, working at about fifty percent. Sleep knocks on his skull, begging to enter, but he won't listen. A bullet lands in the woman's shoulder. Blood drips, but the bullet does not go through.

Out of the corner of his good eye, Gable darts behind another SUV. The peek of a barrel winds around the car, fires off a shot that lands in the woman's leg. The gun gets thrown to the floor. Gable unarmed at the moment. Marcus had tried a defensive strategy, but must take a chance and go offensive. He charges toward the SUV, leaps around the car behind his human shield until he knocks Gable to the ground. The dead woman between them. Fists flying but hard to tell to whom they belong. The smell of a campfire from the woman's chars. He grabs the back of her head and thrusts her face into Gable's, who lets out a shrill cry. Heads knock and Gable gets thrown backwards, the woman's body scooting out from between them. Marcus goes to pull the trigger but Gable does a sweep kick, bringing Marcus down on his shoulder. The pain shoots up his back, paralyzes him momentarily. Gable flips over and waddles toward a gun hanging on the wall, but Marcus grabs him by the feet and pulls him closer. Gable kicks backward, landing a foot right in Marcus's balls. Marcus sees stars and loses the grip on his gun, its clanging sound like a knife in his heart. Gable spins around and claws Marcus's face, digging his nails into Marcus's eyes. One eye just a groove, but the other fucking hurts. Marcus fights back the same way, digging his own nails into Gable's flesh. He feels the wet of Gable's eyes, and he bashes the back of Gable's skull into the hard ground. A trickle of blood seeps, enough for Gable to ease his own grip while Marcus continues bashing his former Boss's head into the cement floor.

The fluorescent lights overhead flicker and for a second Gable morphs into his true self. He's no longer a man of flesh and blood but a being of pure evil, the face red and beating, horns emerging and a smile that licks flames. Marcus witnesses this hallucinogenic transformation. Had Gable made a deal a long time ago with a demon from down under and been in its sway ever since? Gable's mouth gapes wide open and his teeth bare down on Marcus's cheek. A lump of flesh torn out leaving a tiny hole. Marcus can feel the cold air blowing through the opening into his mouth. Gable cackling as he spits out the hunk of Marcus's cheek. They are rolling on the ground. Each time one delivers a hit, the other experiences an even harder blow. They are exhausted, somewhere in between a state of dreams and consciousness, but neither ready to give in. Not until nothing remains.

The lights flicker again, and Marcus's good eye picks up the gleam of a knife. The lights cut out, and he recalls a dream he had in Macau where he went to find Gable.

"This is just a dream," he'd whispered to Gable.

"No," Gable had said. "This is the future. One that I can assure you will occur. You and I in a dark room together, a knife between us sealing your fate."

Gable had taken a knife out of its holder, the blade singing. Just like now, the oracle predicted this. They wrestle more in the darkness, but it's futile.

"A future where I gut you good," Gable says, or either said it in that dream. The two worlds already colliding.

Gable's hot breath in his face, flames rolling off the man's tongue. A knife plunged into Marcus's gut. The impact of the blade the first sensation. Then, a tingle like an electric shock. Marcus's nervous system realizing that thousands upon thousands of circuits have been broken. Heat pours out of him like lava. The hotness piercing, but as the blood seeps out, a cold entity takes over. Teeth chattering, Marcus grasps Gable's lapels as he collapses, his body folding under him. He can see the blood even in the darkness, since it's darker than anything. The vision of Gable morphing back into his human form as he backs away from Marcus, wanting to be as far away from death as possible.

A flash of his life—what happens at the end. Shooting muleys with Gramps when the gun weighed practically as much as him. That week with Annie spent entirely in their hotel room, the sheets smelling of her lemony tang. A mushroom cloud exploding in Siniyah and a dead baby rocking in his arms. The months he gave to heroin. Meeting Gable though Rita Hayworth and going to the Boss's office in the clouds. Choosing the James Dean mask. The missions in New York City, Budapest, the Arctic, bodies he left beneath the ice, and then Marrakesh where he decided to give it all up. Fighting his way to Killenroy where he was reunited with Annie. The time she turned on the shower for him in the cold morning after they made love and told him it needed to warm up. The frozen image of the last kiss she gave when Cagney put a bullet through her skull. These last few days with little Gracie and how he imagined she was he and Annie's child. The footprints left on the white sand beaches of Matagi Island, Annie's tiny and his wide, leading into the ocean that's cold and warm at the same time like his body feels now as it goes into shock, as too much blood leaks out, as the world tints dark—but maybe it's just because the lights went out. Or is it an indication that this is finally the end? Gable cackles as he walks away, as the villain wins, as a final breath expels, and then a quiet pervades like Marcus wanted, like he wished for.

"Any wish fulfilled...for a price," he can hear Gable say until only silence exists.

47

DETECTIVE MONICA BONNER

BONNER TURNS ON THE SIREN AS SHE SPEEDS UP TO Bedford Hills, New York. She's debated whether or not to get other law enforcement involved as she pursues Jay Howell. The benefit would be back-up and proper procedural protocol, but she has a gut feeling that will only scare him away. He'll sense their presence coming miles before they arrive and flee where he'll never be found again. Any chance at rescuing Gracie Stockton will be destroyed. She must go it alone, surprise a career criminal like Jay Howell who'll be expecting helicopters and a SWAT team. She calls Ramirez before she makes a final decision, at home after being released from the hospital.

"How's the shoulder and arm?" she asks.

"Hurts like fuck-all," he says. "But a good excuse to catch up on my TV."

"We questioned the Sinatra guy," she says, seeing the exit for Saw Mill Parkway and making a hard right off the Taconic State Parkway. "He gave up where Jay Howell is hiding. Could be lies, could be for real."

"I assume you're headed there now?" Ramirez asks, and she can tell from his tone that he's not pleased.

"My gut says if I tip the F.B.I. or even bring in back-up, Jay Howell will run. He'll be able to see us coming."

"You haven't told the chief?"

"I'm afraid of what he'll say."

"Bonner, I understand how much you want this. Bringing that girl home. Stopping this monster—"

"We have only one chance at the guy's safe house, then he's a ghost. If there are too many chefs in the kitchen, he'll get a jump on us out of the country. I guarantee, I've seen it before."

She can hear him clicking his tongue. "I don't like you going there solo."

"But you won't tell on me?"

He doesn't answer right away and she knows it's a lot to ask.

"No...I won't. But tell me your mind isn't clouded."

"Clouded? What the fuck are you taking about? I've thrown everything into this case since we got it."

She swerves between two cars, speeding up to get past them by pushing ninety.

"Exactly," Ramirez says. She can hear rustling from the other end. "Fuck these bandages, I'm itching like crazy. Listen, Bonner, I know what it means for you to save this girl."

Bonner wipes her tears away so she can see out of the windshield.

"I know this is our last shot, Ramirez. He's a slip-pery son-of-a-bitch."

"Finding that girl is *not* going bring back your kid," Ramirez says, and the steering wheel slides from Bonner's grip. She rights the car after nearly going off on the shoulder. A truck behind her honks long and hard, sitting on the horn.

"I know that. You don't think I know that?"

HONK! HONK!

"I just wanna be sure your judgement isn't... skewed. Because you're so close to this."

HONK! HONK!

She sticks her head out of the window. "I see you. I fucking see you!"

"What's happening?" Ramirez asks.

"I know it's not Kellan," she says, so quietly she wonders if she's even spoken it out loud. The truck finally passes her, the horns becoming muted. "And I know it's important to me to save Gracie because of him, I'm not stupid."

"Bonner, I would never say..."

Ramirez sounds like he's moving through his apartment, his voice getting softer and then louder again.

"What are you doing, Ramirez?"

"Give me the address."

"What?"

"Give. Me. The. Address. Bonner, I'm your back-up."

"But what about your injuries?"

"They're both flesh wounds, no big. I'll drive with my other hand. If you don't let me help you, I'm calling the chief."

"You stubborn asshole," she says, but she's smiling.

"We started this case together, we gonna end it together."

"All right, 1220 Guard Hill Road."

"Fuck the F.B.I. and their jurisdiction," Ramirez says. "I've never given a shit about them before."

"I'm about fifteen minutes away."

"I'll speed and be there in a half an hour. You'll wait?"

Now she's silent.

"Bonner?"

"I heard you."

"You won't wait."

"I'll just stake out the place. I won't go in. I'll be ready for when you come."

"Okay, I'm out the door. You got this."

She tugs on her bottom lip. "I got this."

"I'm gonna check in when I get close. Be careful."

"Thank you, Ramirez."

"We'll thank each other when this dick bag is behind bars."

His phone cuts off and she's confident with her decision as she heads onto NY-117 South Drive. She's the only car on the road so she turns off the siren since the GPS says she's only a mile away. She grips the wheel tight, hugging the curving road carefully. She passes a horse farm. An amber brown horse gallops in pace with her, its mane tossed by the wind. Would this be the last living creature to witness her alive before she plunges into Gable's domain? Its chestnut eye blinks a stern warning: Many have tried to destroy him only to be led to their doom. It tells her she is not alone. It is with her in spirit. It will keep her strong.

The GPS announces the destination is a quarter of a mile away so she parks the car, puts on a bullet proof vest, holsters her gun, and walks the shoulder the rest of the way. The wind blows cool, making her teeth chatter. Goosebumps appear on her arms. When she reaches the horse farm belonging to Rune Gunnarsson, his horses are involved in a tumultuous dance. A black and brown one wrestle for supremacy, their neighs cutting through the air. She takes out her gun, side-stepping around the property, then hops the low fence. The fighting horses observe but continue their battle. Something has spooked them. There's a tiny house on the farm with a chimney spewing smoke. None of the lights are on. The property extends for acres of rolling greens. She passes the horses and then sees what has spooked them. An older man in a cowboy hat lying on the ground with his throat slit. This must be Rune, and the horses are mourning their master. Out of reflex, she goes to radio it in, but then spies an opening in the ground revealing a large trapdoor. She tries to wedge herself inside but the opening is too narrow until she notices a pulley nearby. Yanking on it causes the trapdoor to fully open, large enough for a car to fit down. With her gun pointing into the dark abyss, she descends.

Below, the fluorescent lights flicker bathing the basement in a washed-out white and then tinting it completely dark. Flashes of the crime scene appear in stages. A woman torched on the ground with a gaping hole in her stomach. A man with his head blown off, bits and pieces clinging to the wall. Another woman still on fire but clearly dead. A man in a James Dean mask that doesn't appear to be moving either. Rows of black SUVs and a wall of guns and ammo.

She hears a scraping sound. The lights click off and then back on to reveal a man dragging himself across the floor and leaving a blood trail. She runs to him.

"Where is Jay Howell?" she asks, as quietly as possible. Her whispers echo, but it sounds like the wind. "Did he do this to you?"

The man is missing an eye, and she thinks of the lady who identified Gracie Stockton's kidnapper as wearing an eye patch. The patch wound up on James Cagney, but forensics later told her Cagney's eye was intact.

The man missing one eye nods. He removes his hands from holding his stomach, as if to show her what happened. Blood starts spilling out an alarming rate.

"No, no, cover up the wound," she whispers. "My partner is on his way. We'll get you an ambulance."

He shakes his head, knowing it will be no use.

"Did Gable run?" she asks. "Where is he?"

His shaking finger points toward a lone door at the far end of the basement. A light pools from its crack, the door slightly ajar.

"Stay put, don't move," she says.

He grabs her arm, begging her to stay, possibly to try to keep her alive. But she shakes him off and pursues the door. Kellan attempts to invade her thoughts. One of her last moments with him when he weighed so little. He was all jutting bones and he asked her why this was happening and she couldn't answer so she just cried and he kept asking and asking, growing belligerent, until a nurse came with a sedative to make him sleep. She wondered if it would be the last time she'd hear him speak and she was right. He lived for another day but his throat had closed up and words were too much of a challenge.

"*No,*" she tells herself, banishing him away. She'll allow him to return at another time, but she's not ready to join him and needs to remain alert. She listens at the door and can hear a murmuring through the crack. She knocks it open with her hip, the gun pointed forward. Inside, Gracie Stockton fights sleep on an orange recliner. The girl whimpers. Bonner eyes the room, but no sign of Gable.

"Oh, sweetie," she says. Motherly instinct rushes over her and she runs to rescue the child.

From behind the recliner, Jay Howell pops up with a gun in each hand and fires a stream of bullets, the sensation like she's trying to stand still while being pummeled repeatedly with a sledgehammer. Gracie attempts to scream, but her voice is blocked and she can only open her mouth in a fixed pose of horror. Bonner gets thrown back, writhing on the ground and searching for the gun that has fallen from her hand. Gable stands over her. He's a regular man, not a mythical beast. Stocky with a ruddy face and thick milk-white hair, his mouth twisted into a grimace. He points the gun between her eyes.

"No, no," she says, the pain too intense to continue speaking.

"*Gable,*" someone hisses from the basement. The shuffling of footsteps behind her. Gable eyes whoever has entered this hell. "The Doctor's here, we have to go."

Gable still has the gun pointed between her eyes. He gives Bonner a smirk then backs up and grabs Gracie.

"Uhhhh," the girl utters, as drool drips from her lip.

Gable steps over Bonner holding Gracie with one arm. The little girl appeals to Bonner to help as she gets whisked away, but Bonner is frozen. She tells the girl sorry with her eyes. She has failed yet again.

With all of her power, she manages to flip over to watch Gable escaping with two men wearing Marlon Brando and Fred Astaire masks. They grab some guns off of the wall and push a giant red button where an elevator door opens. They all wedge inside and ascend to freedom. Bonner gets out her radio and calls for Ramirez who arrives ten minutes later.

He scoops her up in his lap, checking for blood, asking what hurts.

"Bullet...proof...vest," she says, showing him the dozen bullets inches away from killing her.

"Fuck, and Gable?" he asks.

"Gone."

He radios it in, calling for an ambulance too.

"I'm sorry," she says.

"Ssshh, sssshhh, don't talk, it'll hurt your ribs."

"I'm so sorry, Kellan," she says again, as the lights click off and soon the darkness allows her to drift into a welcoming unconsciousness.

48

HELENE

THE POLICE HAVE LEFT, THE HOUSE IS QUIET. Helene learned that the lead officer on the case witnessed her father take a drugged Gracie with him, likely as a hostage. The officer was laid up in the hospital, but her partner stopped by. The FBI has now become fully involved, however there are no leads as to Jay Howell's whereabouts. Helene spoke of business he had in Macau and in Marrakesh too. He traveled so much for his company she could never keep track of where he was jetting off. Her mother was brought in for questioning too, but was too much of a wreck to be much help. Helene tried, mostly numb from the whole experience, caring less about what her father had done and more about how they would find her daughter.

After the questions ended, she sought solace in Gracie's room. Brenton was staying over at a close family friend's because Harrison was still in the hospital. Peter had come over while the police were here. She found it hard to take him seriously with his Zen beads and his clichéd words of hope. He promised to fix her dinner and she was glad to have a few minutes alone.

In Gracie's room, she finds old ballet slippers from when Gracie first started dancing. The shoes so small like tiny pink gifts. She brings them to her nose, breathes in, and then does the same with an old stuffed animal Gracie used to carry around all the time when she was two. It smells of dust, but she catches a hint of her daughter too. She curls up with it on Gracie's small bed.

How could her father have done this to her? She received the letter he sent, but didn't want to read it yet. Doesn't care what he might have to say. He could tell her he loves her a thousand times, but she knows it's all bullshit. His whole life had been a pursuit of money and power; the family was only needed as a cover. His "darling Helly," as he called her just a ruse. We can never fully know another person. Harrison had surprised her as well. She knew he wasn't the picture perfect image of morality, but he'd been complicit with Jay. Her husband was seduced by the Desire Card. And now Gracie is gone, and she could never forgive either of them.

A knock at the door brings Peter inside. He has what looks like steaming soup and she's grateful even though the thought of eating makes her want to vomit.

"I'm going to leave this by the bedside," he says, placing it down and brushing his bangs from his eyes. He sits on the bed causing the corner to sag. His hand on the back of her neck is warm and somehow that annoys her to no end.

"Peter..."

"I'm here for you," he says, kissing her shoulder blade. His breath smells like onions. She's mad because now she's lost the smell from Gracie's stuffed animal.

"I want to be alone," she tells him without looking his way.

"I came in because Harrison is here."

Now she turns over, gives him the evil eye. "What?"

"He's in the living room."

"Fuck," she says, flipping off the bed so fast that Peter almost falls.

Stomping into the living room, she finds Harrison sitting on the sofa, hands folded in his lap. He appears gaunt.

"How did the hospital let you out so soon?" she asks, crossing her arms.

"I insisted."

"You brought these people, these criminals, into our lives," she says.

"Your father–"

"I am aware he's to blame, but that doesn't mean you're innocent."

He twiddles his thumbs, his frown extending. "I know."

"You both have spent your entire lives being selfish," she says. "And now Gracie is collateral damage."

"I'm going to do everything I can to get her back."

She throws up her hands. "And what is that? What power do you have? You are a cipher."

"Helene–"

"You hid from me and the kids all their life. It was always about making more money, having more things. And my father was exactly the same. You two are evil at the core."

She pushes him back against the sofa. She smacks him across the face hard enough to leave a red mark.

"I want you out of this house. I don't ever want to see you again."

A new Helene has emerged, one who cannot return to how naïve she used to be. She's responsible for Gracie being taken because she allowed evil to fester: in the form of her father, her husband. No one else can ever be trusted. She's screaming at Harrison in gibberish loud enough for Peter to run in and take hold of her, linking his hands around her chest. She upper-cuts him with her elbow by pushing her arm from his grip. He saunters off, dabbing blood from his nose.

"I want you out too," she tells him.

"Helene..."

"OUT!"

She picks up a glass bowl from the coffee table and launches it at the wall where it shatters.

"She doesn't mean that," Harrison tells Peter.

"Yes, I do."

"Honey," Peter says, swiping a bottle of pills from off the counter that she's grown accustomed to over the past week. She doesn't want to give in, but will take being numb over wanting to tear off her skin. He taps two into her hand. "Let me get you a glass of water." She shakes her head, pops the pills, and swallows.

"I meant what I said," she says to Harrison, on her way back to Gracie's room. She curls up with Gracie's stuffed animal and takes a whiff, but cannot locate her daughter's scent. She tries again. Nothing. Had she imagined it before?

A knock on the door and Peter comes in again. He sits on the bed and it groans.

"I'm leaving you alone," he says. "And I'll go if you need me to. I just wanted to let you know that Harrison left."

"Good," she murmurs into Gracie's pillow.

"She's going to come back," Peter says.

Helene turns from the pillow, the purple bags under her eyes so large they could have their own zip code.

"No. She's not."

"Honey, don't say that."

"She's my father's now," Helene says, the pills kicking in and drawing out what she believes is the truth. "And he won't give her up."

"They'll find him."

"Maybe someday, but not anytime soon. He had his endgame planned all along. The world is a big place and he's slipped into a crack."

"I'm here for you just so you know."

His still warm hand on her shoulder annoys less, rather comforting instead. Peter, a good man who has stood beside her through this whole ordeal when he could've easily fled. She pats his warm hand with her own.

"I know. And I'm sorry. Don't listen to me when I'm like that."

"You have every right to go ballistic."

"Except what I said to Harrison. He's not welcome in this house."

"I'll make sure of it," Peter says. He goes to get up and the bed groans.

"No, no," she says, pulling him back. "Stay with me."

He curls up on the small bed too, their feet entangled, his nose at the nape of her neck, breathing together, just breathing because right now that's all they know how to do.

49

HARRISON

Bad luck Harrison with the ability to attract gloom and doom. His liver, a good chunk of his money spent on getting a new one, his divorce, the mugging and subsequent coma, and worse of all—losing Gracie. Helene was right to want him as far away from her as possible. But if he's being technical, she's to blame for not realizing earlier what Jay Howell was capable of doing. Still, he'd abide by her wishes, at least until they get Gracie back. No way Jay will keep his daughter forever. Jay's probably figuring out a way across the border and will get her home once he does.

Harrison had spent enough time away from work and initially would've been heading to Haiti to check on the charity he was able to merge with a school in need and see how the "Book Launch" project was going. He might as well hop over to Punta Cana before and try to speak to Naelle. It hadn't gone well the last time because he'd been afraid of the Desire Card following them, but now that wouldn't be a worry. She wouldn't close the door on him when he'd tell her about

Gracie. She'd comfort him when Helene wouldn't. So he finds himself buying a ticket, packing a small suitcase, and heading over to JFK.

Probably not the smartest idea to fly in his condition after waking from a coma, but Harrison had never been a logical guy. He did things on whims. The last time he went to Punta Cana had been on impulse and while it didn't turn out like he wanted, it could have. Naelle was willing to listen, even maybe be with him before he got spooked. It was worth a shot and if he stayed home freaking out about Gracie that wouldn't help bring her back either.

Upon exiting the plane, he's hit with a blast of hot air and realizes he's overdressed. He gets in a cool taxi and gives the driver Naelle's address at Bavaro Beach. Since it was her mother's place, there's a chance Naelle and her daughter may have moved, but Harrison doubted since it would cost money and Naelle had a guaranteed live-in babysitter with her mom. His knees shake as he pulls up to her house. He drags his suitcase outside and onto the winding path towards her villa. If Helene knew he was here, she'd lose her shit even more. How could he fly all the way to the Dominican Republic when Gracie's whereabouts are still unknown? But Helene doesn't understand Naelle's soothing power. If she had a Naelle in her life, she'd become more optimistic about Gracie's return. Nestled in Naelle's giant bosoms, Harrison should be confident that his daughter will be brought home.

He knocks at the door and hears voices inside. An old woman opens it wearing a housecoat and slippers, her face looking like it was physically smashed. She gives a frown that shows some missing teeth and yells at him in Spanish.

"Naelle?" he asks. "Naelle?"

"Mama?" he hears a voice shout from another room.

"*Un hombre gordo*," the mother yells back.

Naelle appears, beautiful as ever. Living in the D.R. over the past year has browned her skin to a dark hue. She's in jeans shorts and a tank top drying her curly hair with a towel.

"Jesus," she says, upon seeing Harrison.

He shrugs like it's a funny joke but she's definitely not laughing.

Her and her mother yell back and forth in a Spanish that's too fast for him to translate. Finally, the mother shuffles into the kitchen.

"What the fuck?" Naelle asks.

"We're safe," he says. "The Desire Card is over."

"You think I care?"

She pulls her hair back into a ponytail and turns off the TV with a remote.

"Why are you here, Harrison? Like, you left me on the beach last year looking like a fool."

"You're not—"

She snarls, her nose trembling. This woman truly hates him. He's the fool to even come.

"You give me whole song and dance about how we're fated to be together. How you'll protect me. And then I close my eyes and you vanish."

"I was afraid."

"You think I give a shit?" She puts her hands on her wide hips. "You are the worst thing that has ever happened to me."

"I've been told that before."

"What's up with your head?" she asks, pointing at his bandage.

"I was mugged."

"*El diablo* sure follows you around," she says.

"My daughter—I told you I had a daughter. She was the same age as yours. She's gone."

"Gone where?"

"I dunno. She was taken."

Naelle eyes the door that's still swinging open and closes it with a shudder.

"*Esté* the Card?"

"It's been exposed," Harrison says. "All over the news. And the leader is my father-in-law..."

She waves her arms. "Look, mister, I'm doing okay now. I waitress at a bar *en la playa*. Yessica is in school. The Card is behind me."

"Gable won't have a hold over us anymore. He's finished. Taking his granddaughter, my Gracie, is the last play he has."

She stares at a fingernail. It doesn't have the silver star decals like he remembers. This time it's painted dark purple and the paint is starting to chip.

"So why are you here?"

"I...I'm lost. I have been. I thought I found myself, but... I don't know what I'm trying to say. You were there for me during the darkest time of my life and helped soothe me. I was hoping for that again."

"Mister, I ain't here to be your pillow."

"I know, I know, that's so... I'm terrible, I know it. And you're wonderful. You always have been. You saved my life before and I thought you could save me again."

She's still staring at her fingernail, refusing to look his way. "What makes you think I want to do that?"

"I thought it was worth coming down here to see."

He's clasping his hands together in prayer, in the hopes she'll find him pitiful.

"Well, I hate to burst your bubble gum, but I have more important things than making you feel good. We fucked, mister. We fucked because it was my job. Then you bleeded everywhere and I called an ambulance. I went to the hospital because I felt bad. Not because I was in love with you or nothing. Then because of you they cut me up to take my liver—"

"I never knew they were gonna do that!"

"Fuck off. Then you got me the money to go home and that's the end of our story. You may have fell in love with me over that time, but I never fell in love with you. I have a *novio*, mister. His name is Manny and he's a *mecánico*. He good to Yessica and never once did he almost have me killed."

"But do you love him?"

"Love? I've given up on love. He good to my baby, he treat me well, that's enough."

"I could treat you well." He steps closer. "I would be great to Yessica. She could have a family back in the States. A brother, a sister." The tears start flowing. "Tell me she's coming home."

"Who, mister?"

"My *daughter*. Gracie. Because he took her, but she's gonna come back." He sniffs up a large piece of snot. "Isn't she?"

"Mister, I don't know what to tell you. The Boss, he don't do nothing out of the kindness of his heart. I know that's not what you want to hear."

"But it's his granddaughter, he wouldn't put her in danger."

"He put you in danger, and your *esposa* too. *Mira*, you need to go. You bad energy."

She shoos him towards the door. He spins around and tries to kiss her, but she pushes him back and slaps him across the face.

"I'm about to call the cops, you hear? Now this is enough. I sorry about your little girl. I am. But it doesn't involve me. Nothing in your life involves me anymore, you hear? You picture us running off into the sunset together, but that is a stupid dream and you are a stupid, stupid man."

She opens the door. The sunlight piercing his vision making him unable to see.

"You are horrible person no matter how sad you make yourself look. I won't pity you, nuh-uh. I had to sleep with ugly men to keep a roof over my head back in America, so I do not have the time to be sad for a rich *cabrón* like you. You've gotten everything you wanted all the time and it's time for that to end. So goodbye, forget me, and leave before I spit on you."

"I'm sorry, Naelle."

"Good, you're sorry. Now go."

She gives a hard shove and he nearly falls over as the door gets slammed in his face. For a second, he waits, just to see if she was playing and will reopen the door and yank him inside. Kiss him with her strawberry lips and bring him into her bosom like he desires. He truly is the biggest fool of them all. For she never opens the door and eventually closes all of her shades. He takes his suitcase that was propped up against the house and drags it down onto the beach. It's late in the day and locals have finished up work and have lain their towels down by the shore. Music plays and everyone seems happy without a care. He's still weeping and sits down in the sand. The last time he was here, a Clark Gable mask washed up into his lap telling him he would always be watched. He thought how unfair that was for the sin he committed. But he deserves a lifetime of being observed by some higher ethical authority. For he lacks the reasoning to do it on his own. Here his daughter has gone missing and all he cared about was finding the woman he assumed he loved. He doesn't deserve her. She was right to have nothing to do with him. He waits until the sun sets and it's a brilliant showing of colors, majestic as it plunges into the ocean. He stands and steps into the waters, the cold licking his feet. He wades farther in until only his head sticks above the surface. Like a child being blessed, he dunks his head back, hoping to emerge anew, holding his breath for as long as can out of fear he's irredeemable.

He stays under for so long he wonders if he'll ever come up again.

50

DETECTIVE MONICA BONNER

DETECTIVE BONNER SPENT TWO DAYS IN THE hospital where she was treated for cracked ribs. Hurt like a motherfucker but she'd had worse injuries on the job. Back in her training days, a methhead shot her in the leg and caused her to limp for about three years. Ramirez visited her with flowers and news from the captain. The FBI wasn't happy at being left in the dark about the Jay Howell raid. While the officers at their precinct had a "way to go" mentality for Bonner going after the dragon alone, the captain hates pissing off the feds because it could poison the well and diminish cooperation, which could seriously sideline other crimes. But the feds are too busy tracking down Mr. Howell and Gracie Stockton to spank her too hard. A couple of weeks of desk duty likely while her ribs heal away.

Once the doctors okay her release, Ramirez drives her home and helps her up the stairs into her third-floor apartment.

"I'm fine from here," she tells him.

"Nonsense," he says, taking away her keys and opening the door. He directs her over to the couch. "Can I make you something?" he asks, already walking toward the kitchen.

"Ramirez..." she starts to say, but he's already passed by her bedroom and seen her shrine to Kellan. A corkboard of pictures from when he was a baby to his last few days in the hospital. Candles sit at the foot of the shrine, the wax melted down to the nubs.

"I've been meaning..." Bonner begins to say, as she winces from the pain. "To take it down."

Ramirez pinches his eyes. "What you went through. I can't even imagine."

"It's not healthy," she says, entering the bedroom and removing a picture. Kellan with a stuffed animal giraffe he used to call Paco. "It's one thing to keep the pictures, it's another to stare at them every day. When I'm not working, that's all I'll do. I'll make Ramen noodles and just waste my day looking at him."

She presses the bandage on her ribs as she sits down on the edge of the bed. "I'm not gonna stop."

"You do what you need to do."

"No, I'm not gonna stop until that girl comes home and Gable is caught."

"Bonner, leave it to the feds..."

"They don't know the case like we do." She's getting excited and she can see the concern reflected in Ramirez's eyes. "They haven't dealt with him face-to-face. I have and lived to tell."

"An indication to let this lie."

"I'll do it without you, the department too. And you can run and tell the captain–"

"Bonner, I wouldn't."

"You can run and tell the captain and if it costs me my job, so be it. Because I won't sleep until he's done."

Ramirez sits on the bed, puts his arm around her. "There's always that unsolved case, the one that nags. I have it too. You just gotta let it be. It makes us stronger for the ones we can close."

"I can close this."

"I believe you *think* you can. But leave it to the feds. Agents in every nearby state and at the borders are on the lookout. They'll get him if they can. And not because you went all vigilante."

"The one-eyed man who survived, he knows something."

"He's in a coma."

"When he wakes."

"Again, let the FBI do their thing. You step on any more toes..."

She pops up, forgetting her cracked ribs. "Ramirez, I'm not gonna say anything more because I don't want you implicated. But I'm not stopping. If you understand my personality at all, you know I'm tenacious. And stubborn."

"So fucking stubborn."

"I don't need you to worry. Okay? This is my decision."

"All right, all right." Ramirez throws up his hands in defeat. "I'm not gonna talk you down."

"Good," she says, smiling. "If you can do anything for me, I'll take that Ramen."

He snaps his fingers and gives her a wink along with a sigh.

"Ramen coming up."

————

After Ramirez leaves and she finishes her Ramen, Bonner washes the bowl in the kitchen before returning to her bedroom. Kellan's shrine remains like she left it, minus the one picture she took off that sits on the desk below. In the waning light, the shrine appears sadder than in the daytime and she cries like she does each morning when she kneels at its altar. She'd taken days off from it while on the Gracie Stockton case, the guilt overwhelming. She could call her mom or Jim to vent, but doesn't want their guidance, or even to pretend to help sate their own sadness. She wants to live in her own despair, have it fuel her to accomplish what needs to be done. Her mind travels to a time before the diagnosis when Kellan was about seven and they had taken a trip down to Muir Woods. Surrounded by the old-growth redwood trees, they munched on trail mix and sipped hot chocolate from packed thermoses. The forest floor covered in redwood sorrel, light slanting through the red alders. Hand-in-hand with her two men, she wanted to freeze time because she'd never been this happy before and knew she would never be as happy again. For she'd lived long enough to know that life has its peaks and valleys and this was a rare moment without any valleys in sight. But they were there on the horizon beyond the trail, ready to swallow them all up. Future years of heartache and resentment, she saw it all and it felt like a stone struggling to slide down her throat. She couldn't breathe, dizzy and having to sit down. Jim was worried but tried not to freak out too much so Kellan wouldn't be scared. She gulped water and lied that she must be dehydrated. But she'd walked into the distance where hell was around the corner waiting.

"Are you okay, mommy?" Kellan asked, and she brushed away any tears and hopped up a little too fast on her feet to prove her invincibility. But she was crumbling. And even after they returned home from San Francisco, she'd been altered. For things were too good not to be wrecked. And a reckoning would come. Swift and brutal and tear them all to shreds.

She thought of that day at Kellan's bedside before he passed. The way the warmth of the sun through the tall trees did nothing to lessen the chill. She had seen Kellan's destruction years before it occurred and there was a slight relief that it had finally arrived and she could breathe from not having to worry about it anymore.

She hasn't realized but during her reflection she's taken down her entire shrine of pictures. The corkboard sits empty but that is good. Now she can focus on catching the elusive Gable. Her mind no longer cluttered with the past. No baggage to knock her off the redwood sorrel path towards her target.

51

GABLE (A.K.A. WILLIAM CLARK)

THE DOCTOR DROVE A TRICKED-OUT VAN REPLETE with a chamber under the floorboards that could fit two bodies lying flat. Holes were poked to allow breathing, unless he was transporting dead bodies. He kept to the speed limit leaving New York State as they headed down to San Ysidro, San Diego. He switched off with Brando and Astaire so they could do the forty-two-hour drive without stopping. Gable tended to Gracie, mildly drugging the girl so she wouldn't freak out. Waking her up just to feed and make sure she remained hydrated. Gable took one last look at the America he was fleeing. He knew it might not be forever, but there was no guarantee he could ever return. Pennsylvania, Ohio, the flat Midwest, places he avoided, corn and soy fields down into Oklahoma prairies, an awe-inspiring stretch through New Mexico and Arizona, rock formations sculpted by the gods, and into California.

The Doctor knew people at the San Ysidro border crossing if they got into trouble. Just in case, Gable wedged below the floorboards with Gracie. She was fully asleep and lightly snored. The Doctor, Brando, and Astaire all had fake papers that should get them through. The Doctor's associate Miguel was notified to correct any problems. San Ysidro widely known as the easiest of crossings allowing half the cars by without inspection. The Doctor was waved past and they were free.

Tijuana hit them like a slap. Gable emerges from his hiding spot to see clusters of houses and parked cars that line the dry riverbed and valley walls. The Doctor has associates in Tijuana, but it would be foolish to stay here. Too close to the border, too risky a chance of being caught. They continue on through the open roads to Mexicali past Yuma and the desert preserve with volcanic peaks down into Sonoyta where The Doctor refuels and pays another associate for guns. In the eighties and nineties, The Doctor did *mucho* business in Mexico, including Gable with a lot of his schemes. Some of his associates have passed on, their children taking over the ship. From Sonoyta, they head to Hermosillo where they ditch the van with another associate, Juan Angel, who will use it for scrap metal. Juan Angel gives them an SUV to continue the rest of the way. After nearly sixty hours of travel, their bodies smell so they strip down and Juan Angel hoses them off and finds them new clothes that don't scream American. His wife cooks them tamales and even Gracie nibbles on one before passing out again. From there, they make one more stop in Ciudad Obregón to refuel and then reach their final destination—Aguaruto in Sinaloa. The Doctor owns a four-bedroom property an hour outside of the city, far from the hustle but close enough to offer Gable business options. The area heavily run by the cartels he has influence with, even though it's waned over the years. Still, they are off the radar of any U.S. law enforcement looking.

When they enter The Doctor's place, Gable carries Gracie up the stairs to her room. It's small but with the right paint job could feel like home. The bed is stripped save for a dusty fitted sheet. He lays her down and then heads across the hall to his own room. He chooses the biggest, a far cry from what he's used to. It will have to do. Outside the view is subpar. Flat lands and the occasional car rolling by. The air hot and dry. This is where he will begin again.

———

Gable can hear Gracie waking so he rushes into her room. Her eyes full of crust, her mouth dry so he gives her water and sits her up.

"Where are we?" she asks.

"I'm going to be honest with you."

She swallows hard, steeling herself for what he will say.

"It's not safe to go home, Gracie. At least not for a while."

"Why?" And then, as if she just realizes. "My head?"

"It's called a sedative. It helped you sleep."

"My tummy hurts."

"That tends to happen too. It will go away."

"What about Mom and Dad?"

"They are okay. They know you're with me. They want you to be here."

"Why?"

"Because you will be safest here. You've been made a target because of me back home, and people will just keep trying to take you again and again."

She's crying, little tears like from a bird. "Can I talk to them?"

"Not for a while. Again, it's not safe. No one can know where we are."

Sniff. "Where are we?"

"Mexico. It's never winter here. Sometimes it rains, but it's never cold. Doesn't that sound good? We're staying at the home of a business associate of mine. This will be your new room. We can paint it pink if you like."

She studies the walls but doesn't seem impressed.

"I like purple better."

"Okay, okay. Purple it is."

She covers her mouth. "But my ballet!"

"Yes, you won't be going to your ballet school anymore. But we are near a very large city. I will find you a new ballet school. You wouldn't even have to go to a real school if you didn't want, just ballet."

This perks her up. "Ballet all day?"

"Ballet all day, baby."

"And Mom and Dad are okay with this?"

"They suggested it. They know you aren't happy in school. In America, you couldn't only go to ballet school. Here you can."

She yawns. "I'm really tired. I want to sleep."

"Sure, sure thing. I'm glad we were able to have this talk."

She's already closed her eyes. He knows he will have to tell her all of this again, many times, and figure out a way so she'd shut up about talking to her parents. He'll write letters from them to assuage her for the next few weeks until the situation feels more natural. If he's ever found, she'll be the best chance he has for getting away. Under no circumstance could he give that up.

He kisses her forehead and shuts the blinds, leaving her in darkness.

————

Gable had Brando and Astaire stay in the house to watch Gracie while The Doctor drove him to Dr. Emilio Flores, a plastic surgeon in Culiacán. The Doctor used the guy for an eye lift around the turn of the century. Most importantly, Dr. Flores could be trusted to keep quiet. They pull up to his office, a slim door in a back alleyway. Dr. Flores had been expecting them and promised no one else would be in the waiting room. When they arrive, Gabel finds Dr. Flores to be a squat man with a tiny tuft of hair, big eyes behind big glasses, and a large belly that sags over his belt.

"So I am to hear you want a complete new face," Dr. Flores says.

The Doctor nods while cleaning his John Lennon sunglasses. "The Boss would prefer to have no resemblance to who he used to be."

"I will not ask why," Dr. Flores says.

"Please don't," Gable says.

"And what you have in mind?"

Dr. Flores holds up a hand mirror as Gable inspects his mug.

"Surprise me," Gable says. "But keep me handsome."

Dr. Flores laughs.

"I'll be in the waiting room when you're done," The Doctor says.

A nurse walks in, pretty with pouty lips and long legs. She preps him for surgery, tells him to count down from ten. He's asleep by five.

As his old face gets removed, Gable dreams wildly of the future. Culiacán a perfect hub for cocaine and even human trafficking. The Doctor would make the introductions. A new Desire Card on a smaller level, big enough so he wouldn't have to dip into his offshore accounts, but not too much to raise any suspicion. He could make do with the offshore funds, but what would be the fun in that? At seventy years young, he was far from ready to retire. He's envisions the business growing as Gracie goes to ballet school while she learns the trade as well. Brando and Astaire would remain his operatives and The Doctor could be his station agent. He could find a role for her too, since a little white girl could come in handy. And he knows she has it in her. She survived these last few weeks with her sanity intact while her brother or her parents would've crumbled. Since they wouldn't be leaving Mexico anytime soon, she could work her way up to being his Number Two. But no masks, never again. They'd need a new form of keeping incognito.

He wakes to Dr. Flores blinking over him and repeating that the surgery went well. Looking in the mirror, Gable's face appears puffy. It will take weeks for it to set and he needs to change the bandages regularly. The Doctor says he will monitor it carefully.

As they drive back, Gable peers into the rearview. Now that the anesthesia has worn off, he can see a dramatic difference in his face. His presidential nose: gone. Shaved down to half the size with half the power. Ears shortened too. The cheeks gaunter, the hairline pulled down. A more ordinary face than he's used to. How it should be. Someone that won't stand out, that wouldn't command a room like he used to. The Doctor's humming "Take On Me" by A-Ha, a favorite of his for the last thirty years, and so Gable starts singing *"I'll be gone, in a day or too-oo-oo-ooo"*.

"What should I call you now?" The Doctor asks, as his humming ceases.

"That's a good question. Certainly Jay Howell is out of the question."

The Doctor lights a cigarette and ashes it out of the window.

"Certainly."

"Gable's over too. But his first name was William. No one in Hollywood called him that. He's been a part of me for so long, it'd be hard to give him up completely. William Clark, that's my new identity. On all my IDs, at home, to anyone, that's how you'll refer to me. So I keep some of Gable around because he's gotten me this far."

"William Clark..." The Doctor says, chewing on the name and approving.

"Poof, I'm reborn."

They see the sign for Aguaruto.

"You know what the town means in Mexican, right?" The Doctor asks.

William Clark shakes his head.

"Place of plants with horns," The Doctor says, flashing a wicked smile. He takes his hands off the wheel to make two devil's horns over his head.

William Clark mirrors The Doctor's joker grin.

"Then I'm home."

52

J.D. STORM

THERE'S A WARNING THAT THE VOLCANO ON Matagi Island will erupt. The villagers are pouring away from the beach in droves. Their small cars fighting down narrow lanes to flee. J.D. Storm doesn't care; he's survived worse. The white sand slips between his toes. Waves rollick. The sun red and flaming as it dips into the ocean like a cherry into a drink. None of this is real.

He checks every so often for another soul along the beach. Even though Annie has died, a shred of him hopes she might be conjured. Her Kentucky twang calling out. Her blonde hair kissed by the sunrays.

"J.D., well if it isn't crazy seeing you here," she'd say. Never calling him Marcus Edmonton because that's not his true self, or James Dean. Born J.D. Storm, and all the nonsense that has happened since eventually brought him back. Gable was still at large, meaning J.D. would never be settled, not until they were both in the dirt.

A rumbling sound courses through the beach, the sand on fire, and the volcano blasts lava over the earth.

The entire village covered as it seeps toward him. He closes his one eye ready for the burn.

When that eye opens, he's in a darkened hospital room. Beeping machines the only noise. His stomach feels like it's been ripped open, a large bandage covering the knife wound. He's about to ring for the nurse, but he's handcuffed to the bed. They'll be moving him right from the hospital to a jail should he survive. No fucking way.

His mouth a dry cave, his body pleading for water but he has more pressing matters. He tries to pull out of the handcuffs. No chance. His good eye passes over anything on the side table he could use. Cup of water, a toothbrush. A dental pick. Bingo.

Stretching, he shifts his body silencing a scream until he's hanging over the side table. Opens his mouth wide and grabs the pick between his teeth, drops it in his lap and shimmies in his gown so it falls by one of his hands. He grabs it and gets to picking, bending it to an approximate seventy-degree angle. Then he removes it and places it back in bending toward the other end. He wiggles the pick until it points in the direction of the locking device, lifting it open. Quickly, he does the same with the other cuffs.

Upon exiting the bed, he collapses to the floor. No clue how long he'd been out. He works the blood back into his limbs and creeps to the door. Outside a police officer sits watch, half-asleep. He doesn't want to kill anyone else ever again, except for Gable and anyone loyal to the Boss. This cop innocent.

Swiftly, J.D. swings open the door, locks his hands around the cop's neck applying the right pressure points and makes him faint. It's the middle of the night and there's only a nurse at the front desk. He swipes the cop's gun and runs for the elevators bare-assed. The nurse doesn't look up, since J.D. can be silent as a ninja. In the elevator, he paces until it reaches the lobby. Then makes a break for the doors, a cab waiting at the entrance. Getting inside, he knows he will need to take the driver's money so he can get away. He sticks the gun in the back of the driver's neck and orders him to floor it. The driver asks where he wants to go and J.D. can't think. There's no one he can rely on. No place to go. The seat is cold against his bare butt. His hand holding the gun shakes like mad. Gable has the kind of resources at his disposal to run anywhere. But J.D. has nothing to live for, nothing to lose. Even if it takes years to find the bastard. He will search, he will hunt, he will be victorious, ending this apocalyptic cycle.

All the chaos he's caused justifying his revenge.

"Where to?" the nervous driver asks. "Where to?"

A PULSE-POUNDING THRILLER THAT ANALYZES GOOD VERSUS EVIL AND QUESTIONS PREVIOUSLY SHED MORALS.

After fleeing from the States when his alias is discovered, Jay Howell—also known as Clark Gable and William Clark—is now an old man wanted by the cartels. As he sets off to disappear completely in the Amazon jungle, those who survived his iron grip are in pursuit to rid the world of his evil for good.

A shaman woman—believed to be the only human alive who can remove the cancer that is the sinister Card organization's influence—calls on JD Storm, Detective Monica Bonner, and Howell's daughter, Helene, to help aid in its demise.

Will these enraged, former victims be successful...or will evil triumph once again?

A pulse-pounding thriller, *Desire's End* closes the chapter on those indebted to this sinister organization in a shattering conclusion.

"An atmospheric riveting thriller you won't be able to put down or easily forget. One of Goldberg's best." —Terrence McCauley, award-winning author of *The Wandering Man* and *The Moscow Protocol*

AVAILABLE SEPTEMBER 2022

ABOUT THE AUTHOR

Lee Matthew Goldberg is the author of eight novels including *The Ancestor* and *The Mentor* and the YA series *Runaway Train*. His books are in various stages of development for film and TV off of his original scripts. He has been published in multiple languages and nominated for the Prix du Polar. *Stalker Stalked* will be out in Fall '21. After graduating with an MFA from the New School, his writing has also appeared as a contributor in *Pipeline Artists*, *LitHub*, *The Los Angeles Review of Books*, *The Millions*, *Vol. 1 Brooklyn*, *LitReactor*, *The Big Idea*, *Monkeybicycle*, *Fiction Writers Review*, *Cagibi*, *Necessary Fiction*, *Hypertext*, *If My Book*, *Past Ten*, the anthology *Dirty Boulevard*, *The Montreal Review*, *The Adirondack Review*, *The New Plains Review*, *Maudlin House*, *Underwood Press*, and others. His pilots and screenplays have been finalists in *Script Pipeline*, *Book Pipeline*, *Stage 32*, *We Screenplay*, the *New York Screenplay*, *Screencraft*, and the *Hollywood Screenplay* contests. He is the co-curator of *The Guerrilla Lit Reading Series* and lives in New York City. Follow him at LeeMatthewGoldberg.com.

Made in the USA
Monee, IL
01 May 2023

32785150R00194